BY LORENZO CARCATERRA

A SAFE PLACE:
THE TRUE STORY OF A FATHER,
A SON, A MURDER

SLEEPERS

APACHES

GANGSTER

STREET BOYS

PARADISE CITY

CHASERS

MIDNIGHT ANGELS

THE WOLF

TIN BADGES

SHORT STORY

THE VULTURE'S GAME

TIN BADGES

TIN BADGES

A NOVEL

LORENZO CARCATERRA

BALLANTINE BOOKS

NEW YORK

Published in the United States by Ballantine Books, an imprint of Random House, a division of Penguin Random House LLC, New York.

BALLANTINE and the HOUSE colophon are registered trademarks of Penguin Random House LLC.

LIBRARY OF CONGRESS CATALOGING-IN-PUBLICATION DATA
NAMES: Carcaterra, Lorenzo, author.
TITLE: Tin badges: a novel / Lorenzo Carcaterra.
DESCRIPTION: First Edition. | New York: Ballantine Books, [2020]
IDENTIFIERS: LCCN 2019012582 (print) | LCCN 2019013011 (ebook) |
ISBN 9780345526472 (Ebook) | ISBN 9780345483928 (hardcover)
SUBJECTS: LCSH: Criminal investigation—Fiction. | GSAFD: Suspense fiction
CLASSIFICATION: LCC PS3553.A653 (ebook) |
LCC PS3553.A653 T56 2020 (print) | DDC 813/.54—dc23
LC record available at lccn.loc.gov/2019012582

Printed in Canada on acid-free paper

randomhousebooks.com

246897531

FIRST EDITION

Book design by Barbara M. Bachman

This one is for Nick.

*He never failed, through good times and during
the difficult days, to bring a smile to his mother's face.
He is a hardworking, kind, and generous young man.*

It is an honor to call him my son.

"I'm a fighter. I believe in the eye-for-an-eye business. I'm no cheek turner. I got no respect for a man who won't hit back. You kill my dog, you better hide your cat."

—MUHAMMAD ALI

TIN BADGES

1.

MANHATTAN

AUGUST 2015

I HATE LAST DAYS OF PRETTY MUCH ANYTHING YOU CAN THINK of—from vacations to the end of baseball season to the final time I'll be able to share a laugh with someone I love. Some last days you can prepare for, knowing there will be the start of another cycle waiting with the flicker of a few months off the calendar. And then there are those days that hit hard enough to send the strongest of us cowering for cover.

That's what my last working day as a New York City Police Department first-grade detective was like for me. Going in, it never entered my mind my career would end before my shift was through. But I imagine no one ever knows when it's their last day of doing anything. Especially not in my line of work.

The day began with my usual routine—a two-hour workout, a cold shower, and two double espressos sipped slowly while I scanned the morning tabloids and overnight police reports. By and large I am a creature of my habits, good ones for the most part, though now and then I'll slip and spend more than I should on a great bottle of wine or play a few more hands of poker despite knowing the cold streak I had been running all night was never destined to warm up.

By 8:00 A.M., I sat on the front steps of my Greenwich Village brownstone, waiting for my partner, Frank "Pearl" Monroe, to drive up. The early-morning sun warmed my face, and it was already starting to feel like one of those New York City August days when the heat-and-humidity combo clouded your vision and made you long for a bitter blast of winter.

By the way, in the event you're wondering how a gold-shield NYPD salary is enough to land a guy a Greenwich Village brownstone, let me set you straight—it isn't. Not even close to it. My cop salary wouldn't cover the monthly expenses. In my case, you can chalk it up to a little bit of luck and a father with a nose for real estate.

"When you go looking for a house," my dad would tell anyone within earshot, "always move toward the cheapest home in the best neighborhood. That's how you end up with a winner."

My father worked as a lugger down at the old 14th Street meat market. He had been a boxer in his younger days, rising up as far as the number-three contender for the middleweight title. A broken right hand and a damaged left eardrum forced him to give up any dreams of being a champion. So instead he got up each morning at 2:00 A.M., regardless of weather, put on his white butcher's smock, and walked to the meat market, which by 3:00 A.M. was lit by floodlights, truck head-lights, and wood-burning fires from rusty iron barrels as workers from more than two dozen companies loaded up freezer shipments to be delivered to restaurants throughout the city. This was decades before the area became the super-chic neighborhood it is today, filled with high-end boutiques, expensive restaurants, and monthly rents that make your legs buckle.

My father made good workingman's money, some weeks clearing as much as five hundred dollars when overtime was heavy, and my mom was even better at socking it away. Back then, in the early 1980s, people like my folks could afford to buy themselves a brownstone in the Village, if they played it right, which my parents did and then some.

The brownstone is a four-story walk-up, and for twenty years my aunt Nancy and uncle Aldo rented the top two floors while me, my brother, Jack, and my folks lived in the bottom two. The mortgage got knocked off years ago, and today I still live in those same bottom two floors and rent out the top ones to a retired shoemaker and his wife, still working part-time at a local bakery. I charge them what they can afford. I'd much rather have quiet and steady neighbors than ones with deeper pockets and friends always in need of a place to crash.

The brownstone has been my home for as long as I can remember, and I imagine it will be until my final days.

MY PARTNER, PEARL, PULLED up to the curb, his late-model fire-red Mustang as shiny as his shaved head. He had a wide smile on his handsome face, Sam Cooke's smooth, sweet voice belting out through the four speakers. I moved from the stoop and slid into the front seat, and before I had my seatbelt latched Pearl had the Mustang gliding halfway down the street. "We still a go?" I asked.

"Checked in with my guy before the sun came up," Pearl said. "If there's a deal going down, then today's the day for it."

"I'd still feel a lot better if we had one of our sources vouch for the guy," I said.

"You worried about him because he's a user?" Pearl asked.

"There's that," I said, nodding. "Plus, he's looking to slice considerable time off a jolt that's sure to land him a serious upstate stretch. Under those conditions, a guy like him will say and do anything to get that sentence reduced."

"I ran his priors," Pearl said, swinging the Mustang toward Sixth Avenue, heading uptown. "Every stretch he did, he did for a job on behalf of Rico's crew."

"Still doesn't make him an inside guy, Pearl," I said. "He's never been in the room when the plans go down. He's a runner. Ready to move when told to move."

Sixth Avenue was its usual early-morning slow traffic crawl, and Pearl turned to look at me.

"This ain't the first time you and me made a move off the word of a stoolie we barely knew," he said. "Hell, not even the twenty-first time. So what makes this particular guy an itch you can't seem to scratch?"

"It's nothing solid," I said. "Just a feeling. A bad vibe. Nothing more."

"Let's work off of what we know," Pearl said. "The source broke it down from first step to last. He gave us the delivery time, the number of the building and the apartment. He told us who would be in there and how much cocaine they would be cutting up. Minus us having a wire dropped behind their television, we're not going to get a better picture of what to expect than what he gave us."

"I'm not saying you're wrong, Pearl. Truth is, you're more than likely on the mark."

"If you're feeling shaky about it, we can hold off. We can take a step back and come at Rico from another direction another time."

I stared out at the now-congested streets crammed with people rushing to work. Most of them walked with earbuds solidly in place, either listening to music or getting a morning fix of gossip. "Let's stick to the plan," I said without turning to look away. "No better way to start a morning than to cause Rico and his boys their share of grief."

ONE HOUR LATER, I was crouched down, my back against a splintered and grimy cement wall, hidden by a stairwell lodged between the third and fourth floors of a dilapidated tenement. My black short-sleeve T-shirt was soaked through, the sweat a cocktail of adrenaline mixed with a dose of fear.

My eyes were slow to adjust to the shadows. I could make out a series of overhead bulbs long since burned out. Blasts of television sound echoed from all sides, a strange brew of Kelly Ripa, ESPN, and Univision. The high volume easily pierced the thin wooden doors that posed as sentries to the neglected railroad apartments.

Pearl was hunched down to my right, his shaved head and base of his neck dripping wet. "Second door on your left," he whispered, gesturing with the gun he held in his right hand. "They should be in the room just past the kitchen."

"How many you figure are in there?"

"Eight at the minimum," Pearl said. "That's a best guess. I could be off by one, maybe two."

I rested the back of my damp head against the cold wall and closed my eyes. I took in a few deep breaths, looking to control my breathing and slow down my heart rate. For any cop, the precious minutes before an anticipated shoot-out or takedown are both exhilarating and frightening. It is during that brief interlude when thoughts of life and death mingle with images of the unknown that awaits.

Those are the moments a cop is at his most vulnerable.

"I always forget how hot it gets in these hallways," I said, opening my eyes. "It's like they save the heat they need in winter for the summer months."

Pearl smiled. "You should have worn shorts. Maybe even a cutoff T to match and a pair of flip-flops. They would have never fingered you for a cop, decked out like that."

I glanced at Pearl and returned his smile. It was a smile I had known since my first week at the police academy, the two of us sitting next to each other, doing our best to listen to a too-eager instructor alerting us to the fact that "there is a ninety-five percent chance the majority of the recruits in this room will go their entire careers without once firing their weapon." Pearl had turned to me and flashed his megawatt smile and whispered, "I guess that means we're all going to be working out of a Staten Island precinct."

"No fun in that," I said. "Might as well put in our papers now, save everybody the trouble."

The friendship started that very minute and has never wavered, the Italian kid from Greenwich Village and the African American from Harlem doing the job we had dreamed of doing since we were old enough to distinguish good from bad. We were both parochial-school boys, from grammar straight through high school; he was happily married and I was even happier being single. We were instant friends and, over time, proved to be the best of partners. Pearl and I worked as one. I trusted him with my life and he put his in my hands every day. And never once did we let the other down.

We were an effective team from the start, and it didn't take long for the brass to notice. We were assigned to foot patrol, first out of the 10th Precinct in Chelsea and then up to Harlem. From there, we quickly graduated to the night watch dispatched out of a squad car. We worked our sector hard, were on a first-name basis with the area merchants, and began to build a solid network of trusted informants, from the hookers on the Eighth Avenue line to the dealers who claimed the after-hours clubs on Eleventh and Twelfth Avenues as their private terrain.

Those connections led to busts, and those busts led to a rapid succession of promotions—a boost to second grade and slots in a plain-clothes unit out of Washington Heights. From there we were assigned as detectives in the South Bronx, where we bumped heads with Luther Wiley and his "Pain Train" crew of drug dealers, up to today, where we were both gold-shield first-graders in an elite narcotics unit going up against the top-tier Colombian drug outfits working Manhattan's upper rings.

During those years and through all those busted-down doors and volleys of bullets aimed our way, Pearl and I grew to be more than partners, more than mere friends with a badge and a gun dependent on one another to survive.

We were family. As close as any two brothers could ever hope to be.

Off the job, we had much in common. We loved sports, jazz, Sam Cooke, Leonard Cohen, and museums—though I preferred the literary bent of the Morgan Library, while he liked the exhibits at the Museum of Natural History. We liked wine and we loved to read—he tilted toward John Grisham legal thrillers intercut with an occasional attempt at a Charles Dickens novel; I read any biography I could get my hands on, tossing in a Linda Fairstein mystery to the mix.

Pearl was married to a terrific young woman in her first year as a resident at Roosevelt Hospital. Her hours were about as long as ours, and while their time together was limited, Pearl made the moments count.

I was just starting to keep company with a lady who co-owned and managed a restaurant a short walk from my brownstone. We cared for one another and gave each other the space required to keep our relationship on solid ground.

Pearl and I complemented each other. Our humor blended with our street savvy, our instincts with our skills, and we each maintained a keen understanding of what day-to-day life was like inside neighborhoods where the criminals often made the call as to who lived and who died on any particular day.

I FLINCHED WHEN I heard a loud bang coming out of the apartment just beyond the stairwell to our left. It was followed quickly by the foul smell of burning drugs. Three rats the size of kittens scurried past us, running in formation down the stairs, frightened more by the smoke than by the noise. "We better get our asses in there before the dumb bastards blow up the entire building," Pearl told me.

I stared at the rats as they stopped, turned, and jammed themselves up against a corner. "You see that?" I said. "They stopped. They always stop when I'm around. It's as if they know how scared shitless I am of them."

Pearl Monroe eased up against the wall and nudged me forward. "How about we get away from the big, bad nasty rats and break through that door and bust us some dealers? Would that help ease your mind?"

"Big time," I said, getting to my feet and checking the clips in both my guns. "But if they follow us up, I'm shooting them first."

I took a final look at the rats and then ran up the half-flight of steps, taking a hard turn around the corner.

Pearl Monroe was right behind me.

2.

MANHATTAN

MOMENTS LATER

A THIN TEENAGER IN A MIAMI HEAT CAP AND A STEPH CURRY jersey walked down the center of a long hallway heading in our direction. Rays of thick sunlight coming through the large window behind him cast him in a warm glow. He was bouncing a basketball.

Pearl held a finger to his lips, signaling for the boy to stay quiet. The kid slowed his pace and kept bouncing the ball, a smile slicing across his face. I was several feet from the apartment door, my eyes on the teenager. "He's not here looking for a pickup game," I said to Pearl. "He's already playing his game."

The teen rammed the basketball under the crook of his right arm, stopped in the center of the hallway, and let out a shout loud enough to be heard for several stories. "Five-O!" he screamed. "Five-O on the floor!"

The next five minutes forever changed two lives and ended several others.

Bullets ripped through the ramshackle wooden door to our left, sending both me and Pearl hurtling face-down onto the concrete floor. The stink of stale urine and ammonia burned our eyes and stung our nostrils. We crawled forward for a few inches and then Pearl rose slowly to his knees. I flipped onto my back, both my guns poised toward the now-shattered door, thin lines of smoke snaking through the slanted openings. Pearl now aimed his weapon at the teenager down the hall. The kid had the basketball resting by his right foot, and his hands gripped a nine-millimeter.

The tight smile was still on his face.

"Whoever steered you into this hall wanted to see you put down," the teen said. "You walked into it, no doubt."

"Maybe so," I said. "But it would be rude to leave now."

"Besides," Pearl said, "we couldn't leave without checking in on our friend Rico."

"Now, let me guess," I said. "Would he be behind door number one or door number two?"

"You need to make the move to find out," the teen told us. "But there ain't no prize waiting no matter which door you pick. There's eight in there and I only see two of you out here. If you're smart, you bolt while you can."

"And it would be wiser for you to be on a court playing a three-on-three," Pearl said. "That'll keep you in the game. Not banging for these losers."

I glanced at Pearl and nodded.

HE HAD HIS EYE on the teen, who'd lost the smile and tightened his grip on the gun. Bracing my legs, I rushed toward the door to my left, ramming my right shoulder full force against the thin wood. The door easily gave way and I half-fell, half-stomped into the foul-smelling foyer of the railroad apartment.

The apartment was lined with low-hanging clouds of smoke and reeked of stale beer and fresh-cooked coke. The hall was narrow, a small bathroom to my right, a brown ragdoll cat coiled next to a cracked and stained toilet bowl. I heard the pump of a shotgun before I saw it, a hot blast coming at me from the first bedroom. Two men, both in their twenties, each with a Rikers cut, walked toward me. They were wearing black sweatpants topped with White Cuban shirts, spraying bullets in my direction as they moved. I crawled into the bathroom, the ragdoll watching me with glazed eyes, and aimed my weapons at the two approaching men. Every shot—theirs and mine—missed its mark.

Forget what you see in movies and TV cop shows. That agile gunman who never misses is myth, not reality. Fact is, the accuracy rate of the best-trained cop in the country is 16 percent. And for drug dealers strung out on their own product, the rate is even lower. It takes as much luck as it does skill to walk away from a firefight, especially one in close quarters. I was banking on a high dose of both as I sprawled down in that filthy bathroom, an indifferent cat my only company.

I poked my head into the foyer and caught a glimpse of Pearl, his hulking body half in the apartment and half out. It was, at best, an untenable situation, and we knew we had to move fast if we were going to step out of the mess we had walked into.

The two shooters closest to me were wedged behind a tipped-over torn red leather couch. The duo closing in on Pearl were stopping to do a fast reload of clips. I could hear sirens wailing in the distance. But they weren't close enough to do us any good.

Three gunmen emerged from a second apartment and were now positioned in the hallway.

"There's too many," I shouted out to Pearl. "Let's pick one end of the hall and shoot our way out."

"I got three fresh ones coming at me from my left," Pearl yelled back. I turned to look at him and saw he had taken a hit, a thick line of blood oozing out of his right leg.

"What about the kid?"

"He's down," Pearl said. "I nicked him in the shoulder."

Everyone held fire, waiting for someone on either side to make the next move.

"How bad you hit?" I asked Pearl.

"I can move."

The two shooters who had been using the flipped-over couch as cover were reloaded and standing now. They were heading toward me, firing rapid shots as they moved, their bullets sending shards of wood flying in all directions. The gunmen behind Pearl stood dead center in the middle of the hallway, lined up three across and firing point-blank into the apartment.

We were flat in the middle of a cross fire.

And it was the first piece of good luck we had caught all morning.

Pearl and I made our move.

I came running out of the bathroom, fired off two quick rounds at the shooters at my back, and moved for the smashed-in front door. Pearl was on his feet, bouncing bullets at the three in the hall. We each hit one of our targets, judging by the loud groans behind me and the sight of a fallen gunman in my path.

We were less than fifteen feet from the open window leading to the fire escape.

I was low on bullets and figured Pearl was as well. The blood from his wound covered his entire leg and dripped to the floor. I had taken a hit just below my right rib cage. From the quick flow of blood, I knew it went a lot deeper than a flesh wound.

The teenager was lying in the center of the hallway, a circle of blood forming a dark pool around his shoulder, his nine-millimeter resting beyond the fingers of his right hand. The basketball was near the side of his head. I jammed a gun into my waistband, bent down, and picked up the nine. "Take deep breaths," I said to the teen. "You caught luck today. Pearl wanted to end you, he would have. Something for you to remember." I turned, steadied my feet, and emptied the nine in the direction of the shooters closing in. Pearl did the same with his weapon, until we were both holding empty guns.

I tossed aside the nine and checked out the damage we had inflicted—two shooters lay dead; two more were wounded enough not to be a problem. The four others were stretched out in the hallway, expecting more firepower to come their way. I nodded to Pearl and we bolted for the open window and the rusty railings of the fire escape.

I got there first and dove through the window, a sliver of sharp wood slicing across the back of my neck. Pearl was fast on my heels.

Below us, blue-and-white patrol cars were screeching to a halt, close to a dozen uniform cops jumping out and running toward the building from every possible angle.

"Looks like the cavalry's finally here," I wheezed to Pearl. "Little late, but at least they showed."

The fire escape was old—half the railings were missing, the metal steps were cracked, and most of them were broken. We raced down them fast as we could, working off pure adrenaline, hearts pumping, senses alert, bodies numb to the pain. I turned a tight corner around a landing between the third and second floors and looked up at Pearl. He was resting his back against an outside railing. "We ducked ourselves another one, Tank," he said, wide smile on his face, blood flowing as if from an open faucet.

I never got a chance to respond.

The third-floor railing Pearl leaned on wobbled, then he began his fall, moving as if in slow motion. I lunged and tried to make a grab for him. I held tight to a rusty bar, and the fingers of my right hand gently brushed against his. Pearl fell three floors and landed with a loud thud against the sharpest edges of an empty old dumpster. I could hear bones break from where I stood. Our eyes met and I looked at his lower body dangling off the side of the dumpster, his strong legs limp and lifeless. Blood dripped out the sides of his mouth and his breathing appeared to be shallow, yet he still managed to give me a reassuring nod.

I couldn't move and didn't want to. There wasn't anything left for me to do now other than to stare at the ruined body of my partner and best friend.

At that moment, I knew neither of our lives would ever be the same again.

And I also knew that for me and for Pearl, this hot August day would be our last as New York City detectives.

3.

WESTCHESTER COUNTY

MARCH 2017

JACK RIZZO TURNED UP THE HEAT IN HIS LATE-MODEL four-door Ford Escape and moved the front wiper blades to max speed. He then spun the seat-warmer knob to five for himself and his wife, Susan, sitting next to him. She was busy checking her texts and emails on her iPhone, trying not to glance out the windshield and see the hard-falling snow building up on the road ahead.

Susan had done her best to beg out of the dinner. The inclement weather was one concern. Her dislike for David and Bella Randolph was a close second. "Why do they always have to play dress-up?" she asked as Jack attempted to quell his wife's unease about the evening that awaited. "It's dinner in their dining room, not a country-club wedding. I swear they are the most pretentious . . ."

"We only have to endure it twice a year," Jack said. "And it's not as awful as you make it out to be."

In truth, Jack hated the idea of going as much as his wife did. He knew they would both be in for a long night of boring talk, bland food, and inexpensive wine poured out of elegant decanters. But David Randolph was his department head and a partner in the accounting firm where he had worked for the past sixteen years, so not going to dinner when asked was not an option.

In the office, David was a demanding and difficult man to work for, always seeking out a path that would eventually lead to criticism rather than praise. He was humorless and short-tempered. On the few occasions where their interaction veered from work-related topics to what was meant to pass for pleasant conversation, the talk centered on either of two topics: David's weekly round of golf with his former Wharton School business classmates or the tedious activities of his beautiful and fifteen-years-younger third wife, Bella.

It was a night neither looked forward to, and Jack hated to have to put Susan through what had become a dreaded twice-yearly ritual. These forced social dinners were the only time Jack and Susan bickered. They had a solid marriage, going on sixteen years now, and he was happiest when in her company. He felt at peace around her, enjoyed the quiet moments spent reading the Sunday papers together, going to the occasional movie or play, or trudging off to watch their son, Chris, play soccer on fall afternoons and Little League baseball in the spring.

They had met at the Elbow Beach Resort on the island of Bermuda and were married less than a year later. Jack was a junior accountant back then, just beginning his climb up the rungs at Curtis, Strassman, and Randolph to his present position as a senior account manager. He earned a hefty six-figure salary and was responsible for managing the funds of two dozen of the firm's top clients. As much as Jack found his supervisor boorish, he loved the work.

Jack had always had an affinity for math and had an innate passion for numbers. He was a devoted baseball fan, fixated on the sport's embrace of analytics more than the actual game itself. His brother, Tommy, was the physical one in the family, Jack the studious. Both habits seemed to have served each one well as adults.

"I hate the idea of leaving Chris alone with this storm hitting," Susan said, still pleading her case, knowing she was waging a fruitless and losing argument.

Jack reached across and put one arm around his wife, eyes still on the road. "Believe me, honey. Chris will have a better time than either of us and hands down a better meal. He's probably already speed-dialed Gino and ordered a large pie with the works. I wouldn't waste much worry on him. He knows how to take care of himself."

The snow had been a light flurry when they pulled out of their Pelham Manor home to begin the drive deeper into Westchester County to the sprawling Bedford estate. By the time they passed Scarsdale the rare spring storm was coming down in a heavy sweep, the wipers of the Escape barely able to keep the windows clear enough to see. Jack shifted into the right lane, slowing the four-wheel-drive vehicle down to 35 miles per hour, his visibility and steering compromised by the thick falling snow.

"How far away are we?" Susan had her cell phone cradled in her right hand and there was a tinge of concern in her voice.

"About fifteen, maybe twenty minutes," Jack replied. "At the speed we're going now, at any rate. The storm isn't going to last long, should taper off in an hour or so. By the time we're ready to head home, the roads will be plowed and sanded."

"Thanks for the update, Al Roker," Susan said, smiling.

"Hey, who needs the Weather Channel when you got me, right?" Jack said, returning the smile. "Actually, it was Chris who gave me the details. A quick click and a swipe on his iPad and I had all the detailed information."

"I bought them a vase," Susan said. "So when David or Bella thank you for the gift, you'll know what it is you gave them."

"We don't have to stay long," Jack promised. "We have the weather and Chris as two solid excuses to get back. Not that we need any. They always seem as eager to be rid of company as they are to have it."

"You'll get no argument from me," Susan said. "If I could get away with eating dinner wearing my coat and boots I would. Anything for a fast getaway."

"I'll give you our usual signal and then we bolt," Jack said.

"Jack?"

He turned his eyes from the road and gave his wife a quick glance. "What's wrong?"

"We don't have a usual signal," she said.

"Good point," Jack said. "Just follow my lead. Soon as I thank them for such a fun night, you make a break for the front door."

"Such a 007 move," Susan said. "What woman could resist?"

THE ROAD HAD TURNED slick, the diving temperature rapidly turning the black pavement into a thin sheet of ice. Jack slowed the Escape down a few more miles per hour, glancing in the rearview mirror to make sure no car was close behind. He gave the brake pedal a soft tap with his right foot and felt the rear of the Escape swerve slightly to the left. He gripped the steering wheel with two hands.

Susan inched forward in her seat. She had one hand on the console; the other clutched the door rest. Jack didn't want to chance another hit on the brakes with the SUV swerving to the right and the left now, the steering wheel no longer fully able to hold the Escape steady.

They were a half mile from the next exit and a quarter mile from a small bridge that would take them over the choppy waters of a lake.

Jack gripped the steering wheel tighter and felt the loss of control. The SUV was sliding from one lane to the next, heading dangerously close to the bridge, approaching it at a sharp and treacherous angle.

Susan didn't speak, afraid that anything she might say would distract Jack. Her fear was palpable, a cold sweat running down the back and sides of her thin body. Jack stayed as outwardly calm as he could manage, focused on the road ahead. He knew he had no choice but to press down on the brake again and see if he could bring the SUV to a slow, sliding halt. The visibility was now down to zero, the snow falling in thick and hard sheets, the wind whipping blasts of it against the hood and windshield.

They were less than three hundred feet from the bridge.

Jack gave Susan a quick glance. "Looks like we're going to miss the cocktail hour," he said, managing a smile.

"There's a silver lining to everything," Susan said.

She was doing her all to keep her teeth from chattering. It wasn't the cold that caused her to shiver. It was the dread she felt. The sudden awareness that this would be one trip they might not live to see through to its conclusion.

Jack kept his gaze on the road, his wipers slowed down from the weight of the falling snow. The steering wheel felt loose and free in his hands, seemingly operating on its own, ignoring any pull or tug he would give it.

Jack took his right hand off the wheel and reached over and stroked his wife's warm face. Her eyes were moist with tears as she looked back at him.

Jack Rizzo then slowly closed his eyes and pressed his right foot on the brake pedal.

4.

TRAMONTI'S

THE NEXT DAY

I SAT AT MY USUAL SPOT, FIRST BOOTH BY THE DOOR, WORKING on my second cappuccino of the afternoon. *The New York Times* was spread across the polished wood of the table, and I was deep into a story about four cops in a small town who had shot and killed a teenager holding nothing more dangerous than a candy bar.

Carmine Tramonti slid into the booth across from me, patted the paper, and nodded when I glanced up at him. "You ever see a candy bar looked like a gun to you?" Carmine asked.

I shook my head, lifted the cappuccino cup to my lips, and took a long sip.

"Right," Carmine said. "Me neither. Which then tells you what about these four cops?"

"How about you tell me what it tells you?"

"Don't mind a bit if I do," Carmine said. "A kid pulls anything on a cop these days and he's going down. And not from a fist, either. These uniform guys will drop him like those shooters dropped Sonny at the tollbooth. No ifs, ands, or buts."

"It's not always as cut-and-dry as you make it sound." I wasn't eager to mount a vigorous defense on a case I had just read about in that day's paper.

"I'll give you that," Carmine said with a slight shrug. "But I tell you what will be cut-and-dry and that's the court case that's sure to follow. Off that, these four badges will walk without a scratch, not a stitch of prison time tossed their way. Just as sure as I'm sitting here. Nothing's changed in all these years. The same movie gets played over and over again. It don't feel right and it don't look right, which to my way of thinking means it just ain't right."

"That's not always how it shakes out," I said. "It looks that way most times, I'm aware. It's easy to sit back and make judgments. But each case stands on its own; each situation can be played out in many different ways. And some of the times, I grant you, the cops are dead wrong. And when that happens the end result is often a dead kid."

"You ever pull on a kid when you were on the job?" Carmine wanted to know. "Let alone shoot one down?"

My mind flashed on the teenager with the basketball Pearl had shot in the tenement shoot-out on our last day as working detectives. "I didn't, no," I said. "But I was there, on the scene, when a kid took a bullet."

"Did he have a gun or a candy bar in his hand?"

"A gun," I said.

"Well, in such a situation that makes him a fair target," Carmine said. "Least as far as I'm concerned. Age and color get tossed out the window on a case of that nature."

"I'm glad we got that settled," I said, eager to change the subject. "How about we move on to the next item on your list of topics of the day?"

CARMINE TRAMONTI WAS THE co-owner of the place and had been since it first opened its doors on August 9, 1974. "Two great things happened that day," he has said at least one hundred times in my presence. "One of my dreams came true and I opened a place of my own in the Village, and then that low-level thief Richard Nixon had his ass hauled out of the White House. It's what you are free to call a win-win day."

Tramonti's was a restaurant/bar/jazz club two doors down from my brownstone. I'm in there just about every day. I stop in for coffee after my daily workout and I come in for dinner at least four nights of any given week. The wine list is top-tier without putting a dent in your wallet. The food is old-school Southern Italian, served family style. And the jazz quartets that are booked start their sets at 9:00 P.M. and are led by musicians old enough to remember what great music should sound like but young enough to play until closing time.

I'm also in there practically every day for one other equally important reason. Her name is Connie Tramonti, the other owner of the place. Connie makes sure the meals are served hot, the wine is chilled to its proper temperature, and no one has to wait more than five minutes for a table they reserved.

We've been together for just about two years now. I was still on the job when we took our relationship beyond the "we're just friends" stage, and she was there to help put the pieces back in place as I weaned myself from cop to civilian. Truth be told, I've had a crush on Connie since we were kids, both of us attending the same Catholic school, around the corner from the restaurant. Connie was at the girls' end, taught her daily lessons by the strictest nuns on the East Coast. I was lumped in with the boys, under the watchful gaze of the more tolerant but equally demanding Christian Brothers.

If I liked to use the term, I'd say we were boyfriend and girlfriend. But since I don't and haven't since I was a teenager, I never call her that. We're together. That works for me and it works for her and those are the only two opinions that matter when it comes to what we choose to call ourselves.

We were always friends, long before we became lovers.

She knew me as well as I let anyone know me, and she never judged. But if she had something to say it was said. Connie often sat with me over a late-night glass of wine as the clock wound toward closing time, the jazz musicians jamming their way through one last set. We would sit and listen to the music and talk if we felt the need. It was the best relationship either of us was looking for. Mutual respect on both sides, along with the freedom to be ourselves.

Connie, I should also mention, is hands-down gorgeous in that classic and simple way that doesn't require hours of makeup and two hours at a salon. She has long light-brown hair and a pair of spend-the-night eyes dark as coal. She's slender and of average height and is quick to dump the dress and flats for jeans and a T-shirt or sweatshirt as soon as the doors to Tramonti's are closed to customers.

As great as all that sounds—and believe me when I tell you it is truly great—they're not the main reasons I'm as crazy for her as I am. It's her smile that never fails to nail me. One flash and it brings light to the darkest of my days and, yes, I know how corny that sounds, but believe me when I tell you—it is hand-on-the-Bible true. Then toss on top of that the fact Connie accepts you the way you are, not the way she would like you to be, and it adds up to the perfect woman for a man like me.

There were reasons we never took our friendship to the next level for the longest time. From my first day as a cop, I never wanted anyone I cared about to be on the other end of that dreaded late-night phone call. I didn't want Connie to hear a stranger tell her I was in emergency surgery at some hospital or, worse, that she needed to come to the morgue and identify my body. Toss into the emotional spin cycle the long hours I worked and the need not to talk about what case I was on or what I had seen that day, and it was difficult for me to see the upside to a long-term relationship.

I never wanted to be in a position where I had to lie to Connie or evade her questions. She was as straight up and direct as they come and deserved to hear nothing but the truth. To this day, Connie has never asked about anything from my past and I've never pushed her on her own history. We have enough in common that there really has never been a need to venture into uncharted waters.

The grind of running a restaurant has kept us both from pursuing our down-the-road dream: spending two years traveling through Italy,

Spain, and France, visiting small villages and big cities, tasting the variety of cuisine and drinking from a wide assortment of wines. Connie has never felt any motherly desires to have children, and I was never eager to have a little Tank Rizzo running around the halls of my brownstone.

There was a second reason I didn't pursue a romance with Connie for a number of years.

And that had to do with her father, Carmine.

5.

TRAMONTI'S

THAT SAME DAY

CARMINE TRAMONTI WAS, IN STREET PARLANCE, A WISEGUY. Not so much these days. He seems content running the restaurant alongside his daughter. He sees to it that the staff doesn't rifle too much cash out of the till, keeping the skim to a reasonable 10 percent.

His younger years were a different story.

Back then, Carmine controlled the betting activity for the five major organized-crime families in the borough of Manhattan. He worked the dollar numbers business along with cash action big and small on every sporting event you can imagine, major or minor—from pro football to baseball to basketball, boxing, and, his least favorite, soccer. "The spread on soccer is insane," he once lamented. "The games are usually two to one or one nothing. That makes practically every game a push. Not worth my time or effort. There's no profit in it. And besides, it's as boring as watching golf on television."

I never made a move to shut down Carmine's gambling operation while I was on the job. Not just his, mind you. I never busted any straight-up bookie, not when all my neighbors and relatives bet the numbers every day, either legally at their local deli or through someone like Carmine. Why did a guy working in an OTB parlor get to collect a salary and go home at night while a guy like Carmine, pretty much doing the same thing, had to face a judge, jury, and a possible 5-to-10-year prison stretch? It never made sense to me. The guys I chose to chase down deserved their cuff-and-convict.

On top of which, I had known Carmine since I was a kid. He and my father were friends.

I knew he was a knock-around guy, but while he could handle any trouble that came his way, he didn't get bent out of shape looking for it. Carmine was an old-school gangster. He kept an eye on the neighborhood and the people who lived there. I was never given a reason to bang heads with him or do any kind of a beat-down on his business.

Now, I imagine what the thinking out there is—Carmine was a criminal and I was a cop. Therefore, it would stand to reason I should be looking to lock him up. But out on those streets, it is never a cut-and-dry situation. If Carmine were a straight-out hard-ass, there is not even a shadow of a doubt I would be on him like any other hoodlum bringing bad to good. But with Carmine, that wasn't the case.

His restaurant, for example, was considered safe turf. It was a place where cops, judges, lawyers of all stripes could break bread, sharing the same space as known members of an organized-crime family. That situation may seem a bit odd to some, but truth is, I know more than a few detectives who picked up solid intelligence late at night at Tramonti's over an after-dinner drink.

Let me give you one example. A dozen or so years ago, a nun was raped and badly beaten in a Lower East Side hallway. The only information cops had to go on was that there were two suspects seen fleeing the crime scene. In less than twenty-four hours, a member of the Special Victims Unit, sitting at Tramonti's bar nursing a cold beer, found a crumpled napkin next to his near-empty bottle. The guy that left the napkin was known to be a high-ranking member of one of the five crime families. The SVU detective unfurled the napkin and on it read an address written in felt tip.

"We had a few leads by that point," he told me years later over din-ner. "We knew we were looking for a Mutt and Jeff team—one tall guy and one short, both white and in their twenties. But we hadn't zeroed in on any known location. Not until that napkin was dropped on that bar next to my beer. Not only was there an address, there was an apart-ment number. And there was one other thing, written on the bottom of the napkin in large black letters."

"What?"

"The words 'three hours,'" he said.

"What did you take that to mean?" I asked, knowing the answer but looking for certainty.

"That's all the time the OC guys were giving us to catch them and bring them in," the detective answered. "Once that deadline passed, the mob would take over. With us, those two animals got twenty-five-to-life sentences. With the OC, they would have been hit with the death penalty."

I smiled. "You know what I would have done if it were me, if it were my case?"

"I can only guess," the detective said.

"I would have waited for the black sedan to show up three hours later, give the driver and passengers a friendly nod as I watched them drive off. It would have saved the city some dough. And saved that young nun the agony of having to relive the horror of that day in open court."

I'm not here to tell you that guys like Carmine are saints. Far from it. If you're a priest and have to listen to his confession, the best advice I could give you is to bring a sandwich and a thermos of coffee. You're going to be in that booth for a long stretch. So, if I had legitimate reasons to bust Carmine's ass, I would have. But never once did he cross my line in the sand.

Initially, Carmine wasn't thrilled with me dating Connie. Hav-ing a cop, even an ex-cop, anywhere close to being family was not high on his bucket list. But I knew he respected me and the way I went about my business. I also think he figured out long before either me or Connie that the feelings between us were strong ones. So, slowly, gradually, Carmine and I became friends. Good friends.

And that's never going to change.

6.

TRAMONTI'S

"I GOT TWO RINGSIDE TICKETS FOR THE FIGHT AT THE GARDEN Friday night," Carmine said, smiling his thanks at the waitress who placed a double espresso in front of him. "In case you'd be interested in going with me."

"Don't you usually go to the fights with Rocco?" I asked.

"He's heading to Florida tomorrow," Carmine said. "He's turning into one of those, what do they call them, snowflakes?"

"Snowbirds," I said.

"Whatever," Carmine said. "Him and Frannie rather play golf and eat dinner while the sun is still out."

A young waiter approached the table, tentative. "I don't mean to interrupt," he said in a voice much younger than his appearance.

"No worries," I said.

He smiled and relaxed a bit. "It's only my second day, so I'm not sure which one of you is Tank," he said.

"That would be him," Carmine said, putting an index finger in my direction. "Me? I'm the guy who pays your salary."

The young waiter looked at Carmine, quick to take in the dark eyes, thick razor-cut silver hair, and an upper body that, while slowed by age, was still muscle strong and instinctively fast. Then he glanced at me. "Bartender says there's a call for you. He's keeping it on hold."

I looked at Carmine and shrugged. I then slid out of the booth and walked over to the bar. I stood by the end of the wood and waited as Barry, the early-shift bartender, passed the landline to me. "Serious-sounding dude," he said. "If you ask me."

"I didn't," I said.

I took the phone from Barry and turned my back, looking out past the mostly empty tables and at the tree-lined street coated with snow.

"This is Tank," I said, and I listened to a male voice on the other end that could only belong to a cop.

I lowered my head and closed my eyes, hearing words I never expected to hear about someone I never thought I would see again.

"Any survivors?" I asked.

I listened, my head still down, Carmine now looking my way.

"Give me an hour," I said. I dropped the phone back in its cradle and left it on the bar. Then I walked back to the booth.

"Could you tell Connie I won't be able to meet her for dinner?" I asked Carmine.

"Done," he said.

"I'll call her from the road. Be back when I can."

"Sounds like bad news. If you need company, my day's free."

"Thanks," I said. "But this is something I need to do on my own."

"Say no more," Carmine said.

I patted him on the back and walked out of the restaurant, heading toward my car, parked across the street.

I needed to go do what minutes earlier had seemed to be the one thing in life I would never need to do.

I had to drive to a morgue in suburban Westchester County and identify the bodies of my brother and his wife.

They had been found in the wreck of a car, hood-end crumpled at the bottom of an icy, shallow lake.

Victims of last night's snowstorm.

A sister-in-law I had met only briefly.

A brother I had not spoken to in decades.

Both now dead.

One of the cops in the town where the corpses had been found was a former NYPD detective working out of a Queens precinct.

That cop badge is like a permanent birthmark: Once you've worn it, other cops can track you anywhere you lay your hat for any reason.

In this case, for me to identify two people—my brother and my sister-in-law—I barely knew.

Or wanted to know.

7.

BRONXVILLE, WESTCHESTER COUNTY

TWO HOURS LATER

PARKED ACROSS FROM FARRELL'S FUNERAL HOME, A CONVERTED Victorian with a wraparound porch. I leaned against the hood of my car—a four-wheel-drive Jeep—my leather jacket opened to the cold air, my head down, my hands jammed inside the pockets of my jeans. I found the blasts of air hitting me from all directions soothing. They helped to wash away the vision of seeing the mangled remains of my brother and his wife lying on morgue slabs, less than thirty minutes earlier.

I identified their bodies more from memory than from visual recognition. I had seen his wife's face over the years in a number of photos my mother kept in a scrapbook and was always eager to show me. She had been proud of Jack. She'd been proud of me. And she never could understand the bitter wall that existed between the two of us.

It seemed like such a long time ago.

My brother and I didn't speak and had seen each other only once in the past seventeen years. I never went to his home and he never came to mine. Our only link for many of those years had been our mother, and that chain was snapped when she died six years ago. Even at her wake and funeral, we steered clear of one another, greeting mourners separately and standing apart during the mass and burial. He was married by that time and had a nine-year-old son, but I managed to avoid his wife and child, as well.

Some families stay close from birth to death, brushing aside the occasional feud that crops up now and then. Some families never discuss any secrets that were buried long ago.

That wasn't the case between me and Jack.

We had no trouble ignoring the normal squabbles that pop up in any family, but neither one of us was able to forget or forgive a family secret we both needed to keep hidden, buried from prying eyes and queries. It was a secret that had, over time, formed a barrier between us. And even if either of us had had the slightest desire to put that past in our rearview mirror, there were simply too many dark memories, too many horrible images buried within the crevices of that barrier for it to happen.

The easiest route was the one we chose—to set aside any thought of family and move on with our lives. Move on as though the other never even existed.

"Who's working on the funeral arrangements?" I had asked the young police officer who accompanied me to the morgue. "Do you know?"

"One of their neighbors, is what I was told," the officer said. "In the meantime, the kid's over at Farrell's now. The chief thought it would be better for him to be there than have him hanging around here."

I stared at the officer. He was thin, tall, with a heavy salon tan and enough gel in his hair to coat my brakes.

"What kid?" I asked.

"Their kid," the officer said. "The boy. Your nephew, I'm guessing. Right?"

I took one final glance at the two bodies resting side by side on their cold slabs, separated from me by a wall of glass. The cop who called me in had done the kid a favor—having me ID the bodies rather than putting him through the visual torture of seeing his parents in such a battered state.

I turned and walked out of the morgue in search of a nephew I had, in the moment, forgotten even existed.

8.

BRONXVILLE,
WESTCHESTER COUNTY

MOMENTS LATER

CHRIS WAS SITTING ON A CUSHIONED CHAIR, HIS ARMS RESTING on the edges of a small wood table. The room smelled of flowers and votive candles, and there was one large bay window that looked over a well-paved parking lot lined with shiny dark hearses. The boy was dressed in a white open-neck shirt, dark jacket and slacks, and brown snow boots. I paused in the doorway and waited until he glanced over at me. I felt as if I were staring at a younger version of my brother.

"Okay by you if I grab a seat?" I asked. "You and I need to go over a few things."

Chris hesitated. Then he nodded.

He had thick brown hair, long enough at the sides to cover his ears, and a handsome face topped by deep-set charcoal eyes.

I pulled back a chair and sat across the table from him. We sat in awkward silence for a few moments.

"I'm Tommy Rizzo," I said. "Your father was my brother."

"I know who you are."

"Did your dad tell you about me?"

Chris shook his head. "He only mentioned you to me one time. Who you are and what you did, I found on my own. I read the stories about you online. From back when you were a cop."

"What did your father tell you?" I asked. "That one time."

"I got into a fight with a kid from my class about two years ago," Chris said. "My dad was called in by the principal to come get me."

"Was your dad upset?"

"Pretty heated at first," Chris said. "He never liked to see me get into any kind of trouble, you know? Then, on the drive home, that's when he told me."

"Told you what?"

"He said you always looked out for him," Chris said. "Made sure no one picked on him at school or anywhere else. You had his back. He told me that the tough kids in school knew if they messed with my dad, then they'd have to deal with his brother."

"I didn't have to do that a lot," I said. "Your dad was pretty good at fending for himself."

I folded my hands on the tabletop and looked at Chris. "I can't guess how tough this has been for you. It's a lot to shove on anybody's plate, let alone a kid who's not even . . ."

"Fifteen," Chris said, rescuing me from having to pinpoint his age. "I'll be fifteen in three weeks."

"Right," I said. "Who's not even fifteen years old. It would be a tough go no matter the age. And I'm not here to make it any easier."

"So why are you here?" he asked. He didn't bother to hide the sudden rise in anger, his face turning a shade of red as he spoke, his hands on the table balled into fists. "Why bother to come see me now? In a place like this? After all these years of not wanting to see me at all?"

"To give you a choice," I said. If he was going to run hot, I was the one who needed to keep the temperature as close to normal as I could.

Chris stared at me, his eyes betraying a mix of unchecked emotion. The kid had some spine to him, a hard shell around what looked to be a vulnerable teenage interior. That was one other thing he had in common with my dead brother—an ability to control the rage that boiled constantly beneath the surface. "Okay" was all he said.

"You got about three years, give or take, before you're seen as an adult in the eyes of the court," I said. "You have no older siblings and your mom, from what little I know, was an only child. And your grandparents on both sides are long since gone. All that ring true?"

"So far," he said.

"And there don't seem to be any guardians lined up to care for you in the event a tragedy like this occurred."

"What makes you so sure?"

"Because then they would have been sitting here instead of me," I said.

Chris watched me but didn't say anything.

"In that case, you're staring at two choices, and neither is going to sound appealing. The first is the court takes you and puts you through the system. What that means is you'd live in foster homes for the next three and change years.

"Now, you might catch a piece of luck and land with a solid family somewhere that will take you in until you're eighteen. They would treat you right and make you as much a part of their family as they could. In my experience, the odds of that happening are not high."

"What's my other choice?" he asked. His voice was raw with tension.

I took a deep breath before I responded. I still wasn't sure I even wanted to put the offer out there. But deep down I knew I needed to give this kid an additional lifeline if he wanted to take a chance and reach for it. Whether I liked it or not, I had to embrace the one fact I could not evade—Chris was my nephew. I was his uncle. And each of us was the only blood family the other had.

"You can come and live with me," I said. "Now, before you react, know I'm about as crazy on the idea as you probably are. Your world has already been tossed upside down. Moving in with me will flip it on its side. You'd be going to a different school, living in an apartment instead of a house, a big city as opposed to a small town. And that's just the little I can skim off the surface. Dig deeper and the picture gets a lot murkier."

"If you were me, which of the two would you choose?"

I nodded, impressed with the question as well as the poise with which it was asked. "I'd probably go with me."

"Tell me why I would do something like that? Go live with some-one I don't know in a place I've never seen? We can pretend we're re-lated, but you're as much a stranger to me as any foster parent would be."

"I might not be the ideal guardian," I said. "In fact, I'd lay even money I would pretty much suck at it. But I'll treat you fair and never lie to you. That much I can guarantee. I doubt you can bank on getting anything close to that from a foster family. But then again, that's not a fact from my end. Just a hunch."

"How much time do I have before I have to let you know?" Chris asked.

"Is there anyone you can stay with for the next couple of days?" I asked. "Until after the funeral?"

Chris nodded. "Marie Andrews has been helping to make the ar-rangements. I can stay with her for a bit."

"Who is she?"

"Mrs. Andrews is our neighbor and my mom's best friend. She was with me right after I got the call about the accident."

"I'll talk to the funeral director on my way out," I said. "I don't want you to worry about any of the financials. I'll make sure that's taken care of."

"I wasn't worried," he said, an edge of anger cropping up again in his voice.

I reached over to my left and tore a sheet of white paper off a pad with the funeral home's design on the top. I pulled a pen from inside my jacket pocket and wrote down a phone number. "That's my cell," I said, handing it to Chris. "You need me, call. Anytime, day or night. Don't worry about waking me. I'm not much on sleeping."

Chris stared down at the sheet of paper, frowning. It looked as if he was wondering whether to ask me a question or keep it to himself. I thought I would bail him out and save him the trouble.

"No," I said. "I'm not coming to the funeral. Don't get me wrong.

There was a time I loved your dad. If I sit back and think about it, I probably always have. Probably loved him more than I ever wanted to admit to myself. But we both decided long ago to stay out of each other's lives. I don't think he would want me to change the deal now that he's no longer alive. And it will be easier on you, too. There will be no need for you to explain to friends of the family who the guy in the corner is and what he's doing there. Does that make sense?"

"I suppose," Chris said, still not meeting my eyes. "But you never did answer my question."

"What question?"

"When do I need to tell you my decision about staying with you?"

"Whenever you make it," I said.

I pushed my chair back and stood. I wasn't sure whether to put my hand out for him to shake, just walk out and leave, or reach for him and hold him in my arms.

"This might be the first and last time I see you," Chris said. "If I pass on your offer."

"Only if that's how you want it to be," I said.

"My name's Chris, by the way," he blurted out. "I wasn't sure if you knew that or not."

"I did," I said.

"And what do I call you?" Chris asked. "Uncle Tommy would sound lame. So is it just Tommy?"

"Tank," I said. "You can call me Tank. Everyone else does."

"So, maybe I'll see you after the funeral," Chris said. Once again, his strong voice gave a hint of a break.

I took a few steps closer to him and rested my right hand on his shoulder. "You're going to have a rough couple of days coming up," I said. "That's no lie and we both know it. But trust me—you'll come out of it and still be standing when it's over. You need to be strong, and I know you will."

"You sound pretty sure," Chris said. He wouldn't look at me, but tears started to well in his eyes. "Considering you don't know me or know anything about me. And, until today, didn't even care to know."

"I'm more than sure," I said. "I'm certain."

I lifted my hand off his shoulder and rubbed it gently across his cheek and looked at him for several moments. "Very certain," I said.

I turned and walked out of the room. I left my nephew alone in the emptiness and silence behind me. He was mere hours away from a wake and a funeral and a final goodbye to the parents he dearly loved.

And a final farewell to the only life he had ever known.

9.

TRAMONTI'S

THAT NIGHT

"YOU KNOW THERE'S ONLY ONE CHOICE FOR HIM, DON'T YOU?"
Connie asked me.

We were sitting next to each other at the bar, my elbows on the
wood, the last of the late-night crowd starting to make their way out
of the restaurant.

Connie was drinking a chilled glass of Pinot Grigio. I was working
on my second Fernet-Branca on the rocks with a lemon twist.

"I had to put both options out there," I said. "It wouldn't be fair
otherwise. To him or me."

Connie stayed silent for a few moments, nodding her goodbye to
an elderly man in an expensive handmade suit, an unlit cigar resting in
a corner of his mouth.

"You think you're ready for this?" she asked, turning back to face me.

"What makes you think I'm not?" I asked. I knew there was more
to her question than a simple yes-or-no answer.

"You're set in your ways, Tank," Connie said. Her voice was soft and
her tone matter-of-fact. "You love your routine. And you handle
change almost as poorly as I do."

I gulped down a mouthful of Fernet and looked at her. Connie was
as honest and to the point as she was smart and beautiful. There were

so many things about her that I loved, it was almost difficult to keep track, but that ability to cut to the point and not dance around it rested close to the top of my list.

"I do like my life the way it is, you're on the mark with that," I told her. "It took a while to get it to that place, as you know, and I'm not eager to see it tossed upside down. On the other hand, I don't see how I have much choice in the matter. I can't leave the kid hanging in the wind."

"Don't read me wrong, Tank," Connie said. "I'm not saying you shouldn't take Chris in to live with you. Far from it. In fact, I think it will be good to have him in your life. All I'm trying to do is point out you're going to have to change some of your ways. You're going to be raising a teenager. My guess would be a pretty angry teenager. A kid who knows about you from newspaper clippings. You can stroll down to the end of the bar and ask my father how easy a job that is for any man. What do you know about Chris other than the basics?"

"On the drive back from the funeral parlor, I put in a call to the next-door neighbor that's taking care of him for now," I said. "She told me Chris is a crime buff. He watches all the TV shows, reads all the books—fiction and non—and sees all the movies. He follows investigations in the newspapers and online. He even is part of an Internet group that selects a cold case and works to piece together the clues to try and solve it. I'm not sure what that makes him exactly, but he comes off as sharp and smart. Reminds me a lot of his father, actually."

Connie cradled her wineglass and nodded. "Yes, the brother we don't ever discuss," she said. "Never in life and not even now, in death."

"Some doors need to stay closed, Connie," I reminded her.

"But no matter how hard we try, some doors can't be kept closed forever, Tank," Connie said. "And that's something you should know as well as I do."

I sipped my Fernet, finding comfort in the harsh-tasting after-dinner drink I have enjoyed since I was a teenager visiting Italy for the first time. I sat there and took in the weight of Connie's words. I had managed for decades to stay clear of my blood relatives, to live within the confines of my own world. Early on I had made a decision and was determined to stick to it: ignore the past; never dwell on it or allow it to creep its way back into my life.

The incident that caused the rift between my brother and me would stay hidden away, never to be discussed or revealed. We made that one promise to each other and had kept it all these years. Over time, I had grown comfortable with the notion I would never have to dwell on it again.

But that is the horrible, unspoken truth about secrets that have been long buried. They have a way of creeping back into our lives. Maybe what they say about the past is true—you can never shake free of it or turn your back on it. The past will always find a way to raise its head.

In my case, my past came roaring back the moment my brother's SUV went over the railing of a bridge in Westchester County.

"If he does decide to come live with me, then we'll both have to adjust our lives a bit," I told Connie. I wanted desperately to steer the conversation away from a topic I had been up to now adept at never discussing.

"By *both* do you mean you and him or you and me?"

"You and me?" I said. "Why would it have any effect on us?"

Connie pushed back her barstool, stood, leaned over, and kissed me on the cheek. She draped her left arm casually across my shoulders. "Tank, you were a great cop." Her voice was low, her long hair covered half her face, and she couldn't have looked any sexier if she had tried. "And you're a good man. Aside from my dad, the best man to ever walk into my life. Everything you've tried to do, you've done well. And if I had to put money on the table and bet, I would put all I have that you'll do just as well with this new job you're about to begin as you've done with everything else in your life."

"What new job?" I asked, confused.

"If Chris says yes to your offer," Connie said, as she walked away from the bar, "which he most certainly will if he's got any sense at all, then, my darling Tank, you are going to be a dad. Like it or not. A dad. Or close enough to one to have to act the part."

I watched Connie approach the last departing customers to thank them and wish them a good night. I then turned back to the bar. I stared into my empty glass and knew with a sudden burst of finality that my life was, once again, never going to be the same.

10.

THE WINTHROP, WESTCHESTER COUNTY

TWO DAYS LATER

I SAT ACROSS FROM MY OLD PARTNER AND FILLED HIM IN ON my brother's accident and the chance I would soon be sharing my home with a teenager.

Pearl managed a smile and a chuckle and shook his head. "You are a lot of things, old friend. But for all the tea in China, I honest to God do not picture you as a Father of the Year candidate."

"To be clear, that would need to be Uncle of the Year candidate," I pointed out. "And trust me, it wasn't anywhere near my bucket list, either."

"Well, you might catch a bit of luck," Pearl said. "The kid can show some common sense and take a pass on your offer."

"It would be a mistake," I said. "I may not be a perfect fit, but I'll be better for him than any group or foster home the powers that be would place him in."

Pearl stared at me for a few moments. "No doubt on that," he finally said.

I missed seeing Pearl every day, working together, busting down doors and chasing leads. If I did have a brother in this world, it would not be the one being buried in a Westchester County cemetery. It would be the man sitting across from me in a wheelchair, fresh off yet another rehab workout.

It had been a long, painful journey for Pearl since his fall from the tenement fire escape. He sustained more broken bones than he had teeth, and his body had been damaged beyond repair. After a four-month stint in two hospitals and an assortment of rehab units, his doctors had recommended he be brought to the Winthrop Institute.

Here, the technicians worked with him on a daily basis, teaching him how to adjust to life in a wheelchair and with partial numbness in his left arm and a shattered right one. He would suffer from persistent headaches for the rest of his life, and no medication had been invented that could ease the constant pain he felt at the base of his neck.

I visited Pearl two, sometimes three times a week. The accident and the needed rehab had proved to be too much of a strain for his young wife. She moved back home to her family in Michigan three months after the tenement incident.

Retirement and disability did not suit either of us. We needed something that would allow us to keep our senses sharp and, in our own limited ways, still stay active in the only profession we had known. We were at a loss as to what that would be and how to achieve it, until an old friend, NYPD Chief of Detectives Ray Connors, came up with the perfect solution.

I reached down and picked up a thick yellow folder from the tiled floor. "How about we put my family situation aside for the time being?" I said. "I got handed another case the other day."

I saw Pearl's eyes brighten. "It's about time," he said. "I was starting to think the chief forgot about us, been so damn long since he tossed one our way."

The New York Police Department maintains a discretionary fund to hire retired detectives in good standing to work on cases it's too swamped to handle or that are deemed too cold to warrant attention. When I was first approached by Chief Connors, I agreed based on two conditions: I never would take more than one case at a time, and I would hire my own crew to help me solve it. The chief thought it through, then agreed. The money was better than good and I was left to my own devices. Chief Connors trusted me and asked only that the case be solved airtight and legal. What he didn't need to know, the chief didn't want to know.

I still consider Pearl my partner and I always will. I include him on any case that is handed to me. Pearl is an important member of my team and I count on his advice and counsel with every job I take.

"You know how it works with the department," I said with a shrug. "A case folder is filed and collects dust until the morning somebody decides to give it a second look before it gets tossed for good. The next thing you know, our bell gets rung and we're back in the ring."

"I was getting tired of reading crime novels instead of helping solve a crime. So, what did we catch today?"

"This one isn't so much cold as cool. Only been a few months. A home invasion that took a nasty turn. The break-in was at a non-doorman building on West Twenty-fifth Street, between Seventh and Eighth. Second floor. From the initial UF-sixty-ones, there were two on the job, physical descriptions on both."

"They question the two or are they in the wind?"

"They were brought in but had alibis that held up," I said. "At least long enough for them to be cut loose and pull a Houdini."

"How much damage did they do?"

"If I had to guess—which at this point is all we can do—they went in not expecting anyone at home. They do a quick smash-and-grab and then get the hell out of there."

"But instead?"

"There were two women in the apartment. One was asleep in a small back room. The other was stretched out on a yoga mat, buds in her ears, listening to music."

"So we're looking at rape as well as robbery," Pearl said.

I leaned over and rested the folder across his legs. "Rape, robbery, and attempted murder. The doers came in probably juiced on some mix of drugs and booze. Toss in the adrenaline rush from the break-in and add on two unexpected young ladies and you have yourself a blood-soaked situation. They did a heavyweight number on both women. They were in ICU close to ten days. They've been out now about two months, maybe longer. But based on what I read in the file they won't ever really fully recover. Physically maybe. But for sure not mentally."

"How come this got tossed your way?" Pearl asked. "A case like this in our day would be a priority one. Hell, a task force would be set up just to go after these two mopes."

I nodded. "I wondered about that myself. But if you look into it deeper, the answer will jump out. The two ladies don't come off squeaky clean. Both have multiple priors. Drugs and solicitation mostly."

"So that means it's okay to beat them, rape them, and rob them?" Pearl asked. "Same old, same old. Nothing ever changes in life except numbers."

"Look, Pearl," I said, "you know the score on cases like this well as I do. Vics with priors make for weak witnesses. Defense lawyers play up the lifestyle and play down the crime. If they're really good, they might even convince a jury the ladies invited the thieves into their apartment and are pissed they didn't cut them in on the action. It doesn't always play that way in court, but more often than not, the two dirtbags end up with a hung jury or a reduced sentence."

"And everybody's conviction rate takes a hit—from the cops who made the collar to the ADA unlucky enough to catch the case," Pearl said. "And nobody is all that eager to see a dent laid into their batting average."

"That's pretty much the long and the short of it," I agreed. "Minus a few interdepartmental turf arguments along the way."

"So tell me, then," Pearl said. The folder was open on his lap and he was scanning the pages. "What happened to turn this case from ice cold to scalding hot?"

"One of the young ladies was a runaway," I said. "Happened six, seven years ago. Her family didn't have a clue where she was or even if she was still alive. They searched for a couple of years and then they gave up the ghost, went on with the rest of their lives as best they could. And then fan meets shit when the young lady's wounds heal and she starts to get back some of her bearings. She tracks down one of the responding uniforms from that night and gives him the name of next of kin."

"And that puts an out-of-town family in the mix," Pearl said. "A mother and father who want answers as to the what and why. And bingo—the case comes back from the DOA file and falls into our laps."

"Better it be us than to have the parents walk off to talk to the first reporter who catches their eye," I said. "Rather than deal with a negative tabloid story, the chief can call it an active investigation, and the department will make sure the folks are kept informed on any progress that's made."

I sat back and folded my arms across my chest. "Read through the folder," I told Pearl. "Break it down and let me know what you think we'll need and who we need to connect with. I'll reach out to the rest of the team tomorrow."

"I can ring up the crew if you like," Pearl said. "I got nothing but time in between therapy sessions. It would seem to me at the moment you got more than enough weight on you."

"Are we back to talking about the kid again?"

"He's still the teenage elephant in the room," Pearl said. "Makes him awfully hard to ignore."

I stood and patted my friend on the shoulder. "Let the kid be my worry," I said. "You get busy on the case."

Pearl gazed up at me. "Anything you say, Papa. Anything you say."

"Not Papa," I said. "It's Uncle. And barely that."

11.

PELHAM MANOR, WESTCHESTER COUNTY

THREE DAYS LATER

CHRIS WAS STANDING ON THE EDGE OF A LAWN IN FRONT OF a red-brick three-story Colonial. He had a pearl-gray backpack slung across his right shoulder and a leather travel bag resting against his left leg. He was wearing a pair of dark jeans, a Philadelphia 76ers hoodie, and new Timberland boots. He had his head down against a swirling wind, and his hands were jammed inside his jacket pockets.

Chris had made his decision.

He had accepted my invitation to come live with me.

I still wasn't sure if he was ready for such a big change, and I also had serious doubts as to whether or not I was prepared for such a move. His call came in just as I was heading out for dinner last night. As soon as I heard the phone ring, I knew Chris had made up his mind and would be heading my way. We didn't speak for very long and I didn't say much from my end other than to tell him I would be by his house in the morning to pick him up.

A lot of what Connie had to say about this was true. I have known only one way to live my life and I had little interest in making any changes. As I eased up to the curb, I looked through the windshield at Chris and wondered if it was too soon for the realization that he was about to enter a new life to have hit him yet. I've been around enough to know the blow he took was not something that could easily be shaken away. In that respect, I decided it might be best to reach out and get him some help. Find someone he could talk to about whatever issues were concerning him, give him space and someone to trust to express any fears and doubts he might have.

Someone other than me.

Chris tossed the travel bag and backpack onto the backseat and then slid into the passenger side. He buckled his seatbelt and glanced at me. "You sure you want to try this?" he asked straight off. "I know you were the one to make the offer, but I don't want you to think this is something you have to do."

"I wouldn't have put it out there if I didn't mean it," I said.

I shifted the car into gear and pulled away from the curb. I glanced back at the house and spotted a woman wrapped in a housecoat standing behind a silk curtain, peering at the two of us. I wondered what, if anything, she made of our situation. A never-seen and seldom-if-ever-mentioned uncle picking up a nephew he hadn't met or known until a few days ago.

It didn't quite have that warm and fuzzy feel to it.

We drove in silence, the radio off, not sure exactly what to say to each other. "You hungry?" I finally asked. I had moved off the Hutch and veered onto the Cross County Parkway.

"Mrs. Andrews wanted to make me some scrambled eggs for breakfast," he said, shaking his head. "But I just had coffee and a slice of rye toast."

"You drink coffee?"

"Not usually," Chris said. "I couldn't sleep last night and I always heard coffee is supposed to help you get going in the morning. So I gave it a try."

"Did it work?"

"I'm pretty tired, so I would say it didn't," he said. He was staring out the passenger-side window. "And the answer to your question is, yes, I am hungry."

"We'll grab a bite soon as you get settled," I said. "I like to shop day-to-day, so if there's anything you like and want to have around on a regular basis, let me know."

"Why do you shop like that? You know, day-to-day? Why not get a week's worth of food? Day-to-day seems like a waste of time."

"Maybe," I said. "But my neighborhood has a great butcher, with the best meat and chicken in the city. Both raw and prepared foods. And if you like rotisserie chicken, you won't find better. The fish store, a bit farther down the street, is just as good, and the vegetable stand is as fresh as a cold shower. So, having all that gives me a chance to decide what I want to cook on that particular day. Then I stop by the top-tier wine store and match the wine to the food."

"So you shop and cook every day? Like one of those guys on the Food Channel?"

"Hardly ever," I said. "But I talk a good game, you have to admit."

"That leaves takeout," Chris said. "I'm not a big takeout fan. My mom and dad weren't, either."

"Not big on it myself," I told him. "I spent too many years as a cop grabbing meals on the run, eating out of cardboard trays. Most of the time, I eat at Tramonti's."

"I'm guessing it's an Italian restaurant," Chris said.

"A very good Italian restaurant," I said. "It's not far from my— our—home. The food and wine are top-shelf. The jazz music is old school, and the owners are people I've come to consider to be more than friends."

"Which makes them what?" he asked. "Family?"

"Something like that," I said.

Chris was on edge. Some of it I could write off as nerves. The rest was welled-up anger and resentment. The anger came out of the loss he had suffered. The resentment, without a doubt, was directed my way.

"You've lived your whole life in one place. A place where you know everyone and everyone knows you, right?" Chris asked.

"Yeah," I said. "That's right. It's not for everybody, I would imagine.

Most people I've come across can't wait to get away from the place where they were born. But it suits me. Maybe it's because I'm used to it. I really haven't known any other way."

"This new family you have," Chris said, "you like them better than the old family you had?"

The kid was coming straight at me, direct and not wasting much in the way of time. A teenager with a lot of questions and a just-below-the-surface anger that could jump out at any moment.

I took a deep breath. "Let's clear the air on a few things, you and me, okay?" I said.

He didn't answer. But then I didn't expect him to.

"How I felt about my parents and your father is my business, not yours," I continued. "We don't know each other well enough for either of us to go there. Maybe in time we will. But I don't see that coming our way anytime soon."

"I was just wondering," Chris said.

"Wondering what, exactly?"

"If my father was as invisible to your new family as he was to you."

"Even more so," I said evenly. "I never talked about him and they never asked. It was an agreement that existed between me and your father and that's where it stays. True then. Truer now."

"Then how are you going to explain me to them?" Chris asked. "You don't seem the type to adopt, and we know from family history you're not the big-brother type. So what are you going to tell them?"

"What I've always told them," I said. "The truth."

"The same goes for me?" he asked, not bothering to hide the bitterness.

"You're free to tell them whatever the hell you want to tell them. They're good people and they'll listen. And they're also smart enough to know not to nose in on other people's business."

We rode in silence for several more miles, letting the temperature in the car cool down a bit.

"Your mom and dad, did they lay down rules for you?" I asked as I snaked through Riverdale toward Manhattan.

"What kind of rules? You mean about homework or watching TV or hooking up?"

The last remark caught me off guard. "Wait a second," I said. "You go out on dates?" I wasn't exactly prepared to veer into a sexual arena with a kid I barely knew. A kid who would be living under my roof.

"I'm going to be fifteen," Chris said.

"Just so I'm clear, then, that's a no on the dating question?"

His cheeks flushed. "We went out as a group. Girls and boys together. To a movie or a ball game. Nothing serious."

"Why the interest in crime?" I asked. I was relieved I didn't have to deal with a teen looking to score with his latest squeeze and was more than eager to bring the subject back to more-comfortable terrain.

"I like solving things," Chris said. "How you put the pieces of a crime together. And if you miss just one, no matter how minor, then the criminal you're after wins. He gets away with the crime."

"It's as much luck and intuition as it is skill," I said. "And having contacts on the street is more valuable than you can imagine. As important as the science is and as crucial as it is to knock on every door—sometimes more times than the person on the other end would like—and follow up on every tip, no matter how off the mark, nine out of ten crimes never get solved, unless someone who knows something drops a dime on someone not expecting him to do so."

"We sometimes work on a famous case that's not been solved for decades," Chris said. "A cold case, you know."

"Yes," I said. "I've heard mention of those."

"Or we pick a case that has been solved," Chris said, "and study how the detectives broke it."

"Who is 'we'?"

"I'm a member of an Internet group, kids my age. Have been for about two years."

"A team of Sherlock Holmes wannabes in Nikes," I said.

"My dad wasn't keen on it," Chris said.

"Why do you suppose that is?" I asked. "Did he think you were going to become a cop like . . ."

"Like you?" Chris said. "That was part of it. He also thought it a waste of time."

"Your mom feel the same?"

"No," Chris said, sparking to the conversation for the first time since he got in the car. "My mom was into it. She loved watching the shows and reading the books. Her favorite was *Forensic Files*. Have you seen that?"

"I'm more a *Criminal Minds* guy," I said. "Especially the ones with Joe Mantegna."

I steered the SUV downtown, heading right into the Manhattan traffic I knew awaited us. I was relieved the conversation we were having had turned to areas of comfort to us. I was neither prepared nor willing to venture into deeper emotional terrain. That talk would happen in due time.

Ironically, I was prepared to discuss the death of his parents and help Chris come to terms with that sad fact. For better or worse, I've had many talks in my police life with too many grieving people to keep count of. So that arena, while unpleasant and distasteful, held, for me, a certain degree of understanding. What I was not prepared to discuss were the reasons why Jack and I had chosen to lead separate lives for such a long period of time. And why, as adults, we were complete strangers to one another.

12.

MIDTOWN MANHATTAN

"**D**O YOU MISS IT?" CHRIS ASKED.

I gave him a quick look. He had been quiet for nearly an hour, as lost in his confused and angry teenage thoughts as I had been in my darker ones, his eyes taking in the crowded streets and the drumbeat of noise that was one of the constants of big-city life.

"Miss what?" I asked. "Being a cop?"

"Yeah."

"There are moments. I see an RMP—a police car—or an unmarked zoom by, siren wailing, I take notice. I wonder what waits on the other end. I miss the rush of making a bust. But I don't break into tears whenever Springsteen's 'Glory Days' pops up on the radio. Being a cop was a huge part of my life for a number of years. And I loved it all— good and bad. But now I'm on to another part of my life. In many ways, it turned out better than my previous one."

"What didn't you like?"

"I was an odd fit," I said. "My partner, Pearl, was, too. We spent time together off the job but didn't pal around with other cops. Didn't drink in cop bars or play the beer-and-bowling circuit. We had our own interests."

"Like what?"

"I love jazz and can find a quartet playing in the city any night of the week. Pearl and me are big sports fans, and we went to a lot of games. I haunt museums. I love wine and travel. I read a lot. And I'm a huge movie and TV watcher. Toss in theater, opera, and hitting the gym every day and it totals out to a full life."

"Is that different from other cops?"

"I'd say yes," I answered. "But that's a guess since, as I said, I never spent much time with them. But here's where me and other cops part ways—I don't like telling war stories; I don't believe today's cops match up with cops I came out of the academy with; I prefer Brunello to a shot of Dewar's and a beer chaser; and I've never been married, which means I've never been divorced."

"And you don't have kids or a family," he said. "At least not a real family."

I was stopped at a light facing the Flatiron building at the intersection of 23rd and Broadway. I glanced at Chris. "Past tense on the kids," I said. "From the looks of it, I have one now. As to family, I believe you make your own, and I have. We may not be blood relatives, but we're there for each other when time and need arise. And it's more than I got from anyone in my family—other than your grandma and grandpa."

"Not even from Dad?" Chris's voice was full of anger again, and I reminded myself how much he was hurting. "You act as if he was a stranger instead of a brother. Which makes me feel less like a nephew than I already do."

"Don't go Hallmark on me," I said, then winced at the anger in my own voice. "There was a time, a long time, when your father and I were close. Then that came to an end and we weren't. It's no more complicated than that."

"You said you and these people you're so close to are always there for each other," Chris said. "If they need help, you'll be there for them, right?"

I nodded. It had started to rain. Heavy drops were blanketing the windshield. I flipped the wipers on.

"But I know there were times when my dad could have used some help, someone he loved to watch out for him. But when it came to him, when it came to covering for your brother, you were nowhere to be found." His tone was like a slap to the face.

"It was the way we wanted it," I said. "You may not like it, you may even hate the idea, but it didn't fall to you to decide. It rested between me and Jack."

"We didn't have family, either," Chris said. "Not even a pretend one like you have. We went away on holidays, different places each year. Dad used to say it beat sitting around a table waiting for a cousin you couldn't stand to bring up some bad business that happened years ago."

"He was on target with that," I said. "A holiday meal well worth the missing."

Chris was an interesting kid, I was deciding. He was neither shy about expressing his concerns nor the kind of chatterbox who makes you want to eat glass. He was exactly as he appeared—a sharp young man who had taken a hard knock and was trying to deal with it. But the anger that simmered below his skin was palpable, and I knew it could erupt at any moment. And when that valve was turned on, I might be the target in its destructive path.

"I don't know if I'll like living in the city," Chris said. "Or living with you."

"Give it time," I said. "It's natural to feel nervous about a new school, making new friends, living in a new place with someone you barely know."

"Mrs. Andrews said I don't have to start the new school until fall semester. They're too deep into spring semester and I would never catch up."

"She's right," I said. "I also thought it would be good to give you time to adjust before throwing you out there. Taking a break seemed like the best way to do that."

"I hate this." Chris was smearing the moisture on the window with his thumb, not looking at me. "I hate all of this. Taking a break isn't going to change that."

"If this is going to have any chance at all," I said, "you're going to have learn to come to terms with those feelings."

"And what if I can't?" Chris asked. "Or what if I don't want to? Then what?"

"If you felt like this, why did you choose me instead of rolling the dice on a foster home?"

"I didn't like either choice," Chris said. "But I thought I'd give living with you a chance."

"You call this giving it a chance?" I said. "You haven't said one nice thing about it since you got in the car."

"Do you still carry a gun?"

"Yes," I said, thrown by his change of subject. "Same one I had when I was on the job. Why?"

"My dad hated guns. He never would allow one in the house. My mom felt the same way."

"I hate guns, too," I said. "But it wasn't a gun that killed your parents. And don't worry. I don't have an arsenal in the basement. Just the one gun I've worn for nearly two decades."

"Can I go to Westchester and see some of my friends?" Chris asked.

"I suppose we can take a ride now and then. Time permitting."

"That's a nice way of telling me to forget that idea."

"I thought I didn't say no," I said. "But you hear what you want to hear."

"You told me everybody calls you Tank. Why is that?"

"It's a nickname that stuck," I said. "My father started calling me that when I was a kid. He said I always bulled my way through, no matter what. Before long, I was no longer Tommy, just Tank."

"Did he have a nickname for Dad, too?"

"He had a few for Jack," I said. "But Numbers was his favorite."

"Why Numbers?"

"Your father was into statistics. Name any sport and he could do a numerical breakdown of any player on any team. He had this amazing capacity for remembering stats, from the best guy on the team to the ones riding the pine."

"That helps explain why he became an accountant," Chris said.

"Maybe," I agreed. "Even though he would have made one hell of a general manager."

"You ever want to do something else?" Chris asked suddenly. "Other than being a cop? Or did you always want to put people in handcuffs?"

I ignored the sarcasm in his questions. "Everybody wants to be something other than what they turn out to be. More often than not, life leads you down one path or another. You either accept it or let it eat at you and turn you bitter."

"Is that a yes?"

"You can take that as a yes," I said.

I eased into a parking space in front of my brownstone. The rain was still coming down in a heavy pour. I pulled a set of keys out of my pocket and handed them to Chris. "Big one works the bottom lock," I said, nodding my head up the steps to the front door. "Take your gear to the second floor. Your room is in the back, on your left, facing the garden. If I'm not back in time for dinner, walk to Tramonti's. That's the restaurant on the corner. Tell the beautiful lady who will greet you who you are and she'll find you a seat. Order whatever you want. It goes on my tab."

"Where will you be?"

"Right now, heading to a crime scene. An old crime scene, so not likely I'll find much. If you need to reach me, you have my number."

Chris stepped out, then opened the rear door and pulled out his travel bag and backpack. He dumped them on the sidewalk and peered in through the open door. "You working on a case?"

"That's right," I answered. "I'm on a case and you have to go to your room, unpack, and get settled."

Chris slammed the passenger door closed. He picked up his bags and made his way up the brownstone steps to the front door. I waited for a minute until he unlocked the door and went inside, then shifted the car back into first gear and pulled out of the spot.

I slid a Sam Cooke CD into the slot and listened for a few moments to his melodic voice. I couldn't help thinking I'd never wanted kids or a family and yet here I now was—a real-life Uncle Buck.

"Maybe Pearl had it nailed right all along," I said to myself. "I must be crazy to be doing this."

13.

CHELSEA

THE NEXT DAY

SHE WAS TALL AND THIN AS A BLADE OF BROWN GRASS. HER face was bruised and her left eye was red and flecked with crust. Her right arm was in a cast up to her elbow, and her left hung loose by her side. She sat on the front stoop of the dilapidated walk-up, a black coat slung across her back. Her torn jeans hid the welts and cuts I knew were on her legs.

I figured her to be in her early twenties, if that, but she looked at least some half a dozen years older. She had on a New York Jets hoodie that was new the last time the team made the playoffs. Her long, dirty bleached-blond hair covered half her face.

Her name was Francine Jackson.

"There's been nobody coming around asking about what happened to us for the longest time," she said. She had a trace of backcountry Southern in her voice. "Now all of a sudden up pops you, ready to ask all sorts of questions. Why the interest? Why now?"

I leaned against the iron railing, across from Francine, not looking to crowd her. "I'm here because my partner and I just caught the case," I told her. "And just so you and me are clear from the get-go, the case was given to us. Me and him, we're not full-active anymore. We get tossed cases now and then."

"What's all that mean in English?"

"We're Tin Badges," I said. "Retired cops who get handed cases when the PD is on overload."

"Cases like mine?" she asked.

"Yeah," I said, nodding. "Pretty much."

"Cases that nobody gives a rat's balls about." Francine's voice was a mix of anger and resignation.

"Look, Francine," I said, "I can't and won't speak of those that stepped in this before me. But I never take a case unless I'm out to solve it. Same holds true for the crew I work with. You can believe that or toss it to the wind. And if I were sitting on your side of the stoop, I wouldn't be giving my words much weight. But it's the truth."

"You getting paid to work this case?"

"You work the streets," I said, "same as I used to. On different sides, maybe, but we work them nonetheless. And we both know out here, on these streets, 'free' died in the war."

She stayed silent for a few moments. She stared at an elderly man walking a playful white Lab across the street. The dog loved the small piles of dirty snow melting in the gutter. "How much of what went down do you know?"

"Read all the sixty-ones," I told her. "Those are reports written by the officers who responded to the call. That plus the witness statements and the crime-scene photos. So I covered what bases had already been covered. That's assuming you and your friend were on the up-and-up when you talked to the cops."

"You think we were lying to them?" she asked, turning to look up at me.

"I'm not saying you or anyone else lied," I answered. "But I have a feeling you didn't draw as full a picture as you could have. Am I off the mark about that?"

"You seem sharp enough to know what the two of us are, right?" she muttered, glancing away. "If so, then you know how cops feel about us."

"Some cops," I told her. "Not all."

"Maybe so, but I only meet the ones who feel the one way. They see us, they see nothing more than junkies and turn-around tramps. You can tell from the look in their eyes. And not one of those cops is going to bust a nut going on the hunt for the two who did this to us. They save their strength for uptown crime. Not for around here."

"I live downtown," I said. "Same as you and your friend."

Francine smiled bleakly. "If that be the case," she said, "might help explain why they tossed you this cold one."

THE FRONT DOOR TO the walk-up swung open and a heavyset man in a long-sleeve T and sweatpants stepped out. He had a shaved head and Rikers Island biceps he hadn't worked on for at least six months. He had an aluminum bat clutched in his right hand. He moved down three steps, his glow-in-the-dark sneakers untied and scuffed. He kept his legs apart and bounced the thick end of the bat up and down against the palm of his left hand. His dark eyes were moist, glistening with a sleepy sheen.

"You want to keep them legs the way you got them, you best move your white ass off this street," he said. His voice was slightly high-pitched, making the threat sound less menacing than he would have liked.

I glanced at him and smiled. "But I'm not finished talking to Francine yet," I said, my voice soft and calm.

"The bitch got nothing more to say to you," he said. "She shouldn't have said jack shit to start off. You got questions you want to ask, you're looking at the one you need to be running your mouth to."

"Back it up, Reggie," Francine said without looking back. "The guy's a cop. Well, sort of a cop."

"What the hell's that supposed to mean?" Reggie asked. "Sort of? Either he is a cop or he ain't one. Which is it?"

"He's been assigned to my case," she said. She looked at me through eyes that had seen more than their share of damage in a short span of time.

I ignored Reggie and kept my eyes on Francine. "What's he to you?" I asked her.

"He's not my pimp, if that's where your mind is taking you," she answered. "Reggie's a friend. Just that. Nothing more."

"He live here?"

She nodded. "Two floors above us."

"Why the hell are you two talking about me like I'm not even standing here?" Reggie shrilled. "You damn fool. You can just as easy be asking me what you been asking her."

"Sorry, Reggie," I said, looking up at him. "I didn't mean to hurt your feelings. But you see, I'm just curious. Francine here tells me you're a friend. And I believe her. The proof is there, right in your hand. You see a stranger talking to her, you take action. Reach for your bat, get up off your couch, turn off the Cartoon Network, and come down to protect her. Like a friend would."

"Damn right," Reggie said.

"But here comes the part where I'm a little confused," I told him. "If what I just said is true, and I believe it is, then why isn't your name— Reggie—on any of the police reports I read? Now, I know the uniforms talked to everyone who lives in this building in the days and nights after the incident. They even did a canvass of the neighborhood. Just in case anyone on the street heard or saw anything. You with me so far?"

Reggie nodded, his small eyes glittering with curiosity.

"So why is it," I asked, "that no one with the name of Reggie and fitting your description was ever talked to?"

"That can be explained," Reggie said. "If I decide to explain it."

"You mind if I take a crack at it first, Reggie?" I suggested. "I've been away from the job for a bit. It'll give me a chance to test how rusty I am. You good with me doing that?"

"Knock yourself out," Reggie said, flashing a gold-tooth smile. "Your dime. Your time."

I turned back to Francine. "You hungry?" I asked her.

"What do you think?"

"How about you, Reggie?" I asked. "Would you sit and break bread with me and Francine? Take this inside where we can get a few warm plates in front of us?"

"Depends," Reggie said. "You buying?"

I rested a hand across my chest and smiled. "Of course," I said. "I wouldn't think of letting you pay. Especially since those sweatpants you're wearing don't seem to have any pockets, which would make you a little light on cash."

"Okay then," Reggie said.

"One more thing before we go," I said to Reggie.

"And what would that be?"

"Leave the bat in the hallway," I said.

14.

FIVE-NAPKIN BURGER

MOMENTS LATER

THE THREE OF US SETTLED ON A QUIET TABLE NEAR THE FRONT window of the fast-food burger restaurant. The traffic flow on the avenue was filled with its usual blend of blue- and white-collar workers; teens walking home from school; homeless looking for a handout or a place to rest; shoppers; street crazies shouting their anger to the sky above; and tourists taking it all in.

Reggie had ordered two double cheeseburgers with the works, French fries and sweet-potato fries, and two large sodas. Francine kept to a simple cheeseburger, fries, and a Coke. I followed her lead.

"Let's pick it up from where we left it," I said.

"What's taking them so long?" Reggie complained. "We should have gone to the Golden Arches. They never make you wait."

"Stay focused, Reggie," I said. "You'll get your food."

"You wanted to know why the police never talked to Reggie," Francine said. "And, truth be told, I wouldn't mind knowing the why to that myself."

A waitress in a bright-red outfit and a slight smile handed over our food. Reggie reached for it as if he had spent the last three weeks as a contestant on *Survivor*. He picked up his first large cheeseburger and took a bite that erased half of what he was holding.

"You chew, Reggie," I said. "And I'll talk. That work for you?"

He nodded, reaching for a fistful of fries.

"I'm going to rule out the cops missed talking to you because you were on vacation," I told him. "I'd lay even money you've never even been on one and the only time you venture more than a mile from your couch is to do a mule run for a local dealer, finish a spin in lockup, or walk to where you can leave with a large bucket of the Colonel's finest. How am I doing so far?"

Francine answered for Reggie. "You read him right on all three," she told me. "As you can see, Reggie likes to eat, and you can guess he doesn't much care for work. Running for dealers is the easiest way man like him knows to get his hands on fast cash."

"What?" Reggie sputtered. "You my accountant now? You don't know my business. You don't know the half of what I do. Let's just leave it at that."

"So what I guessed was wrong?" I asked.

"You ex-cop, so no harm in filling in your blanks," Reggie said. "Not like you can bust my ass or nothing. Am I right?"

"More or less," I said.

"Yeah, I run for some of the locals," he said. "But, shit, you arrest me, you'd have to arrest half this neighborhood for doing the same damn thing. But as far as me being a user? No way, Dirty Harry. I been clean going on three years. And I am not at all eager to ride the white horse ever again."

"What about prison?" I asked. "Dollars to donuts, you have done some time. Nothing major, I'm guessing. Most likely the island rather than upstate."

"They nailed me on a couple of B&E's when I was a kid. Went off to juvie a few times. Then got in for a while with that hard-ass crew from East Harlem. They were big players in the drug business for about a year or so."

"The Colt Forty-fives," I said.

"That's them. Crazy bunch of brothers. But they paid well. With green and with white powder."

"What'd you get pinched for?"

"Was set up by one of them suckers," Reggie said. "Got left holding a couple of loads of hot-and-heavy weapons. Had enough cash on hand back then to pay me a good lawyer. They gave me eighteen months, state time. Most of which I done on Rikers."

"So, comes the night of the break-in at Francine's apartment," I said. "By which time you are clean as clean can be. You can pass the wet-ass test with flying colors. Correct?"

Reggie grabbed another handful of French fries, smiled, and nodded. "You can move on to the Double Jeopardy round," he said.

"Well, I figure you for one of two possibles," I said. "You either set up the break-in, not knowing the two doers were going to lose their shit, or—wait for it—you turned your back and stayed quiet when you heard what was going on two floors below. Didn't know the players and didn't want any part of their game. Friends or no friends. Now tell me, Reggie: Did I get anywhere near the bull's-eye?"

Francine stared hard at Reggie. She was angry now, the idea he might have been in league with her attackers or ignored the commotion not dawning on her until this moment. It was a gamble on my part, but one I thought worth taking. A guy like Reggie will do anything for easy money, and setting up his downstairs neighbors for a quick score would not be out of the question. He may not have known it would go as far as it did, but if it had ended at robbery, it wouldn't have kept him up at night.

I hadn't heard a real reason for him to be in the wind when the cops showed up. And then again, when he spotted me talking to Francine, he could have easily stayed silent, picked up what was said and what wasn't from her later in the day. Instead, he made a show of coming down, holding the bat, looking to put a scare in me. So for the moment, the jury was still out on Reggie.

"Answer him, Reggie." Francine was angry, her face flushed, her hands trembling. "Did you help set it up? Talk truth to me. I can always tell when you're lying your fat ass off."

Reggie had his large back against the cold front window. "C'mon,

Francine," he said. "You gonna listen to this rent-a-badge fool? He's trying to turn you against me. That's what cops do. If I wanted to take what's worth taking from you or Gloria, I wouldn't need to dial anybody else's digits. I would do the deed my own self."

"Then where were you that night, Reggie?" My body language had shifted up a gear from relaxed. "Folks in the building heard noise and a couple of screams. But not you. Then come the sirens and you still do a silent run. RMPs roll up and they make enough noise to rattle the dead. But you still want me to believe you were cuddled up on your couch, eyes half closed, watching *John Wick* for the twelfth time."

"It happens to be the damn truth," Reggie insisted. "I drink more than my fair share, and when I fall out, I am out. Ask anyone knows me! Shit, even Francine will set you straight on that count."

"He's up front with that," Francine told me. "There are guys who when they get too much in them go looking for a woman or a fight. Not Reggie here. He gets a load on, he looks for a bed to rest his ass."

"How's your friend Gloria doing?" I asked Francine.

"Not good as me, and I'm not doing that great. She got it pretty bad. They worked her a lot harder than they did me."

"Why do you think that was?"

She shrugged. "You can't figure what makes crazy do what crazy does. Maybe they liked the way she looked better, or maybe she gave them some lip and they didn't want to hear that. Either way, reason why don't matter all that much, does it?"

"You never know what matters on a case until you know," I said. "You have an address for Gloria? Or a phone number?"

"I can give you both," she said. "She's back home living with her folks. At least for now. But talking to her won't do you much good."

"Why is that?"

"Gloria barely talks to me the times I call," Francine said. "I doubt she'd be eager to run her mouth off with you on the other end."

"No harm in giving it a shot," I said. "Maybe I'll catch her on a good day. Either way, I'll be back to you soon as I have a few more details." I handed Francine a pad and a pen and watched as she wrote down an address and a phone number. "By then I should have my team in place and we'll work on finding these two guys."

"What, you some sort of Super Dick?" Reggie asked. "What makes you think you'll be able to target the duo when all those other cops ended up doing jack shit?"

I pushed back my chair and stood. "Let that be my worry, Reggie," I said. "You just ease up on your drinking and keep an eye on Francine. You think you can get it together enough to handle that?"

"Probably," Reggie said. "But what comes back to me in return for my good deed?"

I pulled a twenty and two fives from my pants pocket and left it on the table.

"Well, let's see," I said. "I would bet your face is out on some outstanding warrant or parole violation. But if I'm wrong on that front, I'll figure out a probable cause and get a search warrant to turn your upside-down place upside down. My odds would be better than good I'll come away with something that should get you tossed back into the system."

"And that's my reward?"

I started heading out of the restaurant. "I'll toss in a case of whatever beer it is you like to drink."

"None of that foreign shit," Reggie said. "I don't pop the lid if it ain't U.S.A.-made."

I waved goodbye to Francine. I started walking toward my car, a chilly wind shooting up the avenue, debris swirling in all directions. On the far corner of 26th Street, a chunky middle-aged man plugged an electric guitar into a small black speaker and began to play and sing a lame version of "I Shot the Sheriff."

Not a single person in the mad rush of human traffic walking past took notice.

15.

THE BROWNSTONE

LATER THAT DAY

WE SAT IN MY LIVING ROOM. POLICE REPORTS AND CRIME-SCENE photos were spread across the wine-barrel coffee table that centered the large space, with floor-to-ceiling windows facing a garden below. After I left the police department, I worked the first case I was handed alone. Pearl did logistics and we brainstormed together, but he was no longer able to work the streets with me. I managed to solve it—an elderly woman from Hell's Kitchen killed by a too-greedy landlord— but it took longer than it needed to and I had to call in too many favors to make me feel comfortable.

After I wrapped up that case, I went to see the chief of detectives. I knew he would be pleased I took a murder off his cold-case file, and I also knew he would be eager to hand over a second case for me and Pearl to work on. The chief—Ray Connors—is a man I've known since I was in uniform walking a beat out of an East Harlem precinct.

At the time, Ray was a rising star in the department. He led an undercover unit that found itself going up against the top-tier drug crews of the day. I was still doing my best to get through a twelve-hour shift without getting killed.

Back in those years, we were allowed to take two-hour naps during work hours. In cop lingo, it was known as "cooping." Most cops I knew would take their regulated snooze in an RMP. My first six months on the job, instead of cooping I would continue to patrol the streets, downing three extra cups of coffee to keep my energy up.

Then a man named Herm Williams approached me one night with an interesting offer.

By the time I met Herm, he was in his late seventies and slow-walked using a thick wooden cane. He always had a lit cigar curled between the fingers of his free hand. But back in his friskier days, Herm had been a top-tier trumpet player and worked the club circuit, playing with some of the great swing bands of his time—including the legendary Thundering Herd of Woody Herman. Herm had also played for years in a band fronted by the drummer Chick Webb, who was, with the possible exception of Gene Krupa, the best stick man ever to sit behind a set.

Unlike many in his profession, Herm didn't drink or drug his money away. Instead, he saved enough to open a bar on 125th Street and Lenox Avenue. It was an old-school saloon, where the beer was served ice cold and the jazz delivered hot and spicy. As a young cop, I loved going into Herm's at the end of my shift. I would sit at the wood bar, polished so shiny you could look down and see your reflection. I went in less for a cold one and more to hear old-timers tell their stories of traveling the country with bands and musicians I had read about in books and magazines.

The neighborhood was rough and tumble back then, not yet gentri-fied as it is today. Herm's place had been broken into four times in the year before I came to know him, and he had grown weary of filling out civilian complaints, talking to one cop after another and never seeing anyone dragged away in cuffs. So Herm, wise old man that he was, had an idea.

"They tell me you don't coop like the other blues do," he said to me one night. We were sitting in a corner of his bar, far away from the regulars, at a small table near the fireplace he never used. "That true?"

"True," I said.

"That because you the kind of man that doesn't need much sleep or because you hate the idea of being locked inside a police car as much as the next guy?"

"You ever been inside a cop car?"

"No, can't say I have," Herm said. "But I can imagine."

"Even the cleanest ones have that smell," I said. "A smell that only years of old coffee containers, sandwich wrappers, and even socks can give a car. Not for me. No, thanks."

"Can't say I blame you," Herm said, with a chuckle. "But none of those issues would cause you grief if you cooped here in my bar, now, would they?"

"You serious?"

"As serious as a bullet wound. We would be doing each other a favor. For me, having a cop coop in my bar might cut down on, if not eliminate, any more of those pain-in-the-ass break-ins. And for you, you get a couple hours of shut-eye in a clean place. At least a lot cleaner than any of them squad cars you guys roll up in."

I took a quick look around. There were no booths. Only a few tables and the long bar running pretty much the length of the place. And a small stage where Herm and his friends would jam on most nights. "Where would I sleep?" I asked.

"There's no room in the back, if that's where your mind is going," he said. "Got me a tiny office, but no couch or anything like that. But that bar gets polished up nice and clean every night after closing time. And it's as comfortable as it looks. I've slept on it many a time myself."

"You want me to coop on the bar?"

"That's what I'm offering," Herm said. "Up by the register near the front door would be the best place. You can use your hat as a pillow. Toss off your shoes and take your nap. I'll even leave a blanket for you on chilly nights."

I thought about it for a few minutes, staring down at my still-chilled bottle of beer. "When can I start?" I said.

THE FIRST THREE WEEKS went off without a hitch. The bar was warm and cozy and I got some much-needed rest. And Herm had what he felt he needed—a cop keeping watch on his beloved bar.

Then, one night, I was just past an hour into my coop. I was sound asleep, my head resting on the back of my police hat, a hand-knitted quilt covering my legs and feet. I had left my shoes and wallet under one of the stools but had kept on my gun belt and holstered weapon. It was closing in on four in the morning, still pitch dark, the street outside as silent as an abandoned house. Then I heard some rustling near my head, by the cash register. I opened my eyes but didn't move a finger. I heard the register ring go off and the bottom drawer slide open. I tried to move my right hand to my gun, but it was numb from an hour of resting on its side. Quietly, I moved my left hand across my body, and even more quietly, I reached for my weapon.

In one swift move, I pulled my gun, jumped to my knees, and aimed it toward the register. The thief was young, probably around the same age I was, and most likely as freaked and scared as I was. "Put your hands in the air," I shouted. "High as you can get them. Do it *now!*"

The frightened thief did as he was told, dropping handfuls of cash as he did. "Where the fuck did you come from?" was all he managed to stammer.

"Move away from the register and face the window," I said.

I slid down from the bar, reached for my cuffs, and grabbed one of his hands. Soon as I had him cuffed, I walked him to the front of the bar. "Don't move," I told him. "I need to put my shoes on."

"Man, what kind of a fuckin' cop are you?" he asked, now as bewildered as he was scared.

"I was good enough to catch you in the act, wasn't I?"

"You got lucky, is all. Sleeping off a drunk on the bar until I waltz in. This is some crazy shit, let me tell you."

"Maybe so," I agreed. "But catch you I did and under arrest you are."

"There is no way this shit will hold up in court," the thief sneered, losing some of the fear and picking up a hint of his street bravado. "My lawyer will be owning your ass."

I had to admit to myself that the thief had a valid point. I could not very well go on the stand when his trial turn came up and under oath tell a judge and jury that I made the bust because the guy was dumb enough to wake me from my nap. Cooping, while the accepted norm at the time, was not official police department policy. Not even close.

I took him into the precinct and had him booked. I managed to write my 61 in a way that overlooked the asleep-on-the-bar scenario. All that was needed to sustain the bust was the clear and unassailable fact that I broke up a robbery in progress.

I was half-hoping he would plead guilty to a lesser charge and walk away with at most a year at the Tombs. Trouble was the thief—whose name was Ralph Jenkins—had a yellow sheet that ran longer than a Stephen King novel. And all before he was twenty-four years old.

So off to trial we went, and I could tell that his lawyer—a court-room agitator name of Wendell P. Garrison—had been properly primed by his client. I was called to the stand. The case was essentially similar to a Western standoff—my word against Ralph's. I needed to make it work and still not commit perjury on the stand.

The assistant district attorney was a sharp young lawyer named Maria Martinez. She was street-smart and I had been honest with her from the get-go. During her questioning of me, she went the Joe Friday route—just the facts and nothing but. The guy was robbing the place. I spotted him and I arrested him.

Then Mr. Garrison got to his feet and walked toward the witness stand, wearing his smartest-looking Robert Hall suit. He must have owned at least three dozen of them. The beat cops who had gone up against him in court always said, "Robert tosses them out and Garrison hauls them in."

"How did you know my client was in the bar, Officer Rizzo?" he asked.

"I saw him at the register, taking out the cash," I said. "Since I knew the owner—and your client wasn't him—I could only surmise there was a robbery in progress. So I moved in and made the arrest."

"And where were you that you could see the register so clearly at such a late hour?"

"I was in the bar," I said. "The owner is a friend and he gave me a key to go in and check on his place while on my beat. I had access and permission to be there. Your client had neither."

"The truth is, Officer Rizzo, that the reason and the only reason you were able to arrest my client was because of the simple fact you were sound asleep on the bar, is that not correct?"

That got the attention of the judge. The guy was old school and sharp. He'd grown up in the projects and had his share of tussles as a teenager before he found the law. He had worked both as an ADA and as a defense attorney. He had been on the bench for more than twenty years.

"Hold the damn line a minute," he said from his perch. "Did I hear what I just thought I heard? That Officer Rizzo here was asleep *on* the bar?"

"Yes, your honor," Garrison said. "Sound asleep until he was roused awake by my client."

"Just so I have it clear in my head," the judge said, "you're telling me and the jurors—let's not forget that they're sitting right over there and hearing every word you say—that your client was indeed robbing the bar?"

Garrison hesitated and realized he had just slipped off the ledge he was trying to walk on. "Well, not exactly, your honor," he stammered.

"That's what I heard," the judge said. "According to you, if your client hadn't been in the bar to rob the place, Officer Rizzo might still be snoring on top of the wood. If that isn't a version of your client's guilt, then I don't know what is."

Garrison stared at the judge in silence for several moments and then glared at me. The starched collar on his white button-down shirt was starting to bend to the weight of the sweat soaking into it.

"You may continue with your questioning of Officer Rizzo," the judge ordered Garrison. "Though, to be frank, I am of the opinion that you have done more than enough damage for one morning. But then, it's your funeral."

"I have no further questions at this time, your honor," Garrison said. He turned and walked slowly back to the defense table, confronted by an angry and confused client.

The judge looked over at me and nodded. "You're dismissed, Officer Rizzo," he said.

As I made my way off the stand, I saw one of the court officers approach the bench. I overheard the judge say to him, "You believe the shit that sucker was trying to sell? A cop asleep on a bar? Bad enough they come up with this bullshit, but then they expect us to believe it?"

"I hear you, your honor," the court officer replied, smiling. "There is nothing they won't say to save their client's ass."

"Amen to that," the judge said.

16.

THE BROWNSTONE

MOMENTS LATER

OPENED THREE BOTTLES OF WINE AS MY TEAM AND THE CHIEF made themselves at home in my living room. The team was more interested in my expensive wine, cold beers, and the case that had been handed down than they were in hearing the chief and me talk about the old days.

I had assembled a pretty eclectic group.

Bruno Madison crouched in to my left, his massive frame sinking into a brown leather couch. He was in his early thirties and one of the bartenders at Tramonti's. A former heavyweight boxer who went the distance with two title holders, he worked at keeping himself in shape and was adept at controlling any trouble that might happen with one drink too many at the restaurant bar. He was, like many boxers, soft-spoken and had a generous heart. Three years back, Bruno took over a deli that couldn't keep up with the rising rents of the area and turned it into a boxing club for neighborhood kids. Bruno was as good with a dollar as he had been with his hands, plus, between take-home and tips, he earned a good salary working the bar. He was a shrewd investor and was always leaving me and Carmine business articles he had clipped from a newspaper or a magazine. "You know how most ex-fighters hear bells going off in their head as they get older?" Carmine once said to me. "Not Bruno. The only bell he hears is the one that opens the stock market in the morning."

Bruno was the muscle of my crew. He also helped me do my tax returns.

Carl Elliot sat on the other end of the couch from Bruno. I'm not sure about his exact age, but I would bet my last dollar he's no older than twenty-five. I didn't do background checks on my team. Their word was good enough for me.

Carl earns his money during the day by playing guitar in various places around the city, usually not straying far from the neighborhood. On his best day, he might pull in twelve dollars, fifteen if the streets are crowded with tourists and he's playing songs other than that dreary folk music he prefers. From his street music, Carl takes in enough to keep his thin-as-a-rail body filled with enough food to get him through a day. But it's how he spends his nights that first got my attention. Soon as Carmine got wind I was going to be working on occasional cold cases for the PD, he directed me toward Carl. "You're going to be under the radar," he told me. "And chief of d's or no chief of d's, shit hits the fan, he's not going to take the hit on his own. Besides, he can only hand you the case and the files. He can't feed you what you're going to need to break it. And that's where this kid Carl can come in handy."

He has an easy smile, thick long brown hair, and two butterfly tattoos, one on each arm. His parents divorced when he was in grade school, and he learned from the earliest age to fend for himself. He lives in a tiny basement apartment on the Lower East Side yet always seems to have room for any neighborhood stray that catches his eye, especially lost or abandoned dogs.

Carl's a fence. He moves everything from the knockoff designer bags and gloves you see on almost every street corner in Midtown to high-value jewelry and cars. Truth is, there isn't anything Carl can't get if you give him enough heads-up time.

He's the team's wrangler. What we need, he gets. All I have asked of him is that he keeps what he does on his own time his own business. With me, he needs to keep it as much on the up-and-up as is possible.

Joey Scalini poured himself a glass of Brunello and sat on the recliner, giving me an easy smile and shaking hands with the chief. Joey is twenty-one, with a killer smile and cobalt-blue eyes and a charming manner. He keeps his black hair short and is always dressed in a long-sleeve T-shirt and jeans topped by a black leather jacket when the weather warrants it.

He works for a mom-and-pop electronics outfit on Sixth Avenue in the Twenties. He's their all-important go-to repair guy, able to fix anything from an iPhone to a laptop to a 55-inch smart TV. Joey has been offered high-paying jobs from a number of big tech companies, since young guys with his skill set are hard to find and harder to keep. But he likes working local and small, and besides, he's not a guy who cares that much about making big money. He just loves playing with the equipment and figuring out how to fix it and, for my purposes, how to break into it.

Joey's my tech guy. He can crack any alarm, key into any high-end system, and break codes on any computer you put in front of him.

Alexandra Morrasa is the last member of my squad of Untouchables and the only one with whom I had a prior history, and not the kind you're thinking. Don't get me wrong, she's drop-to-the-knees gorgeous, which comes in handy with the work she does. She has curly brown hair, wears rings on every finger, and has a silver figure of a wolf's head hanging around her neck. Alexandra runs numbers out of a psychic parlor in Chelsea, one of those shady holes-in-the-wall so many of us walk past and never take note of. She's Romanian by blood and claims to be full gypsy. She has a loyal following who march down the steps of her psychic place and pony up twenty bucks to watch her in action, holding their breath to hear what the future holds.

When I was a kid, my neighborhood had the Italian equivalent of Alexandra. The locals called her the Strega—"witch" in Italian. They trusted her more than any doctor, and shrinks were not even in their vocabulary. The Strega had answers for everything—from a cure for a simple headache to who it was that might have fingered your cousin Bobby and led to his three-to-five-year prison sentence.

Alexandra has ears everywhere and better intel than anyone at the NYPD. She came on my radar when me and Pearl were working a double homicide out of Washington Heights. It was our first year as gold-shield detectives, and a street stoolie tossed us her name and said she could ID the shooters. We drove down to see her, and before we could ask a question Alexandra told us she didn't know who the real killer was. But what she did know was we were looking in all the wrong places.

"Just because the murder happened in a poor area," she told us, "does not mean the shooter is from that area. Or, for that matter, is poor himself. I would look in a better zip code for my killer."

"That's all you got?" I asked.

"I'm not the one with the gold shield," she shot back with a smile. She had the most beautiful charcoal-colored eyes I had ever seen on a woman. "All I have is a bowl and a candle. So, yes, Detective, that's all I have. The rest I leave to you."

On a hunch, we took her advice and worked the case from a different angle. Turned out Alexandra was right. The killer was a hedge-fund guy who would hit Washington Heights looking to score cheap action and cheaper drugs. He had deep pockets, which meant a seven-digit law firm backing his play. On top of that, he had worked out a pretty solid alibi, one he and his lawyers thought would hold up regardless of how many people from the Heights pointed to him as the doer.

"Give it a little time to percolate," I said to Pearl. We kept as close an eye on him as was considered legal and monitored outgoing and incoming calls from his office, his cell, and his home. "This guy has got himself not one but two addictions—he likes drugs and he likes his sex on the rough side. Sooner than later one of those itches has got to be scratched."

"Even if he reaches out for both a hooker and a needle," Pearl said, "it doesn't help shake his alibi."

"You mean where the dutiful wife and the two devoted kids swear he was home making his weekly meatloaf and mashed-potato dinner?" I said.

"That would be the one," Pearl said. "The three of them seemed pretty lockjaw solid on having dinner with our guy."

"The wife will do an IHOP soon as she gets a close-up look at her dear hubby hanging upside down with a red ball jammed in his mouth and a black baton up his ass, all courtesy of his favorite five-hundred-dollar whip-ass mama."

Pearl smiled. "So, once he makes his move," he said, "we ask the wife if she would be kind enough to take a ride with us. Walk her right into the room and show her the kind of man she really married."

"She already knows the kind of man she married," I said. "She's just never seen it with her own eyes."

"What about the two kids?"

"Mom flips, they'll follow right along. No worries there."

"You think he'll be that stupid?" Pearl asked. "Smart guy like him knows the hard heat is on. Must have been told a hundred times by his lawyers to stay away from hookers, heroin, and the Heights. And a double-murder rap hanging over his head to boot. But despite all that, he's going to make a move anyway, knowing it could jack him up for the rest of his life?"

"They are what they are, Pearl. They can't change it. Oh, he'll be a good boy for a couple of weeks, maybe even a month. But he will not be able to hold out. He'll make a play and figure he'll get away with it. All we got to do is be there when he does."

He did and we were and, thanks to the tip from Alexandra, me and Pearl had a page-one tabloid arrest to add to our résumés.

Alexandra is the eyes and ears of my little group, our very own "Page Six" gossip go-to. If something that needs to be heard is said somewhere in this city, then somehow and someway the info finds its way into her little parlor.

CHIEF CONNORS SPREAD OUT the sheets from the case folder. Next to them he rested a stack of crime-scene photos and a legal pad that had the names and rap sheets of what are now termed "persons of interest." I rested a landline on a coffee table and punched in Pearl's number. Once I had him, I put him on speaker, then sat back and handed the room over to the chief.

"Two suspects—Leon Anderson and Rafael Puig—were brought in for questioning," the chief began. "They had, as you can see from the files, thick rap sheets. They also, unfortunately for us, had an alibi that held up."

"Who fingered them initially?" I asked.

"One of the tenants in the building," the chief said. "She said she heard loud noise coming out of the apartment below her, opened her door, and caught a glimpse of two men. Both Anderson and Puig fit the description she gave us."

"Somebody reached out to the witness?" Pearl asked.

"If I had to bet, I would say yes," the chief said. "Either way, she suddenly wasn't sure who it was she saw that night. It was dark, hallway was poorly lit, and she had been having eye trouble the past couple of months."

"Plus, they had an alibi," Bruno said.

The chief nodded. "Not exactly a model citizen, but an alibi nonetheless. Claims the two were with him the entire night, clubbing and hanging out at his place. He held up under questioning and we were left with no choice but to cut the suspects loose. You'll find what you need to know about their alibi in the file."

"He a loner or is he hooked up with any crew?" I asked.

"A little bit of both," the chief said. "Last few months he's been on the payroll of a high-end dealer working out of Washington Heights.

My guess is you look hard enough and you'll find his prints all over this case."

"What about the two suspects?" Joey asked. "Maybe Tank can give them a second look."

"Wish it were that easy," the chief said. "They're in the wind and have been since the night they were released from custody."

"They have out-of-town connections?" Pearl asked. "Family or friends they can bunk with till the heat burns off?"

The chief shook his head. "Nothing like that," he said. "We checked and double-checked."

"In other words, it would be a major waste of our time if we went out looking to talk to them," I said.

"Pretty much," the chief said. "Whoever sent them in to do the job didn't want to run the risk of having them talk about it. Not to us. Not to anyone."

"That leaves the alibi witness and the dealer from the Heights," I said. "We start our work from there."

"This is no easy case I'm handing you," the chief said. "This dealer has a wide reach, and he'll use everything he has to keep the money and the drugs flowing in his direction."

"Sounds like a ripe time to ask for a raise," Bruno said, smiling up at the chief.

"It would be," Ray Connors said. "If I had extra money to give you."

"The detectives assigned the case didn't move on it too deep," I said. "Is that because they weren't any good or they just didn't give a shit?"

"A little bit of both, Tank," Ray answered. "And I figured you might want to talk to them, but frankly I would prefer you didn't."

"Any particular reason why?" Pearl asked through the speaker.

"You already know everything they know," Ray said. "But more than that, I don't want them to know I have people back on the case. That clear enough for everybody?"

"Clear enough," I said.

"Same as always," the chief said. "You'll have everything you need from me, and you only deal with me. There's an envelope under the folder with half your fee. The other half you get once you crack the case. As far as expenses, spend what needs to be spent. And anything I don't need to know, I don't want to know."

"I could use a new computer," Carl said.

"How'd you get your last one?" I asked.

"I found it at the service entrance to the Apple Store," Carl said with a grin.

"This time use the front entrance," I said. "And bring a credit card."

Bruno sat up and nudged me, nodding toward the entrance to the living room. "Looks like we got ourselves some company," he said.

I glanced up and saw Chris standing in the entryway. He had his hands at his side and was studying the faces in the room. My crew stared back at him.

"And who might this be?" Carl asked.

Chris answered before I could. "My name's Chris," he said. "I live here now."

17.

TRAMONTI'S

THAT SAME DAY

CARMINE EASED ASIDE HIS DESSERT PLATE AND REACHED FOR a hot cup of double espresso. Connie sat across from him, nursing her way through her first glass of an Oregon Pinot Noir.

"You think the two of you are ready for the big change?" Carmine asked. He was a tough man, but when with his daughter or his late wife, he always spoke in as warm a manner as he could muster. At the same time, he never coddled either one or dodged uncomfortable discussions. He was out of the old school, and men like him knew only one way to confront an issue or a problem, and that was head-on.

"What big change?" Connie asked.

"You've never played dumb on me before, so don't go starting now," he told her. "The kid. His nephew. The one who's living with him. The clouds starting to part yet?"

"Oh, that big change," Connie said, smiling at him. "It was unexpected, I'll grant you. And Tank's going to have to make adjustments to the way he lives, that's for sure. But I'm confident he's as aware of that as you seem to be."

"Not only him, sweetheart," Carmine reminded her. "You're going to have to make some adjustments yourself. At least if you both want to keep this thing you got between you going."

"What are your concerns?" Connie asked. She took a small sip of her wine and glanced over at a table for four that was growing louder with each drink.

"You and Tank are a lot alike," her father said. "In many ways, you always were. Even as kids. You're both independent, like your space, and like the life you've made for yourself."

"No speed bumps yet," Connie said. "But I have little doubt you'll get to one eventually."

"Look, for a guy who hates change of any kind, Tank handled his leaving the PD the best way he could," Carmine said. "We both know how much he loved being a cop. But when that was taken away, he squared up and set his life straight."

"It wasn't easy, as you well know," Connie said. "The wound he suffered took longer to heal than expected. He never complains about it, but the bullet he took did more damage than we'll ever know. Not even that three-quarter tax-free pension he gets from the department can help soothe that."

"All true," Carmine said. "He had a tough go, no doubt about it. But it helps he's got hobbies and has his own home, locked in and paid for. He's not dragging around a caravan of ex-wives and kids to put through college. And the boss handing him and his crazy pals a case now and then keeps his foot inside the door."

"And you think Chris moving in is going to turn that upside down? And maybe even bring an end to the two of us?"

"That's not where I'm meaning to go with this, Connie. What I am trying to say is putting a kid in the mix, especially a teenager coming in under tragic circumstances, is going to require Tank and you to a certain extent to be something neither of you gave any thought to being."

"And that would be what?"

"A parent," Carmine said.

"You got a good heart," he continued, when Connie was silent. "A lot like your mom. You do a good job of hiding it behind that hard shell, which you need to make a go of a business like this one, but it's there nonetheless. Tank's the same way. That's why you two connect so well. The kid's pretty sharp from what I understand. He's bound to pick up on that and gravitate toward it."

"To be honest," Connie said, "Tank and I haven't had much chance to talk about it. Everything's happened so quickly. The accident and then Chris moving in."

"You and Tank need to find a balance. Not hard to do if you care for each other."

Connie smiled. "You like Tank, don't you?" she said.

"It pains me to say it," Carmine said, returning the smile. "You know, given what I did to make my living, the last person on this earth I thought I would treat like one of the family would be a cop. But, yeah, I do like him. He treats you right and he keeps his life on the up-and-up. And over the years, he's become a good friend."

"Well, he probably won't want it spread around too much," Connie said, "but Tank not only likes you, he respects you."

Carmine downed the last of his espresso and began to slide out of the booth. "Could be worse, I suppose," he said.

"How?"

"He could have been a fed," Carmine said.

18.

THE BROWNSTONE

THAT SAME DAY

"HAVE YOU BEEN HOLDING OUT ON US, TANK?" BRUNO ASKED. "Did you go and recruit a new member of the team and not tell us?"

"This is my nephew," I said. "He's living with me. And my guess is, right now, he should be upstairs watching TV or online with his pals."

Chris took two steps into the room and looked at me. "My group just broke up," he said. "We've been trying to solve a pretty cool case. The oldest cold case in New York City history."

That caught the attention of the team, especially the chief. "John Colman," he said to Chris. "That case may never have closed, but there was no doubt as to how he died and who it was that killed him. Even though his body was never found, so we're working off more legend than fact."

"I'm almost afraid to ask," I said. "Who is John Colman?"

"He was a member of Henry Hudson's crew, working on the *Half Moon* when it sailed into New York Harbor," the chief said. "I forget the year, though."

"It was 1609," Chris said.

"That's it," the chief said. "John Colman was the first man murdered in New York City. At least, the first murder put on the books."

"Someone shot an arrow through his throat," Chris said.

"My guess is that someone was an Indian," the chief said. "Pissed off to see a bunch of white men landing on his property."

"That's one way to look at it," Chris said, stepping deeper into the room. I was annoyed at his barging in but at the same time was impressed by his confidence in a room full of strangers.

"Give me another way," the chief said. He shot me a glance and a nod.

"The crew had just completed a long voyage," Chris said. "Months at sea in tight quarters, with low rations and no guarantee they would ever see land. Under those circumstances, you're bound to make good friends. But you're also going to make enemies."

"So you're thinking one of his enemies bides his time," Joey says. "Once they get to shore, he sees an opening. He uses any weapon other than an arrow, the guilt points to one of the crew members. But an arrow is perfect. It can point in only one direction."

"Not a bad theory, as theories go," the chief said. "So where do you take this next?"

"I'm going to try and find a crew manifest," Chris said, playing now to the entire room. "See if there are any records still around of the crewmen."

"What's your first stop?" Bruno asked.

"The library," Chris said. "I'll find the closest one tomorrow, get a card, and take out a book or two about Henry Hudson and his crossing. That and whatever I can find on the Internet seem the best places to start."

"How often do you do this?"

"It's just a hobby," Chris said with a shrug. "A couple of us read about the Vidocq Society and thought we would form a club of our own."

"Is Vidocq somebody we should know?" Carl asked.

"Eugène François Vidocq," the chief said. "A nineteenth-century detective who used his skills to help solve cold cases. In 1990, a group out of Philly formed a society in his name and attempted to replicate what he did."

"Isn't that what we do?" Bruno asked.

"Not lately," I said. "The case the chief handed us is still cold as yesterday's dinner. Maybe we should get back to it."

"I'll go back to my room," Chris said. He turned to leave. "I put up a few pictures and posters. Figured you wouldn't mind."

"It's your room," I said. "Put up anything you want."

"Mostly framed photos of my mom and dad," Chris said. "There are others, but they're still at our house."

"We'll drive up and get them tomorrow," I promised. "Give you a chance to see any friends of yours might be around."

"Friends I probably won't ever see again," Chris said, an edge creeping back into his voice.

"That's more up to you than me," I said. "I'll come find you later and we'll grab a bite down the street. Talk it over with a meal."

"Let him stay," Joey said. "Another set of eyes and ears won't do any harm."

"And besides, Tank," Pearl piped up on the speakerphone, "the young man is working to solve a cold one from 1609. If he can help crack that, then what's in front of us should be a breeze for young Sherlock."

I took a deep breath and glanced at the welcoming faces around the room. "Grab a chair," I said to Chris. "That's my partner, Pearl, on the speakerphone. This is Ray, the chief of detectives, and you'll get the names of the rest of the crew in short order."

"Thanks," Chris said. He rushed into the dining room and came back in with a rocking chair made from old wooden wine barrels. My father had made that chair decades ago for me and Jack.

It would have made him happy to see his grandson sitting on it.

"Okay," I said, waiting until I had everyone's attention. "Let's get to work."

19.

PELHAM MANOR

T H E   N E X T   D A Y

CHRIS KEPT HIS EYES ON THE ROAD DURING THE DRIVE BACK up to the only town he had lived in, a hamlet in lower Westchester County. He had been living with me less than three days and I was still having trouble reading his moods. He grew animated only when the subject turned to his favorite topics—crime and sports. Otherwise he kept to himself and spoke only when asked a direct question. Some of that I wrote off to his new surroundings and some to just being a teenager. But his simmering anger worried me.

"You excited about seeing your friends?" I asked.

"I suppose," he said, shrugging. "I'll have to talk about my parents and what happened, which I'd rather not do. But they're going to ask."

"They already know what happened," I said. "You don't need to go into any details."

"I don't plan to," Chris said.

"Where do you want me to drop you off?" I asked.

"The Siwanoy playground. I'll show you where when we get to town."

"I'll give you a couple of hours there with them," I said. "Then I'll swing around and take you to your home. You can pick up some more of your things."

He was quiet for a minute. Then he asked, "Has the house been put up for sale yet?"

"The realtor told me it goes on the market next week," I said.

"I hate that someone else will be living there," Chris said.

"I know," I said.

"No, you don't," Chris snapped. "You never had to leave your home. You've been in the same house your whole life. You have no idea what it's like to have that taken away. My mom and dad loved that house. I miss it so much. Every second of every day."

"And that's going to go on for a long time," I said, knowing he meant he was missing his parents but was trying to be too tough to say that. "The kind of loss you had doesn't clear up easy."

"Is that what you used to say to people who lost family members back when you were a cop?"

"Something along those lines," I said.

"It's not much of a help," Chris said.

"Maybe not," I agreed. "But there's not much else that can be said that would be of any help."

"I can get out on the next corner," he said. "The playground is right up that street. You can pick me up there or I can walk over and meet you at the house. Whatever."

I pulled the car to a stop. Chris jumped out, slamming the door hard behind him, walking with his head down and his hands in his jacket pockets.

I circled the tree-lined street, each house seemingly in pristine condition. I pulled into the empty parking lot of the local Catholic church, cut the engine, leaned my head back, and closed my eyes.

I could handle Chris's grief over the loss of his parents. I could help him navigate his way through the changes his life was about to undergo. But there was nothing I could do to tamp down the anger that rested beneath the surface of a teenage boy, especially since that anger was directed at me.

Chris hated me because his father and I never spoke. It was there in his eyes. He hated me because I wasn't there for my brother in his time of need. But what he truly hated was the fact that I was alive and his father wasn't.

I STOPPED IN FRONT of the playground two hours later and saw Chris sitting on a chain-link swing, his head down, his legs dangling, sneakers scraping against the chipped asphalt. Other than a woman pushing a stroller on the other end of the sprawling space, the playground was empty.

"You catch up with any of your friends?" I asked.

"A few," he mumbled, not bothering to raise his head.

"You want to stop by your house?" I asked. "Or would you rather head back home? Save that for the next trip up?"

"I don't have a home," Chris said. "My home's going up for sale, remember? All I have is a room in your home."

I sat on the swing nearest Chris and watched the woman lean down to talk to the baby in the stroller, smiling as she did so. "Where do you want to be, Chris?" I asked softly.

Chris jumped off the swing and glared at me. "Where do I want to be? Where I belong, in my house, living with my mom and dad. With your brother, the one you never talk about, the one you turned your back on. I want to be there with them, but I know that can't happen. So I'm stuck. Living with the man who hated my father."

"I didn't hate your father, Chris," I said, doing my best to maintain my calm. "I just didn't speak to him. There's a big difference between the two."

"Not to me," Chris said.

"Well, then, that's just one more thing you're going to have to learn to live with," I said.

"What if I don't want to live with it?"

"You have no say in the matter," I answered. "What went on between me and Jack stays between me and Jack. You're upset that he died, and so am I. You need to blame somebody for what happened and I'm the best available target. And I get that. But we're going to try and make this work, you and me, despite all that. It's not going to be easy. In fact, it's a lot harder than I thought it was going to be. But get through it we will."

"Why bother?" Chris jeered. "You really shouldn't care about me any more than you did about my dad. Why should we pretend you do?"

I stood and looked at Chris. "Because Jack was my brother and you are his son," I said. "That may not matter to you, but it does to me. You think I didn't care about your father, but you're wrong. And I do care about you. Time will tell if you end up feeling the same about me."

I began to walk away and head toward my car. "It's getting late," I said. "And I need to get back."

"I'm going to stay awhile longer," he said. "I'll take the train back to town."

I turned to face him. His jaw was clenched and his eyes were as red as his cheeks. "You ever do that before?" I asked. "Take the train alone into the city?"

Chris shook his head.

"I didn't think so," I said.

"I'm not ready to leave just yet," Chris said.

"But I am," I said.

"I'm spending the night at my house," he said. "My dad had a contract with a car service, and he let me use it when neither him or my mom could pick me up from a late practice. I'll have them take me back tomorrow. That work for you?"

"It's going to have to," I said, without turning around.

I got into my car, started the engine, and pulled away from the playground. In the rearview I saw Chris walking down a sloping street, heading back to a reminder of a life he loved.

20.

HUDSON YARDS

THE NEXT DAY

I WAS IN THE FRONT SEAT OF MY CAR, BRUNO NEXT TO ME. WE were parked across from the Jacob Javits Center, a cavernous monstrosity that eats up most of the 34th Street end of Twelfth Avenue. There was a toy convention in town, and we were surrounded by platoons of men and women and a few children dressed in everything from *Star Wars* suits to Batman and Spider-Man outfits to one guy geared up to resemble the Incredible Hulk. Which he would have if the Hulk gained two hundred pounds of fat instead of muscle and his skin was spray-can green.

"You ever wonder what a guy like that does for a living?" Bruno asked, watching the not-so-Incredible Hulk walk past the car.

"I would like to think he had a job, assuming he has one at all, where other lives were not dependent on his actions," I said.

"Well, one thing we know for sure," Bruno said. "The Hulk has given up his gym membership."

I turned to look down the street, a line of cars crawling their way toward the entrance to the West Side Highway. I spotted the four men we were looking for leaning against a low wall, drinking beer from large cans inside paper bags, their bodies half hidden by an idling bus.

"There they are," I said, shifting Bruno's attention from the Hulk to our targets. "The guy in the red vest and black beret is the alibi witness."

"What about the others?" he asked.

"Ignore them," I said. "Unless they make it hard to do that."

Bruno got out of the car first and waited while I tossed my laminated NYPD parking permit where any parkie looking to write up a ticket could get a solid look. Keeping my permit was one of the perks I was given for working an occasional cold case.

Bruno and I crossed against the light, walking at a steady pace, eyes on the four across the street from us.

"Even from here, the guy smells like a liar," Bruno said.

"He gave a detailed account of where he went with the suspects and what they did the night of the attack," I said. "He even broke down what they ate and drank."

"You believe any of it?"

"Not a single word," I said.

"So, what are we expecting from our chat?"

"We'll press him a little," I said. "See how far that takes us."

"He'll peg you for a cop, no doubt," Bruno said. "What do I tell him I am, if he asks?"

"We don't need to answer his questions," I said. "He needs to answer ours."

"Is it okay to hit him if he doesn't?"

I laughed and slapped Bruno on the back. Bruno stood well over six feet and weighed a rock-solid 225. He worked out three hours a day and was still young enough to go a dozen rounds with a legitimate fighter. On the street, he was even better. "You won't have to," I said. "One up-and-down look at you and he'll shit right through those torn Jockeys he's no doubt wearing."

"Good to know," Bruno said with a smile.

21.

TRAMONTI'S

THAT SAME DAY

CHRIS WAS SITTING ALONE AT A SMALL TABLE CLOSE TO THE stage. He was savoring a dinner of chicken cutlets with a side of linguini in a thick red sauce. A large glass of Diet Pepsi and crushed ice rounded out the meal. He took a bite of chicken and watched as a burly man approached the table, pulled out a chair, and sat across from him.

"You must be Chris," he said. His voice was warm and his smile even warmer. "I'm Carmine. I'm a friend of your uncle. But that's not all. You know that nice lady that not only gave you a big hug but had the chef put down what looks like a pretty solid meal?"

Chris nodded.

"That's my daughter," Carmine said. "The two of us, we own the place. But between you and me, she does most of the work."

"What do you do?" Chris asked.

"This and that," Carmine said. "Keep an eye on things. Make sure customers are happy, the staff is on the ball, and nobody has to wait long for a meal to get to them."

"Mine came pretty quick," Chris said. He cut into the chicken cutlet and jammed a large piece in the corner of his mouth.

"There you go," Carmine said. "If I didn't own a piece of the place I would go in and ask for a raise."

"Have you known my uncle for a long time?" Chris asked.

Carmine nodded. "He's lived around here since he was a kid and I've been around here forever, so we'd see each other now and then. These last couple of years, since he's been off the job, we've seen a lot more of each other."

"If you knew Tank when he was a kid," Chris said, "you must have known my dad, too."

Carmine reached out and rested a large hand on the boy's smaller one. "I did, and I liked him a lot," he said. "And I'm very sorry for what happened. Not just to him but to your mother, too."

"Thanks," Chris said, his voice lower, sadder. His eyes were wet with tears and he reached for his napkin to give them a quick wipe. "I miss them so much, but I figure it's better to keep that to myself."

Carmine stayed silent for several moments, giving Chris time to compose himself. "We've all lost someone we love, someone we miss," he finally said. "It's a shitty part of life. When my wife died—Connie's mom—I cried every day and night for a year, maybe closer to two. There are nights I still cry and it's been years since she died. You never get over that kind of a loss. It'll be with you the rest of your life."

"What are you supposed to do about it?" Chris asked.

"Learn to live with it," Carmine said. "And you will, in time. And then always keep alive the good memories. Hold those front and center. Your folks will always be a part of you and you'll always be a part of them. Not even an ugly thing like death can change that."

"Did Tank ever talk to you about my dad?" Chris asked.

Carmine shook his head. "No," he said. "And I never asked."

"Why not?"

"If he wanted to talk to me about Jack, he would have," Carmine said. "But he never did. You accept it. It's part of the many things one friend does for another."

"I suppose," Chris said. "I wish I knew why they lived as if they weren't brothers. Something had to have happened."

"Let it sit for a while," Carmine said. "You two need to get to know each other. Trust each other. All this is new to you and to Tank. Going to take some adjustment time. There's a lot about Tank I don't know and don't feel a need to know. Same is true about me. We have a don't-ask-don't-tell policy."

"I think they did away with that."

"For the military, maybe," Carmine said. "But not for me and Tank. We live our lives by it."

"I read as much about him as I could," Chris said. "I wanted to meet him but never thought I would. And I never counted on living in the same house with him."

"No one did," Carmine said. "And there's a lot that needs to get done. You need to get signed up for your new school. Move the rest of your things out of your parents' place."

"Do the schools here have baseball teams?"

"You bet," Carmine said. "Good ones, too. And, on top of that, I sponsor one of the neighborhood club teams. I'll make sure you get on the squad. Tramonti's could use a good bat and glove."

"Thanks," Chris said.

"Well, I guess we pretty much covered everything," Carmine said. "Not bad for a first-time sit-down. But there is still one very important item left to discuss. And we should get to it ASAP."

"What's that?"

"What would you like for dessert?" Carmine asked.

22.

HUDSON YARDS

THAT SAME DAY

THE GUY IN THE RED VEST AND BLACK BERET WAS NOT IN A mood to talk. At least not to me and Bruno. He was playing tough to impress the three younger men around him. He was bantamweight short and in semi-decent shape. But the drink and the drugs had stripped the tone from his muscles and the bounce from his legs. All he had left now was a big mouth and a gun lodged against the side of his left hip.

"Who the hell you supposed to be, stepping into my face, asking me about people I might or might not know?" he asked. "I don't mess and I don't fool. So how about you and Mr. T turn around and walk back the same way you walked over?"

"I get it," I said. "You're tough. And your friends must be impressed by that."

"Damn straight," he said. "And they're gonna be even more impressed when I kick your ass up and down both sides of this street, you don't get out of my sight."

"That's not going to happen," I said. "We both know that. I'm going to ask some questions and you're going to give me some answers. Then you and your musketeers can go play spank the monkey the rest of the day. But if you don't, your day will take a very, very dark turn."

"I'll bring you down, you try to fuck with me," he said. The words were gruff, but his eyes told me all I needed to know. He had no idea who we were and how far we would go.

"That gun will be deep inside your ass before you let off one round," I said. "And while that's going on, my pal will make sure your three friends will be pissing blood until the end of the summer. So do we play or do you pay?"

Red Vest looked hard at me and then at Bruno. I wasn't eager to have a street fight, especially one that would attract attention from tourists and eventually cops. But I was betting the odds I wouldn't need to take it that far.

We all stood in silence for a few moments, taking in each other, engulfed by the noise and the crowds.

Red Vest broke the quiet. "You got five minutes to ask your questions," he finally said.

"Let's start with your name," I said.

"They call me Mano."

"That means 'hand,' right?" Bruno asked. "I hope your last name ain't Job."

The three musketeers behind Mano laughed. Mano's face flushed and he glared at Bruno.

"Okay then, Mano," I said. "I'll make it quick. Your two friends. The ones you say were with you the night they raped and robbed two women in Chelsea. They're in the wind. Thought maybe you have an idea where I can find them."

"I'm their friend," Mano said. "Not their daddy."

"Did they cut you in on their action?" I asked. "Or did you cut them out and take it all for yourself?"

"Neither one, loser," Mano said. "They were nowhere near Chelsea and had nothing to do with the two lying bitches. As for me, I don't need women to give me money and I don't need to rip off a woman's clothes to get my share."

"You're a player, I can see that," I said. "And what fine young lady—crack whore or debutante—wouldn't want to be on the roll with you?"

"Now you're listening," Mano said with a nod to his friends. "You want these two fuckers so bad, find them yourself. You supposed to be like a white John Shaft. Then do your thing and round up the dogs."

"That might be a waste of time, Mano," I said. I stepped closer to him, inches from his face, smelling the cheap cologne on his neck and corner hooch on his breath. "Rumor has it that your two pals aren't in the wind. They're in the ground. Put there by one of their friends. I'm betting you're the odds-on favorite to be that friend. Is any of that true?"

"You talking shit now," Mano said. "And your five minutes were up five minutes ago."

"You're right, Mano," I said. "I'm wasting those minutes talking to the last link on the chain. Now, here's what me and my friend need you to do. Run and tell the man that holds the lock and key to the chain I need to speak to him. Is your head clear enough for you to understand that?"

Mano tried to laugh it off, but he was too nervous to sell it well. "I'm my own boss, sucker," he said. "Why you think there's somebody I work for?"

"Because guys like you always need somebody to tell them what to do and when to do it," I said. "I figure that somebody was the one who asked you to find two fools dumb enough to listen to what you were selling. So you dug up the two scumbags who broke in and raped the girls."

Mano was sweating now and his three friends took a few steps back, no longer eager to be connected to their street runner. "Just words. No proof."

"Listen, moron," I said. "I'm not taking you in, for two reasons. One, I can always find a loser like you. Two, I need you to talk to your boss. So, are we cool?"

"I don't even know your damn name," Mano said. "How am I supposed to tell anybody that somebody's looking for him if I don't know who the fuck that somebody is?"

I glanced at Bruno and smiled. "Finally, you asked a question worth an answer," I said to Mano. "Tell him Tank Rizzo needs to see him."

"And that name is supposed to scare him?" Mano asked.

I tapped Bruno on the arm and we both turned and started to walk back to our car. "It won't," I said. "But eventually it will."

23.

MADISON SQUARE GARDEN

THAT NIGHT

THE NEW YORK RANGERS WERE UP 3–1, EARLY IN THE THIRD period. Chris was already on his second hot dog and itching to get to the giant bag of peanuts he had crunched in the side of his seat. We were sitting six rows from the ice. The tickets were courtesy of a friend of Carmine's who, despite doing a three-to-five-year stretch for some pump-and-dump scheme the feds caught wind of, refused to give up his prime-time seats.

I found going to a game to be not only a good place to see a favorite team but also to talk things out with a friend or to kick back, relax, and think out my next move. Instinct told me the case the chief handed us had more layers to it than would at first appear. On top of that, I wanted some time alone with Chris. Get a feel of how he was handling the changes tossed his way.

"Never been to a hockey game," Chris said.

"Figured we could use a break. And I wanted to see this kid on the Blackhawks I've been reading about. See if he's as good as the writers say."

"They move fast," Chris said. "It's hard to tell one player from the other."

"It's about speed and precision," I said. "And working as a team.

Anybody tells you it's guys fighting on skates doesn't know anything about hockey."

"Were you always a hockey fan?" Chris asked.

I nodded. "Played in a roller-hockey league when I was a kid. Your dad did, too. And one of the perks was going to Westchester a couple of times a month to see a Rangers practice. I got to know a few of them. Great guys—always giving us sticks, pucks, tape, Rangers gear."

"Were you any good?"

"Good enough to stay on my feet and get in some solid hits," I said. "Your dad had some moves, but he used to get crushed up against the boards. He was the youngest guy on the team, and the bigger players tried to use it to their advantage."

"And, of course, you came to his rescue," Chris said, his words dripping with sarcasm.

"Yeah, I did," I said. "You don't sound happy about it, but Jack sure as shit was."

"That's probably why he never signed me up for hockey," Chris said. "Instead, we were co-owners of a Rotisserie baseball team. You know, fantasy baseball."

"I know what Rotisserie is," I said.

"We were in a league for the last three seasons. Called our team the Continental Ops. That's a character that—"

"Dashiell Hammett created," I said, finishing his sentence. "You weren't kidding about being a crime buff."

"I love reading about crime, watching the shows and movies. But now I can't think about anything beyond making it through high school."

"Why is that?"

"Well, I'm supposed to be living with you until I'm done," Chris said. "We're barely making it through our first week, so I'm not sure it's going to last that long. And who knows how I'll do in this new school."

"One day at a time would be a good motto," I said.

"And even if I make it to the end, college is out of the question," he said.

"You'll do fine in the new school," I said. "If you want to, that is. As for college, you can go to any school in the country that will accept you."

"I'm not taking money from you for college."

"You won't," I said. "Your mom and dad will be footing the bill."

He turned to look at me. "What do you mean?"

"Got a call this morning from a guy in White Plains," I said. "He managed your family's estate plans. Besides the house, which he says is worth between 1.2 and 1.5 million dollars, with 300,000 dollars left on the mortgage, your parents socked away 550,000 in cash and bonds. That goes to you."

"Really?" Chris said.

"Really," I said. "And they had heavy insurance policies on their lives."

"How heavy?"

"Two million dollars each," I said. "That's four million in cash, tax free. He's checking to see if it's double that since they died in a car accident. If so, total it up and you're richer than anybody in this arena, including some of the players."

"They never talked about money," Chris said. "I knew my dad made a decent salary because of the house, the private school, and the vacations we took."

"It's a lot of dough," I said. "If it's handled right, it will only grow. You and I will meet with the estate lawyer next week. Then, if it's okay by you, I'll reach out to a friend of mine does investments—safe ones, not Bernie Madoff bullshit—and have him put some in trust funds, some in a bank, some in stocks and bonds. Spread it around."

"Can I spend any now?" Chris asked. "I can pay for food and rent."

"I don't want any money," I said. "I took you in because you're my nephew. You and me are looking at the only blood family we've got. You may not like that, but it's a fact, and the sooner we face up to it, the better we'll get along."

"I'm not going to make any promises," Chris said.

"No surprise there," I said. "Would be nice if you loosened that chip on your shoulder a bit, though."

"Is that what you would do if you were me?" he asked.

I stayed quiet for a few moments, focusing on the last-minute action on the ice.

"Probably not," I said. "I'd have that chip on my shoulder the rest of my life. But I would do a lot better job of hiding it from people who were looking out for me."

"Whether I liked them or not?" Chris said.

I turned to look at him. "I don't give a rat's ass if you like me," I said. "Same holds true for Connie, Carmine, and the crew. No one is looking to be liked. We got all the friends we need."

"What are you looking for, then?" Chris asked.

"Respect," I said. "The same respect they've shown you. That's all you owe anyone until they do you wrong. And no one you've met, starting with me, is ever going to do you wrong. We've earned that respect."

"And what have I earned?"

"Not a damn thing," I said. I stood and eased my way out of the aisle. "Let's go. This game is over."

24.

THE WINTHROP

THE NEXT DAY

"WE'RE ON THE SAME PAGE," PEARL SAID. HE RESTED THE file folder on the small table to his left and reached for a cup of Dunkin' Donuts iced coffee. "This case has a lot of what they want us to see in it. But it has even more of what they don't want us to see."

"I figured it wouldn't take you long to smell it out," I said. "This uptown dealer moves a lot of dope and takes in even more money. But he's never anywhere near it. Not the money. Not the dope."

"Which only means he figured a way to hide it in plain sight," Pearl said. "He could be warehousing it or using safe drops."

"A warehouse eventually gets found," I said. "It's the first place a narc goes looking for."

"He not only moves drugs, this guy," Pearl said. "He's got himself a working stable of women spread from the Heights to Chelsea. He's taking in cash with both hands."

"And these women must all work out of apartments they live in," I said. "Once again, leaving no link to the dealer."

"What, then, if our two and two equals out to the apartments used for sex are also the best places to stash the drugs?"

"It's a smart play," I admitted. "Money and dope can be moved around without anyone taking notice."

"But where does he stash the cash?" Pearl asked.

"This guy doesn't like to touch anything," I said. "He uses mules and drivers to move the drugs. And I would bet that there's a banker out there that makes sure his cash is put in a safe place."

"In which case, the two who broke into Francine and Gloria's apartment went in looking to score both cash and drugs. And when they didn't find either one—"

"They trashed the place and did a number on the ladies," I said. "But they were fueled more by fear and anger than lust. They had to figure whoever sent them wouldn't believe the dope had vanished. He would have to think—"

"They stole the stash. Lied about it and were looking to put it out on the street and cash out."

"The dope was missing, that's for sure," I said. "But my five to your ten tells me the girls weren't in on the lift."

"But my ten to your twenty tells me somebody on the drug boss's crew did the taking," Pearl said. "Francine and Gloria might have turned a few tricks to earn extra cash, but nothing in that file or their history fingers them as lifters."

"They knew enough not to shit where they eat," I said. "They were probably getting a hundred, even two hundred a month, to have the place used as a stash drop."

"You ruling Mano out?"

"On the lift, most likely," I said. "It's a coin toss whether he was the one who was given the job of icing the two rapists. If it wasn't him, he knows the name and the face of the hitter."

"You lay any of this out for the chief?"

"Not yet," I said. "Chances are better than good that our dealer has dozens of these shelter drops spread throughout the city. You remember that guy we nabbed our first year working plainclothes?"

Pearl smiled. "Who could ever forget. Mongo with the bongos.

That fat bastard was moving four hundred large of coke a month. He had fifteen shelter drops in one borough alone."

"Took us a while to piece together. And it wasn't because we were new at it, was it?"

Pearl lost the smile and shook his head. "No. He had three of ours on his payroll looking out for him. Giving him a heads-up whenever our heat got close to his stove."

"Until we know all the players in this particular game, we keep clear of the chief," I said.

"What's the play?"

"Alexandra has her ear to the ground," I said. "If there's loose talk on the streets, she'll get wind of it. Joey is going to wire up that Chelsea tenement, from phones to laptops. Bruno is going to tail Mano and figure which uptown dealer he works for. And Carl's going to outfit us with a surveillance van and two clean cars, in case we have to follow multiple crews."

"What do you need from me?" Pearl asked.

I took a deep breath and stared at my best friend. "You got the hardest job of all."

"Bring it on, my brother from another mother," he said.

"Carl's going to bring you some state-of-the-art computer equipment," I said. "Probably tomorrow."

"And once I have these nifty toys?"

"If there are dirty badges in this, you need to find them, Pearl," I said. "Use the databanks, use your contacts. Go down any road you can think of. If you need anything to help you—from cell phones to a wiretap—just say the word. And you have to do it without anyone smelling you out."

Pearl looked down at his hands and then back up at me. "You must think there are," he said. "You wouldn't be going to so much trouble otherwise."

"The chief throws us a case you and me could have cracked while we still were in uniform," I said. "We could have caught those two hair balls that same night. But it was never closed and he let it sit for a bit.

And then hands it off to us. Why? We're not charity cases and we didn't go asking for a job."

"He knew we wouldn't stop until we cracked it," Pearl said. "And we would go down every road we needed to go down. No matter where it led."

"He went with his gut on this one," I said. "Just like we're doing. He would love to be proved wrong and so would we. If all we're dealing with is a top-drawer drug crew, that would be fine with me."

"And if it's more than that?" Pearl asked. "If it hits closer to home?"

"Then they'll go down," I said. "Every last one."

Pearl shook his head. "Most cops when they retire, they head to Florida and play golf and chase rich old ladies around Atlantic Avenue. But not us."

I stood and leaned over and gave Pearl a tight hug. "We're not like most cops, partner. But if you're looking to score with an old lady, I can stroll through the White Plains Mall and see if I can scope out one or two for you."

25.

WASHINGTON HEIGHTS

THAT SAME DAY

THE SMALL SOCIAL CLUB WAS SQUEEZED BETWEEN AN ABANDONED lot filled with garbage, old tires, rusty pipes, and large rats and a four-story tenement with three boarded-up floors. The club consisted of two rooms cluttered with Big Bob's leather furniture, a pool table that would have been considered old when Fast Eddie Felson was playing the Fat Man in nine-ball tournaments, and a jukebox that played only hip-hop and Tom Jones songs. There was a makeshift kitchen in one of the corners, a fridge filled with cans and bottles of cold beer. Across from the fridge was a working toilet, with three rolls of paper resting next to the cracked water line connected to a basement pipe.

There were six men in the room.

They were all smoking—cigars, cigarettes, or blunts—and five of them were slurping from sweaty bottles of Bud. No one in the room was over forty, and all were packing guns and knives. They were dressed in a similar style—knockoff jeans, tight and hanging low at the waist, T-shirts in a variety of colors, and bandannas wrapped around their necks. Each man had a string of tattoos on his arms, neck, and fingers.

Their attention was focused on the man sitting in a recliner in the center of the room. Cradled on his lap was a plate filled with a fat sausage-and-fried-pepper hero, and a longneck beer was wedged in the side of the recliner. He had thick jet-black hair and eyes that were the color of crows. A large scar ran from the edge of his lower lip to his Adam's apple.

His name was Juan Marichal Gonzalez. He was born in the Dominican Republic and his mother had named him after her favorite baseball player—the Hall of Fame San Francisco Giants pitcher Juan Marichal. This particular Juan Marichal did not, however, play baseball.

This Juan Marichal was the biggest cocaine dealer in Washington Heights and the third-most active in the tri-state area. He started—as the high-end dealers almost always do—as a runner for Harlem drug lord Nick "Baby Face" Arnold. Juan worked his way up the ranks, and within five years he had a street crew of forty moving his drugs. He named his brands after Al Pacino movies, including "Carlito," "Dog Day," and "Heat." He even named one high-potency blend "Serpico," just to piss off the narcs who were hot on his trail but could never get close enough to slap on the cuffs.

On the street, he was known to dealers, junkies, hookers, and cops as "Gonzo."

And right now, Gonzo was pissed off.

"It's not bad enough that a chunk of my stash is wiped away," he said to the men assembled around him. "Then those two morons Mano sent to get the stash go batshit crazy and bring the boys in blue into the mix. And now I hear there's a Tin Badge starting to sniff in places his nose shouldn't be. So tell me, how the fuck does that shit happen?"

The youngest of the group stepped forward. "It's his case now," he said. "It was a handoff from the PD. Talk is he was a hard-charging cop in his time and he was brought in to find out who beat those girls."

"But he wasn't brought in to come after me," Gonzo said. "Or my drugs. There is no way this off-the-job fool could know how I work my business."

Gonzo had, over the years, established a network of twenty-four apartments where he could have his drugs cut, bagged, and stashed. All the apartments were in tenement buildings and the drugs would be moved by teenagers on their way to and from school, packets left in trash bins, under rubbish, in empty paint cans. The kids would stash the cocaine in their backpacks, as many as six triple-wrapped bricks a trip, and then toss them through the open windows of a series of parked cars. Once the kids had cleared out the drug stash, Gonzo's street crew would get into the cars and drive them to the sale site.

Then, Gonzo used delivery trucks to collect the cash and bring in fresh loads of uncut drugs. It was a well-oiled, well-organized operation and one that netted the dealer a six-figure monthly income.

Gonzo had eyes on those streets, as well.

Heavily armed men stood watch from a corner gas station or from inside a cramped bodega. If anyone made a move on the cars or the carriers, the gunmen would come out ready to do some damage. A crew of younger kids were paid five dollars each to keep an eye out for RMPs or unmarked Chevys, yelling out the standard "Five-O" if they spotted a cop circling the block. The call had been in use for decades now, since the first version of *Hawaii Five-O* with Jack Lord landed on TV screens.

"He must have somebody with muscle inside One PP," the young man said. "How else you figure guy like him gets handed this case? Or any case?"

Gonzo sat back and shut his eyes, rocking gently in the recliner. "This Tin Badge," he said. "He got a name?"

"Don't know his full name," the young man said. "I just know what they called him back when he was on the job."

"Which is what?"

"Tank," the young man said.

Gonzo sat up in the recliner and opened his eyes. "Tank?" he said with a giggle. "Like the ones they got in the Army? That kind of tank?"

"I guess so." The young man shrugged.

Gonzo grabbed the longneck and jumped to his feet. "Let's keep an eye on this Tank," he said. "Find out as much as you can about him. We got friends with badges, too, remember? Have them earn the money I give them and scope this fucker out. A guy like him is trouble, and I don't need or want trouble come knocking on my door."

The group of men started to head out of the social club. Gonzo stood in the center of the room, watching them leave. He reached out and grabbed the young man by the arm and held him close. "Hang back," he said. "Let them go first."

Once the last of the men left, closing the black windowless door behind him, Gonzo let go of the young man's arm.

"I been keepin' an eye on you," he said. "You got a head on you, smart enough to connect the dots. I don't have too many around me like that. Could make good use of you, if you up for that."

The young man nodded. "Anything you need," he said.

"You're Luis, right?" Gonzo asked.

"Yes, that's right," he said.

"You had a brother was an on-the-come guy, few years back," Gonzo said. "I get that right, too?"

"Yeah, Edwin," Luis said. "He was good, worked with some of the crews on Pleasant Avenue. He just wasn't lucky."

"Prison or bullets?" Gonzo asked.

"Both," Luis said. "Did a stretch up at Attica. When he came out, he wanted to give going legit a try."

"Didn't work out?"

"He tried," Luis said, almost cringing at the memory. "I guess it was too late for him. He got in with the wrong crew for the wrong reasons. And it got him killed."

"That list is a long one," Gonzo said. "Long enough to fill a cemetery. None of us go into this life looking to cash out on the pension and health insurance."

"What do you need me to do?" Luis asked. He was anxious to get the conversation back on track.

"This guy, this cop, Tank," Gonzo said. "See if he's close to anybody. A wife, daughter, best friend, like that. Just in case we need to do some pushback against his ass."

"I'll get right on it," Luis said.

"That's the second thing I need you to do," Gonzo said.

"What's the first?"

"It was Mano this Tank reached out for, right?" Gonzo said.

"Yeah," Luis said. "Stopped to talk to him on the street. Him and some other guy."

"That Mano, he sure likes to run his mouth. I don't want him ever talkin' to this guy Tank again. I don't want him talkin' to anybody again. Is that as clear as a blue sky to you?"

"Got it," Luis said in a low voice.

He stared at Gonzo for a moment and then turned and walked out of the dark social club.

26.

THE CLOISTERS

FOUR DAYS LATER

I LEANED AGAINST A RAILING A FEW FEET FROM THE PARKING area and stared at the magnificent stone façade of the Cloisters. I always found it to be one of the most peaceful as well as beautiful places in the city, a tranquil oasis a short turn off the Henry Hudson Parkway.

It's also a great place to enjoy a quiet lunch with my crew. It is seldom crowded, and even when it is, most of the traffic heads inside to check out the artifacts and the art.

Bruno, Carl, and Joey were huddled around me. Two large grocery bags rested next to me, filled with sandwiches, containers of roasted peppers and artichoke hearts, a few bottles of Pellegrino, and some iced coffees. "Let's walk until we find a quiet spot," I said.

We settled on a grassy patch under a weeping willow. I started dishing out the food along with napkins and utensils. "You sure we're allowed to eat here?" Carl asked.

"Probably not," I said. "But I've been doing it for years, and the next time I get busted will be the first time I get busted."

Bruno carefully unwrapped a chicken cutlet and hot-cherry-pepper hero and took a large bite. The others reached for their lunches and began eating as well. I flipped the lid off a container of iced coffee and took a long swig, then slipped a piece of paper out of the rear pocket of my jeans and unfolded it.

"Bruno tailed Mano long enough and far enough for us to get a handle on our dealer," I said. "Goes by the street name Gonzo. And Pearl was able to locate eight of his drop apartments. Most are on the West Side, starting in the mid-Twenties on Seventh and heading down to what used to be the old meat market."

"Alexandra is closing in on three more of his stash places," Joey said. "She's got some Wall Street guy on the hook. All the money this guy reels in goes right up his nose. He's going to need to hit two Lotto jackpots just to keep up."

"And I'm sure she's telling him at least one of those jackpots is in his future," I said.

"That girl can spin that psychic shit with the best of them," Bruno said.

"I've got the place where the rape and robbery went down wired up," Joey said. "Soon as you tell me where the others are, I'll do the same there. Works to our advantage that they're close to each other."

"How so?" I asked.

"The equipment is pretty high-tech and pretty expensive, so the chief better not stiff me on the bill," Joey said. "I can park the surveillance truck as far as half a mile from the farthest location and it'll pick up chatter as if it's parked in front of the building."

"Any chance we can wire up Gonzo's den?" I asked.

"That's going to take a little time," Bruno said. "Gonzo never ventures far from his Washington Heights tenement. He needs something, he sends somebody to fetch it."

"Pearl's digging into Gonzo's background," I said. "I'll have him get us the name of his lawyer and see if he owns any property either here or on the islands."

"How much do Francine and Gloria fit into this?" Joey asked. "Not to mention their friendly neighbor Reggie."

"Gloria is clean," I said. "She was unlucky, is all. I spoke to her mom and she barely lets the girl out of her sight. Francine is trying to get off the dope and out of that life, but as you all know that's the hardest quit there is. Plus, you have to figure she needs whatever money comes her way in return for letting them use her place as a drop."

"And Reggie?" Carl asked.

"Jury's still out," I said. "He might know something about something. But he seems more scared than tough to me."

"But there is a connection between him and Gonzo," Bruno said.

I looked at Bruno and put down my container of iced coffee. "What is it?" I asked.

"Reggie was facing a gun-possession rap about three years back," Bruno said. "He had a legal-aid mouthpiece just out of law school and a judge who wanted to get on with his day. So he hit Reggie with a heavy bail."

"To a guy like Reggie, heavy bail would be about forty dollars," Carl said.

"Well, this was forty dollars plus nine thousand nine hundred and sixty dollars more," Bruno said. "Making for a grand total of ten large. So it looked like a summer on Rikers for our man."

"But instead?" I asked.

"Instead, up steps a guy with deep pockets who said he would put up the bail," Bruno said. "Which he did and our pal walks out a free man."

"What happened with the gun rap?" I asked.

"By the time it got to court, Reggie had a lawyer with a nice suit and some skills," Bruno said. "They gave Reggie community-service time."

"And who paid for the new lawyer?" I asked.

"None other than Gonzo himself," Bruno said.

"How'd you dig all this up?"

"Didn't have to lift a finger," Bruno said, a smile spread across his face.

"Then who did?" I asked.

"Your nephew," Bruno said. "Chris. He got on his computer, chatted up some of his online buddies, and in less time than it takes to brew a pot of coffee, he had the dope on Reggie."

"You ask him to do that?"

"No," Bruno said. He sensed a shift in my voice and toned down his excitement. "He came to me with it."

"How did he know to look for him?" I asked. I was as confused as I was angry. "Even if he got a look at the case folder that night in my living room, Reggie's name was nowhere near it."

"I asked him that," Bruno said.

"And he said what?" I asked.

"He said he and his online buddies did a search on the building where the break-in occurred," Bruno said. "That gave them the names of the folks living there. Reggie was listed as an emergency contact for Francine on her rental agreement. They ran a scan on Reggie and came up with his lawyer. A guy named Albert J. Burnett. They checked out some of his other clients and one of them happened to be Juan Marichal Gonzalez. Also known as Gonzo."

"Might be something there," I said. "Or it could just be Francine went and asked Gonzo to do a favor for a friend and he delivered. In return, Reggie paid Gonzo back by working as one of his mules."

"You ain't mad about this, are you?" Bruno asked. "The kid did us a solid. He wants to be involved. And if this is any indication of what the boy can do, then why the hell not?"

"It might make his transition go smoother," Joey said. "Boy's been through some serious shit. He's just trying to find his place."

"He looks up to you," Carl said to me. "Even if he doesn't act like it."

I glanced away, not sure which way to go with this. On the one hand, having Chris help out the team would give him a sense of belonging and a taste of once again having a family.

On the other hand, he was a kid, a pissed-off one, and we were both feeling our way around each other. Having him work on a cold case, potentially a dangerous one, might not be the best route to take with a fragile and rattled teenager.

"You're all in agreement on this?" I said.

"Don't see any harm," Carl said. "Don't see any foul."

"That includes Alexandra, as well?"

Bruno nodded. "She's already read his cards," he said. "You listen to her and the boy is a combination of John Douglas and Sherlock Holmes."

"And no doubt lurking somewhere behind this are the happy faces of Carmine and Connie," I said. "Except they're both smart enough not to leave behind trace evidence."

"So does this mean Chris is a go?" Carl asked.

"Not saying yes and I'm not saying no," I said. "I want to give it some thought. Run it by Pearl, get his take. Unless that base has already been covered."

"It has," Joey said. "Him and Chris have been feeding each other tons of computer info. Pearl says the boy can find hot spots he never knew existed."

I shook my head. "Not one no vote in the group," I said. "Why am I not surprised?"

"It's your call, Tank," Carl said.

"Fair enough," I said. "In the meantime, let's keep working the case. Be nice to have all of Gonzo's stash apartments in our scope by end of the week. We need to be on his ass twenty-four/seven."

"What's your next play?" Bruno asked.

"It might be time me and Gonzo had a face-to-face," I said.

"He eats in the same place every night," Bruno said. "A chicken joint a block from his home."

"How many armed go with him?"

"One, sometimes two, never more than that," Bruno said. "He always sits at a table in the back, facing street traffic. He goes in late, when the place is empty. And the cheap bastard never pays and he never tips."

I helped pack up the empty sandwich wrappers, Pellegrino bottles, and coffee containers. "He's no different than any other lowlife gangster," I said. "All crass and no class."

27.

TRAMONTI'S

LATER THAT NIGHT

I SAT ACROSS FROM CONNIE AND CARMINE. WE WERE AT ONE OF the front tables, every inch covered with food platters, wine and water bottles and glasses. It was a Friday night; the early dining crowd had left and the second wave had just begun to arrive. There would eventually be a third seating, but that crowd came to listen to jazz and would wash down the rhythmic music with drinks and maybe a sampling of appetizers.

"The kid seems to be settling in, no?" Carmine asked. He cut into a thick veal chop, swirling the piece in sauce and waiting for me to respond.

"In some ways," I said.

"Where do you see the problem?" Connie asked. She was the only one not eating, content to pick at a breadstick or a carrot slice while she nursed a white wine and kept an eye on the customers coming in.

"He's got a lot of below-the-radar anger," I said. "Most of it directed at me. Which is understandable but not that pleasant to endure. He's still feeling his way. Trying to piece it together. Could take a while."

"He seems to get along with the team," Connie said. "Especially Joey."

I nodded. "Chris wants in on the crew," I said. "Found out he's been helping them a bit on the side. Actually, more than a bit."

"Helping them how, exactly?" Carmine asked.

"Working computers for the most part," I said. "He seems to know what he's doing. I mean, I thought Pearl was good. Even he admits Chris runs rings around him."

"So that's a good thing," Carmine said.

"That's just it," I said. "I don't know if it is or not. Granted, he's smart and sometimes he comes across as older than he is. But bottom line is he's still a kid. And we're not working a pretend online game here. We're dealing with real people and real crimes, and when we get close to these folks they'll do anything they need to do to stay out of jail."

"You're worried he might get hurt," Connie said.

"Everything he had or knew has been yanked away," I said. "He's in a whole new world now."

"He's working computers, Tank," Carmine said. "He's not riding in an unmarked looking for bangers. He's either in your home or here in a back booth. Both places seem pretty safe to me."

"He likes to eat dinner with Pop," Connie said with a smile. "Pop won't admit it, but he's always wanted a grandson to hang with."

"I can only imagine what the hell you two talk about," I said.

"The usual," Carmine said with a shrug. "He helps me pick out my racing bets for the day, then we move on to baseball. It's no surprise he's great on a computer. The kid understands statistics. Name a ball-player in either league and he can give you a complete breakdown. Tells me his dad had the same skill set."

"He did," I said.

"You remember how ticked I was the Yankees didn't keep Robinson Cano, right?" Carmine said.

"Hard to forget," I said. "Heard about it every day for months."

"Well, after Chris broke down his numbers in his three years with the Mariners, I'm sorry I said word one," Carmine said. "You take a peek at those numbers and not signing him was the best move Yankees ever made."

"Is this your way of saying it would be okay if I let Chris work with the guys on the case?" I said.

"Yes," Connie said, answering as Carmine nodded. "But only to a point."

"I'd keep him invisible," Carmine said. "The guys you're chasing will see you and see your team. There's no reason for them to see the kid. That could only lead to trouble, in my book."

"Him wanting to be on the team, I get that," I said. "And if that was all of it, I suppose I would be less anxious about it than I am."

"What else is it you think he wants?" Connie asked.

"He's looking to prove himself to me," I said. "Get me to trust his abilities."

"Okay so far," Carmine said.

"Once he proves that, he can come to me with a lot more confidence, a lot more wind at his back," I said.

"Come to you with what, Tank?" Connie asked.

"I passed his room the other night. He had all the clippings about his parents' car accident and the follow-up stories written about them spread out on his bed."

"That's understandable," Carmine said. "They're about his mom and dad."

"He also has the police reports on the accident and the medical examiner's findings," I said. "He's got detailed information about the car they drove that night. He's got breakdowns of the organizational chart of the company where my brother worked. He's got stacks of corporate folders, everything from what the company invested in to who they invested with, how much, and when. In addition, he's got printouts of every article he could dig up about the company limited to the years my brother worked there."

"And what does having all that tell you?" Carmine asked.

"It tells me Chris doesn't think his parents died in an accident," I said. "It tells me he thinks they were murdered."

Carmine and Connie stared at me and stayed silent.

"It also tells me one more thing," I said. "One more very important thing."

"What?" Connie asked.

"It tells me Chris is going to ask me to work with him," I said. "Solve the case and prove him right."

28.

CHELSEA

THREE DAYS LATER

ALEXANDRA'S PSYCHIC HEALING CENTER WAS LOCATED IN THE basement of a dilapidated brownstone in the West Twenties off Eighth Avenue. Two of the rooms were hidden by thick velour drapes. The main room was where Alexandra greeted her curious customers. The room was dark and dimly lit. The walls were lined with six framed posters—three were portraits of gnarled old women dressed in peasant garb, staring out with eyes meant to convey mystery; two were drawings by famed illustrator Frank Frazetta; and one was a print of an Andy Warhol painting of Ludwig van Beethoven.

Alexandra was in a long flowered cotton dress, her shoulders and back covered by a black hand-woven shawl. She sat at a small circular table surrounded by three chairs. In the center of the table was a large silver bowl filled with water, oil, and an assortment of fragrances. Next to the bowl were two decks of playing cards—one Italian, the other from Romania.

Alexandra was sipping hot ginger tea from a saucer when the door to the room opened. She gazed over the lip of the saucer at two men— both tall, one muscular and lean, the other overweight and sweating profusely. They both were wearing knockoff jeans and smelled of cheap cologne. The fat one had on a black T-shirt too small to cover his belly.

The muscular one had on a white button-down shirt, the sleeves rolled to the elbows. Alexandra figured he would be the one doing most of the talking. Neither one seemed to be the type looking to have their fortune told.

"You the fortune-teller lady, right?" the muscular man asked. He gave her a snake-smooth smile and stepped deeper into the room.

"That would be me," Alexandra said.

"Okay if we sit?" he asked, reaching a hand for one of the chairs.

"It is if you want your fortune told," Alexandra said.

"That depends," the muscular man said, still holding the smile. "How good are you at looking into the future?"

"I can tell you one thing right off," Alexandra said. "Maybe that will help give you a clue."

"Let's hear it," the muscular man said.

"Here's what I see in your immediate future," Alexandra said. "You both are going to have twenty fewer dollars in your pockets in less than a minute's time."

"Why would that be?" the fat one asked.

"That's what I charge to look into this bowl or at any of these cards," Alexandra said. "So if you want to know what else the future holds for you, pony up. Otherwise, find the door again and close it on your way out."

The muscular man pulled the chair back and sat down. He rested both hands on the table and looked at Alexandra. "We didn't come here to hear about our future," he said. His voice was calm, relaxed, but the tight ripple in his arms and neck betrayed his tension. "We came here to tell you yours."

Alexandra sat back in her chair, hands on her lap, and took a deep breath. "Say what you came to say, then get out of my sight," she said.

"Way I see it, your future is not looking too pretty," he said. "Not for you. Not for your cop or ex-cop or sometime-cop friend. And not for anybody else who goes in with him. Not that crippled black badge holed up in rehab. Not that restaurant he eats in, with the pretty lady running the show. And not even that kid who's been hanging around him and your pals. You see where I'm coming from?"

"I not only see, I know," Alexandra said. She gave off not the slightest hint of fear, though the back of her dress was now stained with sweat. "You and the Lord of the Onion Rings behind you are messenger boys. So now you can go back and tell your master you delivered the message."

The muscular man lost the smile and glared at Alexandra. "We ain't finished just yet," he said. His voice was no longer calm, now coated with anger. "You might be right—to your eyes we're nothing but what you say we are. But there's more to our message than words."

"We need to make sure your friends not only hear what we asked you to tell them," the fat man said, "they need to see it, too. You hear me, pretty lady?"

Alexandra smiled. "You going to cut me, that the plan?" she asked. "Leave a slice for all my friends to see?"

The fat man chuckled and jabbed a stubby hand into the muscular man's back. "Hey, maybe this bitch really can see the future."

The muscular man leaned across and grabbed a handful of Alexandra's hair. He gripped it tight and lowered her face closer to the table. With his free hand, he reached behind him and took a long, serrated blade from the fat man. He turned to grip the handle of the blade and then looked at Alexandra. "What does the future tell you now?" he asked her. "You going to lose an ear or just have half your face sliced?"

The muscular man flinched when he felt the muzzle of a .38 jammed into the left side of his neck. "I may have a scar; the stars aren't clear on that yet," she said in a low voice. "But for sure you will not be alive to see it, that much I know."

The muscular man held the blade inches from Alexandra's face. "You're not going to shoot me," he said, with as much bravado as he could muster. Behind him, the fat man stood frozen in place, unsure of what move, if any, to make.

"That blade moves another inch and so does my finger," Alexandra said. "I'll be scarred for life and you'll be dead. And no worries, fat boy. You'll be dead, too, before your chubby fingers touch the door."

The standoff lasted only thirty seconds, but to the three in the room it felt like hours. "Okay," the muscular man said. "There's no need for anybody to get crazy here, right?"

"Let go of my hair," Alexandra said, "and then let the knife drop from your hand. Once you do that, put both hands over your head, free and clear."

"While you still hold your gun to my neck?"

"That's right," she said. "That's the only play that'll get you out of this with your head still connected to the rest of your body."

"What kind of fuckin' fool you take me for?" the muscular man said.

"The kind of fuckin' fool who wants to leave here in one piece," Alexandra said. "So unless I got that wrong, you'll do exactly what I told you to do and you'll do it now and you'll do it slowly."

The muscular man was soaked in sweat. The fat man still held his ground, waiting and watching to see whether his partner would do as the fortune teller told him. He looked into her eyes, her steady hand on the gun, her finger gripping the trigger, and he had no doubt she would blow off his head without hesitation.

"Do what she says," the fat man said. "We came here to deliver a message. Not to die doing it."

The muscular man took a deep breath, his eyes staring into Alexandra's, his body starting to ache from the awkward position. He slowly released the grip he had on her hair and then let the knife fall with a thud on the table.

"That's the way to keep living," Alexandra said. "Now raise the hands nice and slow. And if you make the slightest move toward my gun, I will blow your head right into your fat friend's arms."

The muscular man lifted his hands toward the ceiling. With one swift and smooth move, Alexandra removed the gun from his neck and pushed his head back toward the chair. She then grabbed the knife and dropped it onto her lap.

"There now, that's better," Alexandra said.

The muscular man pushed back his chair and stood. He tapped the fat man on the shoulder and nudged him toward the door. "We'll meet again," he said to Alexandra. "I have no doubt about that."

"You're probably right," she said. "But that is for another day."

"Don't forget to deliver the message to your friends," the muscular man said. He started to move toward the door, the fat man at his side.

"You're both forgetting something," Alexandra said.

"And what would that be?"

Alexandra held up the gun, aimed it at them, and smiled. "You both owe me twenty dollars. Toss the bills on the table and then get the hell out of my place."

"You can't be serious?"

"Money on the table or blood on the rug," Alexandra said. "To tell you the truth, it's all the same to me."

29.

ONE POLICE PLAZA

THE NEXT DAY

THE OFFICE WAS LARGE AND SMELLED OF POLISHED LEATHER. There was a couch lining one side of the wall across from a small conference table. Two leather wing chairs faced a massive mahogany desk. Every free inch of wall space was covered with framed photos of former detective chiefs and tabloid headlines of cases cracked by the team installed by the man currently sitting behind the desk. There were three floor-to-ceiling windows that overlooked an array of federal buildings and courthouses along with a steady stream of traffic coming off the FDR Drive.

I waited as Chief Connors poured us each a cup of black coffee in an NYPD mug. He looked up as he filled the cups. "I don't think I need to ask you how you take your coffee," he said with a smirk.

"Just like old Sister Timothy," I said, smiling at the memory. "Dark and bitter—like my life, she always would say when asked."

The chief sat back in his black leather swivel chair and took a sip of hot coffee. "Heard about what happened to one of your team," he said. "Sounds like she handled it well. Maybe I should think about recruiting her."

"She's good," I said. "And she was lucky. The two they sent couldn't find a couch in a living room. Next time she might not be as lucky. Or the next time it might be some other member of the team who isn't as good with a gun."

"I finished reading your report before you walked in," the chief said. "You're making fast progress, and this case is leading down a path I didn't expect."

"That good or bad?"

"Depends," the chief said. "A B&E topped by a rape and assault. That, I had no doubt you and your cronies could handle. A drug dealer with a few dozen backing his play might be more than you want to take on."

I took a deep breath and stared at the chief. "You know what would help me an awful lot?"

"What?"

"If I had the full picture of what this case is about."

"You think I'm holding back on you?" the chief asked. "Or you think you've been set up? I've known you a long time and I know how that brain of yours works. Which direction is it taking you this time?"

"I don't know this guy Gonzo from any other honey-dripper out dealing and pimping. And, better yet, he doesn't know me. Agree?"

"No arguments," the chief said.

"Yet, in no short order, this guy finds out I have a team in place I work with," I said. "That I have a teenager living with me who eats in the same restaurant I do. That there's a woman running the place I keep company with. And this next part is even more amazing—that I have a partner in a rehab facility. Now, I ask you, Chief, how did this Gonzo suddenly get so smart?"

"You think he's got ears inside the department?" the chief asked.

"He's got ears somewhere," I said. "And those ears either carry a badge and a gun or have a briefcase and a law degree."

"That's a pretty big jump to make, Tank," the chief said. He finished his coffee and rested his mug next to his phone. "I'm the only one knows you get assigned a case from time to time. No one else."

"We both would like to think that," I said. "The cases get wrapped up, perps get arrested, that means other cops who weren't in on the case catch the bust. I never take credit for the arrest. The cops that do then have to deal with the DA's office, and that brings legal into the loop. Paperwork is filed, charges are put in front of a judge, pleas are made, sentences doled out, sometimes even a body or two get left behind. You might be the only one who knows I get assigned. But you're not the only one who knows I work the cases."

"But this case has been the first and only one to cause you or your team any grief," the chief said.

"True," I said. "But this is the first and only case that goes deeper than what was in the initial folder. This one touches harder hands, and from the way it's shaping up there's sure to be bloodshed along the way."

"I can take it off your hands," the chief said. "Just say the word."

"Maybe if the offer had been made before yesterday, I would have given it thought," I said. "But not after what happened. They reached out and touched one of my team and made threats I can't let pass. They're in my scope now."

"You better remember one thing before you start to go off the rails," the chief said.

"I know what you're going to say," I said. "I'm not what I used to be. I'm slower, off my game a bit, maybe even more than a bit. I got a rag-tag crew, not exactly a full-geared SWAT team backing me up. I've thought about that and more."

"Have you thought about Connie and Chris?" the chief asked. "Crew or no crew, Tank, it's you that's going to have to deal with this. You think about that. And I'll think hard on whether or not I should let you get any deeper into this shitstorm."

I rested my cup of coffee on the edge of the chief's desk and stood. "You take me off or leave me on, I'm still going to butt heads with Gonzo and his gang."

The chief rocked back and forth. "The case is still yours. And if you find you need an extra backup, I'll be there for you."

I smiled at the chief. "You're not what you used to be, either," I said, shaking his hand. "Let's try and remember that."

"When you stop and think about it," the chief said, "who the hell really is?"

30.

THE WINTHROP

"I'M NOT GOING ANYWHERE," PEARL SAID. "BESIDES, IF THESE fuckers can track me here, they can track me down the next place you rest my ass."

"You are one stubborn bastard," I said.

"I learned from the best," Pearl said, flashing a smile. "Working by your side day in, day out."

"How tight is security up here?" I asked.

"There's cameras where you would expect them to be," Pearl said. "Entrances, exits, stairwells. I would imagine they're on a twenty-four-hour spool, so whatever was seen yesterday is erased by what's seen today."

"What about the guards?" I asked. "They armed or just baton and pepper spray?"

"It's a low-key place," Pearl said. "Local police cover the area. No need for security to carry. The guards monitor the halls and the front desk is covered. They are in radio contact with central PD."

"Regardless, they want to get to somebody, they can get to somebody," I said. "You know that well as I do."

"Well, if that's one of your concerns, partner, you can wipe that off the blackboard," Pearl said. "Anybody comes after me, they're gonna have some heat coming back their way."

"Wait," I said, unable to hide the surprise in my voice. "You still have your gun?"

"Who the hell else would have it?" Pearl said. "I earned the right to keep that and my shield."

We were outside one of the therapy rooms, under the shade of a tree that had seen better days. I sat on a bench, Pearl next to me in his wheelchair. He was dressed in short sweats and a cutoff hoodie, fresh from his latest workout routine.

"Where do you keep it?"

"That's my little secret," Pearl said.

"If need be, how fast can you get to it?"

"Fast enough to waste a shooter or two," Pearl said. "I've learned how to maneuver this chair pretty well after all the time I've been in it. So don't think of me as a sitting duck. Especially if I take my wheels down one of those sloping paths."

I turned and gazed casually around the grounds, meticulously maintained. It was a beautiful and sunny afternoon with a mild breeze, a nice break from the cold spell we'd been having. I spotted the gray Chevy sedan parked four slots away from where I had left my car. Pearl read my body language and followed my eyes.

"You were tailed coming up here?" he asked.

I nodded. "I spotted them on the Henry Hudson. Didn't make an effort to lose them. Figured it would be easier to deal with them here than to do a *French Connection* chase into Westchester."

"How many?"

"Two from what I could see out of the rearview. That was confirmed while I was waiting for you to finish your session. One Hispanic, the other white. They split up once they got out of the car. I figure one's above us somewhere, watching. The other is down below, probably doing the same."

"How do you want to play it?" Pearl asked.

"How about I take you for a spin around the grounds," I said. "Get a better look at the place. Wait for them to make their move. We'll know soon enough if they're here to observe or to take us down."

"This case turned nasty in no time flat," Pearl said.

"It seemed cut and dry," I said. "But there never really is such a case to be found."

"Now we're smack in the middle of a high-level narcotics operation," Pearl said. "Is that coincidence, bad luck, or a setup from old friends want to see us fall?"

"Let's rule out coincidence," I said.

"Which leaves what on the table?"

I shook my head. "Just what's ahead of us. We didn't set out to crack a drug ring, but that's what we need to do. If we manage that and come out alive, we'll have our answers."

"The two detectives originally assigned the case check out clean," Pearl said. "They made mistakes in judgment but nothing that would point to them having their hand out. They were new to the precinct, and the squad was spread thin when they got there. The case seemed one that fell through the cracks. At least on the surface."

I stood behind Pearl, grabbed the handles of his wheelchair, and began a slow walk down a winding path. "Fell through cracks or tossed aside, still doesn't add up," I said. "We talked to a couple of our old contacts. They led us to Mano and that opened the door to Gonzo and his crew. Didn't take long for us to put some of the pieces together. You would think someone in the squad could have done the same, if they wanted."

"That's a big if, my brother."

I spotted one of the men following me as I rounded an array of trimmed hedges. He was tall and slender, dressed in jeans and a blue blazer. He had on white Nikes and a Yankees cap. Pearl saw him at the same time I did.

"Are you sure that's one of the guys drove up behind you?" Pearl asked.

"Without a doubt," I said.

"Then let me ask you this," Pearl said. "Does he look to you like a guy gets his weekly take-home from a drug dealer?"

"Not one bit," I said. "He might take cash from a dealer, but his paycheck comes his way through direct deposit."

"Which makes him what, then?" Pearl asked.

I stopped and held the wheelchair in place. Beads of sweat formed at the base of my neck.

"It makes him a cop," I said.

31.

GREENWICH VILLAGE

THREE DAYS LATER

CARMINE TRAMONTI SAT IN A GARDEN CHAIR IN THE BACKYARD of his restaurant. There was a small table next to him, filled with a bottle of Biondi Santi, a wineglass, an ashtray, and slabs of pecorino cheese. He had a lit Cohiba cigar in his mouth and the *Daily Racing Form* folded in half on his lap. He held a blunt pencil in his right hand, ready to circle his betting action for the day. He was wearing his customary outfit of sharp-creased khakis, black three-button polo shirt, a Yankees windbreaker, and black moccasins. Carmine never wore socks, regardless of the time of year.

He reached over and grabbed the bottle of wine, a 2008 vintage, and poured himself a glass. He held the glass in his hand and stared out at the freshly planted vegetable garden surrounding him. He raised the glass skyward in a toast. "To you, my honey," he whispered. "I miss you each and every day. And your garden misses you even more. Even from the grave, you still take good care of me. You will be amazed at all the different fruits and veggies that will be sprouting out of the ground. Then again, baby, maybe not."

The underground sprinkler system was not yet on and the garden was still a few weeks away from being in full bloom, the various plants and trees soon to glisten under a warm sun. Carmine took a sip of wine and sat back, lifting his face to the sky and closing his eyes.

It was then he heard a footstep on the gravel path.

Carmine didn't move, just listened and waited. He heard a second footstep and then a third. He figured he had less than a minute to determine if it was one man out there or two. He knew whoever it was probably had scaled the red brick wall surrounding his backyard and waited in silence for him to come out. That meant they had studied his routine and learned his habits.

That meant they were pros and had come prepared to either deliver a message or do him harm.

This was not, Carmine knew, a mob setup. The mob wanted you dead, they didn't hide in a fruit-and-vegetable garden and wait for the right moment. They walked up to you and came up blasting. Besides, the mob had no beef with him. He had gone in old school and come out the same, leaving behind no waves.

These were either junkies looking to make a quick score or bangers trying to shake him down. They could even be muscle from the crew Tank and his band were in a tangle with. But guessing wasn't going to give Carmine an answer. He rested the wineglass on the table and took a long puff on the cigar and then put it on its side in the ashtray. He took a deep breath, stood, and walked toward the garden.

"If you're looking for some fresh fruit, I recommend the peaches," he said. "Best this side of Naples. But you'll need to come back in a month or so to grab a taste."

A young man tossed aside a handful of leaves, stepped on a row of tomato seedlings, and stopped a few feet from Carmine.

"We didn't come here for peaches," he said. He held a semiautomatic pistol in his right hand.

"Who is we?" Carmine said. "I left my glasses in my office. All I see is your-not-so-pretty face."

A second man came up from behind Carmine and jammed a pistol into the center of his back. Carmine didn't flinch; instead, he smiled. "I see you brought along a date."

The first man stepped closer to Carmine. He was in his late twenties, a runner's body with enough artwork on his arms and neck to fill a wall. "We're going to talk and you're going to listen. Do that, maybe we let you live."

"You may not want to, though," the one behind him said. "Once we're done working you over, you may just want to lay down and die."

Carmine turned his head slightly to the left, catching a glimpse of the man holding the gun to his back. "Everybody dies," he said in a low voice. "It's just a question of how, where, and when."

"You hear that?" the man with the gun said to his friend. "Sounds to me like we got a tough guy on our hands." He nudged the gun deeper into Carmine's back. "Is that right, old man? You a tough guy?"

"I used to be," Carmine said.

The first man nodded to the man with the gun and waited as he eased away from Carmine and moved three feet to his left. "Listen to me, onetime tough guy," the first man said to Carmine. "Tell your friend to back off, stop playing detective and causing grief to people he shouldn't be bothering. He does that, no one gets hurt. Other than you. I come across loud and clear?"

"I'm old," Carmine said. "Not deaf."

The first blow, from the blunt end of the gun, landed against the back of Carmine's head. The force sent him to his knees, hands clutching at thick mounds of soil, his vision blurred. The first man reared back and kicked Carmine hard, the edge of a thick black boot landing square against his chest. Carmine fell in a heap, gasping for air, mouth and nose covered with dirt. The duo then closed in on him and rained a violent series of hard kicks against Carmine's head, neck, arms, back, and legs. It lasted for several minutes that ticked away like hours. When they finally stopped the beating, they were each spent. They bent over, resting their hands on their knees, gasping for breath. They glanced down at Carmine, who wasn't moving but was still breathing.

"Make sure our message gets delivered," the first man said. "You don't want us to come back here."

The man with the gun started to laugh. The first one looked over at him and asked, "What's so funny?"

"Got an idea," he said. "We fucked the old man up, right?"

The first man looked down at Carmine and nodded. "Looks that way," he said.

"Then how about we fuck up his little garden, too?"

The first man looked around at the freshly planted and mulched rows of vegetables and trees recently freed from their winter wrappings and shrugged. "I like the way you think," he said.

The duo spent the next fifteen minutes ripping apart vines, crushing tomato plants, and knocking over a row of still-frail young fruit trees. By the time they were finished, the garden was completely ruined.

Carmine lay motionless amid the debris, his back soaked with sweat and streaked with dirt and stained with the ruins of a garden that had once been tended with great care by the love of his life.

32.

THE WINTHROP

THAT SAME DAY

I EASED PEARL AGAINST THE SIDE OF A TREE AND LOCKED THE wheelchair in place. "We got company in front of and behind us," I said to him.

"The one up top has been using the hedges as cover," Pearl said. "He's been tracking down since we started moving."

"They're either here to talk or to take us. And neither one of them is moving like they want to chitchat."

"Could be looking to put a scare in us," Pearl said. "Make us take a step back."

"I'm going to go down and meet our friend below. You sure you can handle the one above?"

"If I have to, I can take them both," Pearl said. "That help calm your concern?"

"He's all yours, Sundance," I said.

I faced the man at the end of the hill and raised my arms to eye level. "You got something you want to say to me?" I asked.

The man smiled. "They sent me to tell you to keep your nose out of Gonzo's business. But my guess is that would be a waste of words, knowing what I know about you."

"You know about me?" I asked. "How's something like that happen?"

"No hard thing," he said. "For one, it would be tough to forget the man put my brother away for twenty years plus."

"I did that to quite a few deserving souls," I said. "I remember them all, though. Most likely I'd remember your brother if I had a name to go along with the time served."

"Hidalgo," the man said. "His name is Ronnie Hidalgo. He was head honcho for the Park Avenue Snipers. You and the spook in the wheelchair went toe-to-toe with them in the Wild West years."

"He had a unique way of dealing with witnesses," I said. "He would blind them, eliminate any chance at a visual ID. Killed a bunch, too. You ask me, he got off easy with the twenty and change he got hit with."

"Not saying he was a saint," he said. "But he was blood. You know how that goes?"

I stared at the man for several seconds. His attitude, his outward calm, even the way he stood and moved his hands, told me my initial reaction was on the money. "How'd old Ronnie feel about seeing his little brother go to work in a blue uniform? I can't imagine gangbangers like having a cop in the family. Unless you were there not to serve but to protect."

"He stayed off my turf; I stayed away from his," he said.

"In other words, he padded you up," I said. "Cash flowed your way; information was whispered in his ears."

"It worked for a bit," he said. "I was only on the force less than three years. Hated the hours and the money sucked. Then I had to sit by when you and your pal pinched Ronnie and sent him to live in a cage. That was tough for me to watch. Promised myself one day I would get a taste of the get-even."

"And you're thinking today's that day?"

"Good a day as any," he said.

"You got a name?" I asked.

"Tomas."

I looked around the grounds. There were a handful of passersby, all a safe distance away. I had my gun tucked in the center of my jeans, resting against my spine. I had the sun to my back and there were hedges on either side of the path. I couldn't risk turning around to check on Pearl, not without giving Tomas an advantage I couldn't afford to let him have.

"This could end easy, for you and for me. Get back in your car. You and your friend up the hill. Go back and tell Gonzo we were warned. Collect your dough and head home, live to die another day."

"You put my brother away," Tomas said. "Some of his friends, too. Now it's time for you to go away. For good."

"I've never shot a cop before, ex or otherwise," I said. "Not even a dirty one like you. Then again, you weren't a real cop, were you? You were your brother's inside man. Nothing more than a snitch for some scratch. Now you're running errands for Gonzo, drinking from his water bowl."

"It got me what I wanted," Tomas said. "A face-off with the one and only. Gonzo wants you out of the way. He's betting I'm the man to do it."

"A sucker's bet," I said.

I reached for my gun and jumped into a row of hedges. Tomas was caught off guard by the sudden move, hesitated, and then started running toward me, pulling his gun as he ran. I lay flat on the ground and aimed my gun in his direction. Tomas fired two shots into the hedges, both zipping by above me, slicing off chunks of a maple tree to my right.

I jumped to my knees and aimed my gun at Tomas. He was about fifteen feet from me and walking close to my side of the hedges. I popped out of the hedges and fired one round. It caught Tomas just below his throat and brought him to his knees. He was still holding the gun.

"Drop it," I said. "You took a hit, but it won't kill you. You pull on me again and the second one will."

Tomas raised the gun, ready to fire a third round.

I didn't hesitate and fired the kill shot into his chest.

His hand fell to his side and the gun dropped to the ground. His head slumped and his upper body twitched in a series of spasms. His shirt was drenched with blood, and thick red bubbles formed at the corners of his mouth. I could hear the death rattle in his throat.

Behind me, farther up the hill, two shots rang out. I turned and saw the back of Pearl's wheelchair. Tomas's partner was stretched out a few feet from the base of the wheels. He was facedown and not moving.

I raced up the hill, rushing to Pearl's side. His old .38 was clutched in his right hand. "You good?" I asked.

Pearl pointed to the dead man close by. "Doing better than he is, that's for damn sure."

"The RMPs are heading our way," I said, the sounds of police sirens wrecking the quiet of a lazy day. "You sure you're allowed to have that gun?"

"A disabled man needs protection," Pearl said. "As you can plainly see."

"Before the uniforms get here, friend to friend, tell me where you keep it?"

"Stays our secret?" Pearl asked.

"To my grave," I said.

"Safest place I know," Pearl said. "In my Depends."

"In your what?"

"Depends," Pearl said. "You know, adult diapers."

I shook my head. "No shit, really?"

Pearl smiled. "No shit," he said. "Not this time, anyway."

33.

NYU MEDICAL CENTER—ICU

LATER THAT NIGHT

I SAT ACROSS FROM CONNIE, A SMALL HOSPITAL BED SEPARAT-ing us. Carmine lay in that bed, connected to a half dozen tubes and machines monitoring his body and sending drugs into his system. His face was heavily bruised and bandaged, blood seeping through the white gauze. He had a concussion and several cracked ribs, and one of his lungs had been damaged. His breathing was labored and his hair, always carefully combed, was disheveled.

I got the call about Carmine from Bruno.

I had been at White Plains police headquarters dealing with the fallout from the shooting, answering the same half dozen questions over and over to an array of confused and concerned uniform person-nel. A phone call from the NYPD chief of detectives was enough to get me out of the room and back on the road. I checked on Pearl be-fore I left, filling him in on what had gone down with Carmine.

"Get to him," Pearl said. "I'm fine here."

I nodded. "Get some rest. I'll be back soon as I can."

As I raced to the hospital, my team was already on the scene, keep-ing an eye on Connie and checking in on Carmine.

I reached over and clutched Carmine's hand. I was a bundle of anger and regret. He was in that bed because of me. I glanced at Connie, her beautiful face sad and drawn, and knew she was thinking the same thing. It wouldn't be lost on any member of my team assembled in the corridor, either.

I stood and walked to Connie's side. I reached for her hand and held it softly in mine. "I never meant for this to happen," I said to her. "I know you know that. I just thought you needed to hear me say it."

Connie nodded, her eyes welling with tears. "But it did happen, Tank," she said. "And I could ask you to let it go, walk away from the case. But I know it's not in you to do that."

"I might surprise you," I said.

"A trip to Paris would surprise me," Connie said. "You asking off a case would shock me. But you're not walking away. It's who you are, Tank. And who you'll always be. Just like him." She nodded toward the bed at her father.

"How do you mean?"

"You two get along so well because you're so much alike," she said. "That's one of the reasons I love you so much. You remind me so much of Dad. Granted, you were a cop and, well, let's just say he wasn't."

I wiped a tear from her cheek. "Let's just say."

"He's going to come out of this," Connie said. "And he'll get stronger and better. I'll see to that."

"We all will," I said.

"But he's not going to let this sit," she said. "Any more than you can. He's going to reach out for some of his friends and he's going back to being what he once was. He put that life behind him long ago, promised my mom on her deathbed that he would lead an honest life. But that promise is now out the window. He'll leave that garden the way it is—destroyed—until the day he gets even or they get him."

"If that's what you believe and that's what he's going to do," I said, "he won't be doing it alone."

"He's not what he used to be, Tank," Connie said. "Older, slower, damaged, up against younger, stronger, and not afraid to die. Not even a gambler like Carmine would give winning odds on that bet."

"He's beaten the odds before," I said. "We both have."

"You need to think about more than yourself," Connie said. "More than about me. You need to think about Chris. He needs you and you need him."

"I thought it best for now to give him some alone time."

"He and Dad have gotten pretty tight," Connie said. "Carmine taught him how to bet the daily double and signed him up for boxing lessons at Bruno's gym."

"I heard," I said.

"Dad gave him several books to read," she said. "It was a pretty mixed bag—couple of sports bios, a few *Classics Illustrated* comics, and one about Meyer Lansky."

"Sounds better than the summer reading list he would have gotten from his new school," I said.

"Chris hides it well, but he's scared," Connie said. "He's reaching out to you, through the crew, through Dad, through me. He wants to be part of this, be included, and from what I've heard he can be a help."

"He's come up with some useful information," I said. "But you need look no further than that bed to know this is anything but a connect-the-dots case."

"I'm not saying to put him in the middle of a street fight," Connie said. "Except for Bruno, you never put anyone on your team in harm's way, not intentionally. Do the same for Chris. Don't baby him. That's the last thing he needs."

I smiled at her. "Didn't take you long to figure out how to read a boy's needs," I said.

Connie looked from me to Carmine, asleep on the hospital bed. "I've been reading the needs of boys, big and small, most of my life," she said.

"Where is Chris?" I asked.

"Joey took him to the cafeteria," Connie said. "He didn't want to leave until he gets to see Dad."

I leaned over and wrapped my arms around Connie and held her for a few moments. I bent down and kissed the top of her head and then walked over to the side of Carmine's bed. I rested one hand on top of his and lowered my head and whispered soft words in his left ear. His burly fingers gripped my hand and held it tight. I stood back up and smiled down at him.

"What'd you say to him?" Connie asked.

"Boy talk."

"I was afraid of that," she said.

34.

NYU MEDICAL CENTER—CAFETERIA

MOMENTS LATER

SPOTTED JOEY AND CHRIS SITTING AT A CIRCULAR WHITE Formica table in a corner of the large dining area. I stopped to get a large coffee and walked toward them. The other tables were filled with relatives and friends of patients chatting quietly, eating salads and sandwiches, while their damaged loved ones were being attended to. A smattering of doctors, nurses, and hospital staff were spread around the tables, enjoying a few quiet moments in an otherwise emotional and hectic day.

Chris was winding his way through a bag of Sun Chips, and Joey was drinking a diet soda.

"Okay if I sit in?" I asked.

"Help yourself to some pizza," Joey said. "Guy at the counter said it was as good as if it were made in Naples."

"Naples, Florida, is maybe what he meant," I said.

I turned to Chris, who couldn't mask his concern for Carmine. "How about you?" I asked him. "The guy at the counter try to convince you the hot dogs came from Germany?"

"I had a grilled cheese and these chips," he said, holding up the bag.

I glanced at Joey and tilted my head, signaling him I wanted to be alone with Chris. He caught the move, grabbed the pizza plate, and stood. "You two finish up," he said. "I'm going to grab a coffee and bring it up to Connie. Think she might want a salad or a sandwich to go with it?"

I shook my head. "I'll call the restaurant and have them send up some food. Ida will cook one of her favorites. I'll call in something for you and the rest of the crew, too. Is everyone still here?"

"Except for Bruno," Joey said, starting to walk from the table. "He wanted to check on the restaurant and work the bar tonight. Just in case."

"He shouldn't be there alone," I said. "I don't think they'll make a move on the place. Probably waiting to see how we choose to go after the number they did on Carmine. But it would be better if Bruno had some backup."

"No worries on that end," Joey said. "Two of Carmine's buddies came by earlier and told Connie they'll have the place covered until her dad is sitting back in his booth."

"Rocco and Carlo," I said. "Those three were inseparable back in the day. Had more action going on the streets than a dozen of the crews working today."

"Drugs?" Joey asked.

"Never went near that," I said. "That's why they lasted long as they have. Kept it simple—numbers, sports betting, high-stakes poker, some money on the street. Made themselves a lot of cash and were smart enough to keep most of it."

"I guess the restaurant will have at least two paying customers eating there tonight," Joey said.

"Not likely. Rocco and Carlo are crime, and as you well know by now, crime don't pay."

They both laughed. "How about you and me do a walk-and-talk?" I said to Chris. "Get some fresh air and stretch our legs."

"Okay."

"If we pass a hot-dog stand, I'll toss in a hot pretzel with plenty of mustard," I said.

"I read somewhere the best pretzels are made in Belgium," he said.

"Not the ones we're going to get," I said, leading the way out of the cafeteria. "They're made in the Bronx. If we're lucky."

"Is that a good thing or bad?" Chris asked.

"It's a coin toss," I said. "Just like life."

35.

NYU MEDICAL CENTER— ENTRANCE

MOMENTS LATER

WALKED OUT OF THE HOSPITAL, CHRIS CLOSE BEHIND ME. WE turned right, past two parked ambulances and an elderly man sitting in a wheelchair, seemingly relieved to be alone even for a brief moment.

"The guys told me what a help you've been on the case," I said. "Even Pearl's impressed, and that happens about as often as a lunar eclipse."

"You okay with it?"

"At first, not really," I said. "I was pissed and surprised. Then I sat on it for a while and came around to their thinking."

"So I can keep helping?"

"I'm going to pull the team off the case," I said.

"Why?"

"It's taken a dark turn," I said. "Me and Pearl are the only ex-cops, and the two of us will work it alone. I'm not putting anyone else's life in danger."

"We could still work the computers," Chris said.

"There's one target in this investigation, and I don't need a computer readout to tell me who it is."

"You can't go after him alone," Chris said.

"He touched people I care about," I said, looking at Chris. "People I love. First Alexandra, head-on. Then a threat to Pearl. And now the beat down they gave Carmine. I can't let that sit. I can't allow anyone to hurt the ones I love."

"Did you feel that way about my dad, too?" Chris asked. "Or did you stop loving him when you two stopped speaking?"

The question caught me off guard and I stayed quiet for a few moments before I answered. "No one hurt your dad. He had an accident, on a night he shouldn't have been driving."

Chris lowered his face, and I could tell from the sag in his shoulders that he was fighting back the urge to cry. "You're wrong" was all he managed to say.

"About what?"

Chris stood in front of me. "I've read the police reports about my mom and dad. I saw what the medical examiner wrote up."

"The reports are pretty cut and dry," I said. "Unless it's a homicide or a rape. It's facts and little else. You want detail and plot points, pick up a John Grisham novel."

"You know how much Dad loved cars," Chris said. "He raced them as a kid and he was always working on them, every weekend. When I was old enough, he let me hang with him in the garage and at the tracks, teaching me as much as I could absorb about cars and engines."

"I remember," I said. "It was more than a hobby; it was a passion. In another life, Jack would have been a Formula One driver instead of an accountant. But none of that has anything to do with what happened to him and your mom."

"It has everything to do with it," Chris said. He held his ground, his voice tinged with a hard edge.

"Which adds up to what to you?"

"My dad was too good a driver to be knocked off a bridge by an ice storm," Chris said. "He doted on his cars and was obsessed with safety. He always anticipated any type of road condition and went out prepared to handle it."

"Maybe," I said. "But Jack wasn't driving on an Indy Five Hundred track. He was on a parkway, crossing a bridge that iced up and a road that hadn't been salted or sanded. Mario Andretti couldn't have kept that car from smashing through the guardrail."

"We'll never really know," Chris said. "Because nobody bothered to check the car. All they saw was wreckage. No one looked at the brake lining or the pads."

"And if someone had?" I asked. "What would they have found?"

"That there was something wrong with the car," Chris said. "Someone had worked on it to make sure my parents had an accident on that road. With or without a storm."

"So you're telling me it wasn't an accident?"

"It was murder," Chris said.

Chris rushed into me. His arms reached around my waist and he buried his head in my chest. His body heaved and moaned and the tears came gushing out. All the pain and anguish he had held in came out in an avalanche of sorrow.

I looked up toward the clear sky and closed my eyes.

Chris was opening a door I had sealed for decades. We who keep our past hidden do so for valid reasons. None of those reasons have to do with hatred, jealousy, or hard feelings.

They have to do with fear.

I thought I buried that past years ago.

But now I felt the cold hand of fear touch me once again.

I stood there in the middle of the street, motionless, a crying boy clutched to my waist as I felt the walls of my past close in on me.

36.

CENTRAL PARK

THE NEXT DAY

He was sitting on a park bench, halfway through a twelve-inch Subway sandwich. He had a container of coffee resting on a wooden slat to his right. He hadn't changed much since I last laid eyes on him six years ago, a little rounder in the middle and a little less on top. But the face still looked rugged and the eyes, even from a distance, gave off a feeling of menace. He was a sergeant when we first ran into each other. I was working a homicide, and he was running a plainclothes unit bordering my precinct.

We despised each other on sight.

I made it my business to steer clear of him, and he did the same with me. He rose up the ranks quickly and hit captain before he turned forty. His rocket-like rise had little to do with cracking any major case. A peek at his arrest record gives no indication that he made any, in fact. But he was always Johnny-on-the-spot to recommend a restaurant to a higher-up, going so far as to book the table himself and strong-arm the manager into giving the boss and his wife a great meal without a tab, letting them know it was the captain's treat. Soon enough, he was hanging with the deputy chief as well as the then-commissioner himself, joining them for weekly dinners at some of the city's finest, with no worry of a bill ever hitting the table.

His name was Frank Rumore. Among the cops he was known simply as "Zagat."

The word about him was he was running a pad, taking in a few hundred a month in dirty cash from each of three high-end drug dealers. I always did my best to stay away from stained badges, refusing to be smeared and lumped into their company. I'm no saint, not by any means, but I didn't become a cop to line my pockets with a criminal's excess cash.

There are a lot of ways to make easy money. None appealed to me. I know all the excuses cops who take use—kids coupled with tuition and medical bills; multiple marriages tied to alimony and lawyer bills; too heavy a mortgage and too expensive a car; a taste for fine wine and exotic vacations. I never bought into any. You need money, get a second job or lease a cheaper car and hit Tar Beach on your two weeks off instead of the Peninsula hotel. You dig your own holes in life and you should be able to figure a way—an honest way—to dig yourself out.

Plus, I didn't need the money. I had the brownstone, thanks to my parents. While I got it free and clear, my parents made sure Jack had the education he wanted without the weight of loans and a down payment on his first house. He also got all the insurance money when they died.

I SAT A FEW inches away and waited for him to look at me. He didn't seem surprised to see me. He gave me a smirk and a nod. "Didn't think you ventured far out of your neighborhood these days, Tank," he said, taking a huge chunk out of his Subway hero. "You bored or you got something on your mind?"

"Don't tell me you believed that guy on TV who told you that crap would make you lose weight," I said.

"He's in the slammer now, that guy," Frank said.

"That's his worry," I said.

"And what's yours?" Frank asked. He wiped at his chin with a handful of napkins clutched in his right hand.

"I need a favor."

"If you're looking for me to do it for you, you're pissing on the wrong tree," Frank said. "I didn't care for you when you were on the job, and I care even less since you've been off."

I slid closer to Frank. "I'm only going to ask once. And I expect you to say yes."

"Hey, take a good walk for yourself," Frank said. "I ain't doing shit for you."

"You must have pocketed how much dirty money by now?" I asked. "You were on three pads when I was on the job. Lord only knows how big the number is now. I'm thinking three, four hundred thousand easy."

Frank glared at me, balled up his Subway wrapper, and flipped it into a large paper bag. He reached over and picked up his coffee and was about to stand and walk away. "You can't leave now, Frank," I said. "You're going to miss the best part. It's the part where I pick up a phone and whisper a few words to the right ears and—wait for it— you get nabbed by Internal Affairs and the DA's office, and, before you know it, adiós to all those great restaurants and fabulous meals. Farewell to all that dough you got stashed, not to mention your pension. No more condo in West Palm, and wave bye-bye to the wife and that Upper East Side widow you've been slipping in nights to see."

Frank looked at me, face flushed red, hands balled into fists. "That ever were to happen, you would end up along the BQE, seagulls pecking at your flesh."

"Maybe so," I said. "But I won't be the one in the orange jumpsuit in a place where a Subway foot-long has an entirely different kick to it."

"What the fuck do you want?" Frank said, spittle forming at the edge of his mouth.

"I need a name," I said.

"Whose name?"

"The name of the top cop Gonzo has on his pad," I said. "I know it isn't you—too uptown and your name wouldn't mean anything to him. But I figure, just like all the good cops seem to know each other, all the bad ones do, too. No doubt you've had many a meal with the man. Give me his name and I'll be on my way."

Frank shook his head. "You've got some pair of balls coming to me this way. I should run you up on charges."

"You would if you could," I said. "But a hair ball like you wouldn't know a DD-five from a can of DDT. So cut the Bogart and give me the damn name."

"I think you're all bluff," Frank said. "You're not going to go rat me out to the Internal guys or to the DA."

"Maybe you're right. Maybe I wouldn't go see them. Maybe I'd take a walk in my neighborhood and stop by for an espresso and see Mike Ruffalino. Mr. Mike knows me since I was a kid. He knew my old man, too. So what if I tell him that a cop he's been giving money to for a gang of years is running his mouth?"

"I never put his name to my lips," Frank said, suddenly on the defensive.

"Mr. Mike doesn't know that," I said. "What if I tell him you've been playing him for a fool and laughing about it with your friends? And the info he gets back from you for all that cash is nothing more than street gossip? He might as well toss those bills in that basement furnace he's always running at full throttle."

"He won't buy it," Frank said. Sweat was forming at the corner of his neck and the sides of his face.

"You want to bet your life on it, Frank?"

He stared at me for a few moments. I could feel his stale, warm breath, his dry tongue lashing against his lips.

"This can't get back to me in any way, understood?" Frank said.

I nodded.

"I mean nobody, and that means nobody can ever know it came from me," Frank said.

I leaned over and put my lips to Frank's left ear. "Give me the fucking name," I whispered. "Now."

37.

WASHINGTON HEIGHTS

THE NEXT DAY

GONZO STOOD WITH HIS BACK TO AN OPEN WINDOW. HE WAS wearing Nike running shorts, a knockoff pair of Air Jordans, and was sipping strong black coffee from a mug with a headshot of Princess Diana across the front. He was shirtless, and his upper body glistened with sweat despite the cool morning breeze sweeping in, sending the white curtains fluttering.

He looked at the four men spread out across the large room. "I don't ask for much, am I right?" he asked them. "All I ask is to get this Tin Badge off my back. That's it. And, instead, what do I have in front of me? Two of mine down, and him and his team still sniffing my ass. That ain't right."

"He went to the hospital to check on the old man," one of the men said. "Seeing him in that bed might be enough to chill his shit."

"You're fuckin' wrong, Pedro," Gonzo said. "What do you do? Wake up and take stupid pills with your coffee?"

"How you figure wrong?" Pedro asked.

"First of all, seeing that old man in a hospital bed is not going to make the cop back down," Gonzo said. "It's going to piss him off."

"Okay, so he doesn't take a step back," Pedro said. "He makes a forward move. Don't matter either way. So long as he stays in our scope."

"Touching the old man like you did," Gonzo said, "without running it by me first was not a smart play."

"You asked us to reach out and touch his family," Pedro said defensively. "This guy Tank don't have much family. Just that band of losers and the old man, the kid, and his woman. We thought the old man was the best way to go."

"He's not just any old man," Gonzo said. "Back in his day, he was a major OC player. He had his own crew. Now, maybe he's been out of the life too long a time. Maybe when you look and see an old man is all you get. That the case, then we're standing on hard ground."

"You think he's still connected?"

"Once you go into the life, you don't get unconnected," Gonzo said. "Not like he worked for Verizon, retired, and pulls down a pension. No such thing as an exit door for the mob boys."

"I hear what you're telling us, Gonzo," Pedro said. He gave a quick look at the other three men in the room and caught them nodding their encouragement. "But even so, the only ones he could drag back into a fight have gotta be other old men. And the way he got worked over, he might give serious thought to sitting this one out."

Gonzo stared at Pedro for a few moments. He took several long sips of his coffee and reached for an open pack of Kools. He pulled out a cigarette and cradled it in his palm. "There's some truth to that," Gonzo said. "But this guy Tank is going to need more pushback. I've butted heads with guys like him. I know how they think, how they figure ways to reach for me the way we reached for him. Never think he's going to walk from this."

"There's still the girlfriend," Pedro said.

"And then there's the kid," the older of the three men said. "And we can get to both if you say the word."

Gonzo smiled. "Those are solid choices, no doubt. And I'm not saying no to the idea. In fact, far as I'm concerned, you can reach out and hit his whole fuckin' team. But I think you should add one more piece to this little puzzle. One that will save us hours of time as well as grief."

"You're talking about the cop, right?" Pedro asked.

"I'm talking about the cop," Gonzo said. "He goes down and this shit goes away."

"We tried once, and him and the cripple put our two men down," Pedro said.

"Send two more," Gonzo said. "And two more after that. I don't give a shit how many you have to send—you put an end to that cop. Hear me?"

All four men nodded.

"Then hear this part, too," Gonzo said. "If that cop don't go down, I will make damn sure the four of you do."

38.

THE BROWNSTONE

LATER THAT DAY

I STOOD IN THE CENTER OF THE LARGE LIVING ROOM, MY TEAM sitting and standing around me. Connie and Chris were there, as well. The landline was resting in the center of the wine-barrel coffee table, on speaker, Pearl listening on the other end.

"The case I signed on for is now closed," I said. "The two suspects in the break-in and rape are presumed dead and buried. Which means, as of today, your job is finished."

"You're forgetting something," Joey said. "Or should I say some-one?"

"I'm not forgetting anything, Joey," I said. "You didn't sign up to take on Gonzo and his crew. None of you did. That's my case now, and this is one I'll work alone."

"Did I just hear you're going to work alone?" Pearl's voice boomed off the speakerphone.

I shook my head. "I stand corrected. When I said I was going to work it alone, of course I meant along with Pearl."

"That sounds a whole lot better," Pearl said.

"We can't let you do that," Carl said.

"Look, in the past, cases me and Pearl have been handed involved knocking on doors, breaking down files, working the phones, and putting together a timeline," I said. "Basic legwork. This one's a bit more complicated."

"By complicated you mean dangerous," Connie said. "And you and Pearl have been out of that end of the job for almost two years."

"Maybe so," I said. "But we're the only two who have ever been in it. The rest of you never have had to do it."

"Why don't you let us make that decision?" Alexandra asked.

"You handled yourself well with those two who stepped into your shop," I said to her. "But they came to you on your turf and you caught them by surprise. The next time they won't be as careless."

"You can't take on Gonzo and his crew by yourself or with Pearl's help," Bruno said. "There's too many of them, and they can come at you from any direction at any time."

"You need a team, Tank," Carl said. "And like it or not, we're the only team you've got."

"So instead of handing us our walking papers and a group hug," Joey said, "how about we spend our time putting together a plan to nail these bastards before they get a chance to do more damage?"

"I don't want any of you to get hurt," I said.

"In that case, whatever plan we come up with better be a damn good one," Joey said.

Connie moved next to me, one arm around Chris's shoulders. "The chief is not going to let you go at it alone, so you might as well pencil his name on your lineup card. And then there's my dad."

I turned to look at her. "He needs to heal and get well. Last thing he needs is to go head-to-head with Gonzo."

"Doing that is the fastest way for Dad to heal," Connie said. "He's not going to take the beating he did and shrug it off. Nothing any of us can say or do is going to stop him from calling in old friends and putting them on the street."

"It's not just Gonzo we need to concern ourselves with," I said. I was slowly resigning myself to the fact my team was going to be in this battle whether I wanted them or not.

"There's a dirty cop in the mix," Pearl said. "Most likely more than one. And believe me when I tell you, a dirty cop will do anything to anyone to avoid getting a pair of cuffs slapped on his wrists."

"They're as dangerous as Gonzo and his posse," I said. "Even more so, since they can use the law against any of us."

For a few moments everyone remained silent, lost in thought, casting furtive glances at one another. Finally, Joey stood and faced the crew. "Just so we're clear," he said, "we'll have mob guys on our side and a few dirty cops working with Gonzo and his dealers on the other side?"

"That seems to be the way it's laying out," I said.

"Then I was wrong a few minutes ago when I said we needed a damn good plan," he said.

"What do we need, then?" Carl asked.

"We need a great plan," Joey said. "A *Dirty Dozen* kind of plan. A can't-miss, can't-fail plan."

"That is exactly what we need, Joey," I said.

Chris moved away from Connie, looked at each member of the team, and then turned to face me.

"I have a plan," he said.

39.

LOWER MANHATTAN

THE NEXT DAY

I WAS WALKING AGAINST A RED LIGHT WHEN I SPOTTED THE idling car.

It was a dark-green Chevy Impala with out-of-state plates, hub-caps missing on the front and rear tires. The windows, front and back, were down. I could only spot the wheelman from where I was but figured there to be more than one rider in the car. It was early on a weekday morning, the sun getting ready to rise above the WPA-built structures housing the bulk of Manhattan's criminal-justice system. The street traffic was light, and the cool breeze making its way through the maze of buildings would soon surrender to the demands of a spring day.

I was halfway across the street, waiting as a slow-moving Jeep headed toward the light, when I saw the car ease out of its parking slot. I made it to the other side of the street and stood between two parked cars, each with an NYPD permit hoisted against the windshield, and waited. The car came toward me slow, the driver's eyes on me, his left hand hanging out the open window, a handgun wrapped around his fingers. The driver, a young Hispanic male in his early twenties, looked my way and smiled.

The man sitting in the backseat had one arm dangling out the window and resting against the side of the car. He was holding a semiautomatic weapon, his finger curled against the trigger.

I did a quick scan of the street, noting some of the pedestrians slow-walking to their offices, holding cups of hot coffee and small bags stuffed with bagels or muffins. Most, I figured, were lawyers, both defense and prosecutors, heading in for another day of legal battle. A few I took to be reluctant jurors summoned to do their duty at forty dollars a day. Then there were the stragglers, always easy to spot, dressed in their best clothes, off to face a judge and either end their day free on bond or bound for a bus ride to a jail cell and fresh-issued prison wear.

I figured a few in the crowd to be cops, either NYPD or federal agents, gearing up to tackle a new case or a mountain of paperwork and dozens of phone calls, designed to break down an existing investigation.

I stared at the two in the car, pulled my gun out of its hip holster, and held it against my right leg. I braced myself against the two parked cars and waited for the shooters to make their move. I caught the driver's eye and held the look as he raised his gun and moved the car toward me. They were looking to hit me where I stood, between the two parked cars. I wasn't going to give them that chance.

I jumped away from the cars and into the street, standing in front of the approaching Chevy Impala. The two shooters raised their guns and I raised mine, aiming it at the windshield. They were close enough for me to see their faces. The gunman in the backseat leaned out of the car to get a better position. The driver held up his gun, but I saw the flinch in his eyes when I took aim directly at him. "Run me down or shoot me down," I shouted to the driver. "Either way, I will take you out before I fall."

The driver brought his gun hand back into the car and stepped on the gas. I jumped out of the way, barely avoiding the front end of the Impala. The shooter in the back was struggling to get to the other side of the car and was unable to get off a shot. The car screeched to a stop and the shooter in the backseat jumped out, crouched down, and fired two rounds in my direction.

I dove behind a parked RMP and raised my gun above the hood, taking aim at the shooter coming my way. I looked to my right and saw three uniform officers running toward the gunman and the Impala, their weapons drawn.

"Ten-thirteen!" I shouted to them, seeing one of them nod in my direction. It's the distress call for a cop in jeopardy. "The driver is armed, as well. Take them both in alive if you can. In body bags if you can't."

The three uniforms surrounded the car and were soon joined by a half dozen other cops, some in plainclothes, shields hanging around their necks. I stepped out from behind the RMP and walked toward the two shooters, the driver still sitting behind the wheel of his car. I looked over at one of the plainclothes detectives and nodded at him. "Nice to see you again, Tony," I said to him as I walked toward the front of the Impala.

"All this and no coffee, Tank," Tony said. "Some pal you are."

I looked at the two shooters, my gun raised. "There are at least eight cops taking dead aim at you. And I underline the word 'dead.' Drop your weapons and do it slowly. And cut the engine on the car. You do that, you live to see another morning."

The gunmen glanced around and then slowly lowered their weapons. The driver cut the engine and stepped out of the car, his hands raised above his head. They were surrounded by cops in seconds and cuffed. Tony stepped up next to me. "Be honest, now," I said to him. "What's better to have first thing in the morning? A cup of coffee off a street cart or a nice bust on your record?"

Tony smiled. "Anything else we can do for you this morning, Tank?" he asked.

"Get these two losers of out my sight," I said. "And buy each cop you see here a coffee and a buttered roll."

"Your treat?"

"Don't get crazy," I said to Tony. "The chief of detectives will pick up the tab. Send the bill up to his office."

I watched them leave, the two suspects lost in a sea of cops, and stared out at the passing traffic, lost in a swirl of my own thoughts.

Was this case worth the risk it came with? Was taking my team into a battle they might not be ready for worth it? There were a thousand drug runners like Gonzo on the streets of the city. Would taking down one make much of a difference?

If I walked away, Gonzo would hold fire for a while. He would lie back and savor the victory, pretend our battle was at an end. And then, in a month, maybe in a year, he would make his move.

A career criminal was once asked by the great FBI profiler John Douglas why he kept committing crimes when he knew the odds were stacked in favor of his getting nabbed. The guy, in cuffs, in the backseat of John's car, being driven off to yet another stretch in prison, shrugged and said, "We are who we are. And nothing can ever change us."

Gonzo is who he is. A killer, a pimp, and a drug dealer. He knows no other way, and nothing will change that.

And I am who I am. A wounded ex-cop, a Tin Badge, looking to take him down. Nothing will ever change that.

Not until one of us dies.

40.

ONE POLICE PLAZA

LATER THAT MORNING

I LEANED AGAINST THE WINDOW, LOOKING DOWN AT LOWER Manhattan, the long, imposing shadows of the cement structures shrinking the crammed streets and the pedestrians to microscopic size. The chief of detectives was to my right, sitting at his desk, reading the report I had handed him minutes earlier. Prior to that, I had filled him in on my run-in with two more of Gonzo's cowboys on the street near his office.

The chief rested the report on his desk and removed his reading glasses. He rubbed the worry from his eyes and stared at me in silence for several moments. "This is some pickle jar you squeezed open," he finally said.

"I'll handle it from my end—the how and the when I'd like to keep to myself for now. But you need to wash out the dirty laundry that's mixed in with Gonzo."

The chief looked down at my report and flipped to the third page and shook his head. "How'd you manage to dig up his name?" he asked.

"Are you at all surprised he's on the take? He's probably had his hand out since he first stepped out of the academy."

"He's in line for a promotion, the bastard," the chief said. "I got three glowing letters of recommendation about him two weeks ago."

"Have the IA boys check out the three who wrote the letters."

"You're certain he and his partner are involved this deep with Gonzo?" he asked.

"Might even go deeper than the drugs-and-skin trade," I said. "It's not in that report because I'm not nailed-down certain. But the smart money tells me they're the ones who took care of the two who raped and beat the girls in Chelsea. If I'm right, that's a murder one tossed on top of bribery, corruption, prostitution, and any other charges the DA can stick to their ass."

"That would total out to life without parole," the chief said. "And you know what that means, especially to a cop?"

I nodded, still gazing out the window. "They'd rather die on the streets than be taken in doing a perp walk."

The chief walked over and stood next to me by the window. "Are you up to this, Tank?" he asked. "Taking on a crew like Gonzo's is rough enough. Toss in these dirty bastards and you and your guys will be up against the wall. You're going to need more than what you have on your side."

I looked at him. "I have more on my side. You may not like where it's coming from, but they're very good and they're extremely motivated. In their day, they've gone against tougher."

The chief walked to a small table in a corner of the room and poured out two steaming cups of coffee. He came back and handed me one. "I'm guessing Carmine has been reaching out to his old crew," he said. "They're rough and tumble, I'll grant you. But they're way past prime time."

"They've been hard knockers all their lives," I said.

The chief smiled. "I remember that crew of his. I spent years trying to nab them and never could make anything stick."

"I came close once," I said. "Thought I had one of Carmine's uptown pals dead to rights on a truck-hijacking charge. Had it all scoped out, even had two eyewitnesses eager and ready to testify."

"How did it go south?"

"The two witnesses changed their tune, claimed it was a misunderstanding," I said. "And then the owner of the truck company decided not to press charges. I figured their lives were threatened. Wasn't until years later I found out Carmine had stepped in and bought a stake in the truck company, bailing the owner out from under a ton of debt, and the two witnesses took their wives on a cruise to the Greek islands. They claimed they won some sort of contest."

"That's the difference, Tank," the chief said. "Back then you had organized crime, you knew the players, and they knew the game. Today you got disorganized crime. Guys making it up as they go along, lungs and brains clouded by white powder and pills."

"Maybe so," I said. "But it's what's in front of us and what needs to be handled."

"I'll move on these dirty cops soon as I get the heads-up from you," the chief said. "Until then, I'll make sure they're kept busy so as not to have much free time to help their boss."

"It won't be long," I said. "Two, three days at the most."

"Anything you need, just get word to me," the chief said.

We shook hands and I started for the office door, then stopped and turned. "There's only one thing we're going to need before this is over," I said.

"What's that?"

"Body bags," I said. "Lots of body bags."

41.

THE BROWNSTONE

LATER THAT DAY

WE WERE ASSEMBLED IN MY LIVING ROOM. THE ROOM HAD been turned into an operation control center. A large-screen computer covered the top of my wine-barrel wooden desk and there were two other computers resting on top of a foldout black poker table. Chris and Joey were sitting on reclining chairs manning the computers as the rest of the team stood around them to watch. The landline was on speaker with Pearl listening in on the other end.

"Let me hear it," I said.

"We started with his cell phones," Joey said. "He has a few; all the drug dealers do. They get as many as eight phones and burn them every couple of weeks. This makes tracking incoming, outgoing, and texts harder but not impossible to retrieve."

"And it was a major help to have access to TARU," Chris said.

"What's TARU?" Bruno asked.

"An NYPD special unit," I said. "Officially known as the Technical Assistance Response Unit. They have the capability to download the history of any phone, no matter how old. Cutting edge and hard to crack into. Or so I was led to believe."

"Damn," Pearl said. "I sure am glad Joey and Chris are on our side of the fence. That shit's walking into Stephen Hawking's territory."

"What did it give you?" I asked.

"We printed it all out," Chris said. "It's on the dining room table. A copy for each of you. And we sent an encrypted PDF to your cell, Pearl."

I exchanged a look with Bruno.

"Give us the short form," I said.

"He talks in code," Joey said. "But we understood enough to pick up half a dozen more of his drug drops. So, with the eight you picked up when we first jumped on this, we have fourteen of his locations. Shouldn't take us much longer to pick up the rest."

"Good," I said. "I'll let the chief know soon as we break. We'll have those raided and shut down. That should put Gonzo on his heels a bit and do damage to his cash flow."

"We can do more than damage it," Chris said. "We can take his money."

No one spoke for several moments, our eyes focused on Chris. "How can we do that?" I asked.

"His money comes in early-morning deliveries," Chris said. "Same time morning papers are dropped in front of homes and apartments. Every morning, seven days a week."

"Who makes the deliveries?" Carl asked.

"He uses bread trucks," Chris said. "Gonzo has distribution routes in the Bronx and Manhattan. They deliver bread to bakeries and delis and the cash to predesignated locations."

"How'd you find this out?" I asked.

"Cell chatter," Chris said. "And back and forth texts."

"Then we searched data for the name of his distribution companies," Joey said. "It took a few hunt-and-pecks, but we found them. And we zoned in on the GPS tracking devices in the trucks he uses."

"We had to get VIN numbers," Chris said. "Soon as we hacked the DMV, we were able to pinpoint plate and registration info."

"Didn't you need a name to do that?" Alexandra asked.

"We put in Gonzo's name first," Joey said. "We struck out on that one."

"But then we put in Juan Marichal," Chris said. "He was named after his mom's favorite player. Figured we would give that a shot."

"He was a great pitcher, I grant you," Pearl said.

"Everything Gonzo owns is registered under that name," Joey said.

"That's good work, both of you," I said. "I'll put the chief on the truck routes, as well. That should put another dent in his armor."

"That would be only for one night's take," Joey said. "But there's one more piece to add to the mix. A piece that will leave Gonzo with empty pockets."

I looked at Chris. "What's the final piece?"

"We have the name of his banker," Chris said.

42.

THE BROWNSTONE

I SAT ON THE EDGE OF CHRIS'S BED. HE WAS LYING DOWN ON top of the blankets, in bare feet, black sweatpants, and a New York Knicks T-shirt. A bottle of orange Gatorade rested on the nightstand, next to a reading lamp covered with decals from the Yankees and Mets and a framed photo of his parents. I glanced at the picture, my brother holding his wife close, a younger Chris nestled between them.

"You've done amazing work," I told him. "I'm not saying it to put a smile to your face. It was a top-shelf job."

"Thanks," Chris said. He was fresh out of the shower and his hair was matted and damp. "I was afraid I was going to screw it up."

"Are you kidding?" I said. "Tom Cruise in one of his *Mission: Impossible* movies couldn't have done better. What you and Joey came up with is going to help freeze Gonzo's cash supply and put a hurt on his drug operation."

"It's not hard, really," Chris said, his face turning a shade of red. "You just need to know where to look and what to look for."

"Not many people can do that."

"Some stuff I picked up from online friends," Chris said. "A little more from reading Harlan Coben novels and a little from Mark Harmon."

"Mark Harmon?" I said. "The actor?"

Chris slid up in the bed. "You can pick up a lot of information from *NCIS*. You watch it?"

"I will now."

"Joey and I can pinpoint the banker," Chris said. The more time I spent in his company, the more he reminded me of Jack. He stayed focused on the task, never lost sight of the job that needed to be done. "We can map out the banks where he does his business and where he keeps Gonzo's money."

"That would be huge if you can narrow it down," I said. "We can bring in the feds and have them block Gonzo's offshore accounts."

"There's one thing me and Joey are having trouble figuring out," Chris said. "Maybe you know somebody who can help?"

"What do you need?"

"The banker gets cash from Gonzo through deposits in a few Florida banks and then has them moved out of the country," Chris said. "He moves the cash from bank to bank until it can't be linked to Gonzo. We need someone who knows how he does that."

"A money launderer," I said. "Somebody who takes dirty money and turns it clean."

"If we had somebody, we could figure a way to find all of Gonzo's cash."

"Get some sleep," I said. "By this time tomorrow, you'll know so much about money laundering, even Mark Harmon would be impressed."

43.

ALBERTO'S GRILL — WASHINGTON HEIGHTS

LATER THAT SAME NIGHT

THE USUALLY CROWDED BAR WAS DOWN TO A DOZEN OR SO regulars. It was known in the neighborhood as a cop bar, a place where the shots and a chaser went down in minutes after the end of a tour. There are dozens of cop bars spread throughout the five boroughs, and they all have the same look and smell—stale beer, a pool table that's seen more than its share of bad games, and a guy behind the wood who knows enough to stock the place with the drink of choice of most cops. It's not complicated, usually boils down to a shot of Dewar's straight and a cold longneck bottle of Budweiser.

Cops have one of the highest divorce rates of any profession. Shrinks and pollsters, not to mention too many of the TV shows Chris likes to watch, often lay the blame for this statistic on the stress of the job and the difficulty we have in talking to those closest to us about what we do. The reasoning behind this theory is we look to spare them the emotional anxiety we go through on a daily basis. So we bottle it up and keep it locked inside. This thinking is also used to explain the high rate of suicide among active and former law-enforcement members.

I never bought into those theories. Instead, I lay the blame square on the fact cops spend too many hours drinking in dark bars rather than being at home with their wives and kids. If stress and emotional angst were the primary reasons for divorce and suicide, then why don't the same stats apply to surgeons or high-powered attorneys? Cops love to hang out with other cops, and the best places to do that are bars and bowling alleys, and both places serve booze.

I was never much of a bar guy. First of all, I prefer wine to hard liquor, and if you've ever been in a cop bar you know better than to ask for a glass of their finest red. I also like to have an excellent meal to go along with my wine, and you won't ever find that in a cop bar unless you think a burger and fries or a Reuben sandwich is high-end cuisine.

Besides, I was never stressed by the demands of the job. I felt energized by them. The same held true for Pearl. We wanted nothing more than to nab the guy or the crew we were chasing, and we never thought about the dangers we faced in having to do what was needed in order to make that happen.

If Pearl and I were addicted to anything, it wasn't booze. It was the adrenaline rush that came from doing the job the way we thought it should be done.

I walked up to the bar and nodded at the bartender. He was a muscular young man in his midtwenties, with a smile spread across his handsome face. "This is one of the last places I expected to see Tank Rizzo," he said to me. We shook hands and I returned the smile. "What brings your ass this far uptown?"

I turned and scanned the bar and caught the look on the faces staring my way. "I don't suppose you have a bottle of Fernet-Branca on one of the shelves there, do you, Jimmy?" I asked.

"If I did, this place would empty out in a heartbeat and I'd die broke," Jimmy said. "Would you take a beer instead? On the house."

"A beer it is," I said. "As cold as you can make it."

He grabbed a mug from under the wood and poured out a draft with a short head. He slid it across to me and leaned across the bar. "My dad talks about you all the time," Jimmy said. "He misses you and

Pearl. Misses the job, too. He hasn't been able to find something to keep him busy."

"It can take a while," I said. "He'll figure it out. Meantime, give him my best and tell him I'll give him a call soon as I get out from under."

"He'd like nothing better than to have a drink with you," Jimmy said.

"As long as it's wine and not beer," I said, holding up my mug. "No offense."

"None taken," Jimmy said with a laugh. "I barely touch the stuff. Probably because I'm around it all day. All I see are empty mugs and barrel bellies. Neither one suits me."

I looked over to my right, by the pool table, and saw a burly man in his midthirties starting to make his way toward me. "Could you do me two favors?" I asked Jimmy.

"Anything."

"You still keep your dad's nightstick under the bar?" I asked.

"You bet."

"Slide it up on the wood," I said. "Put it where I can reach it in case I need it."

"What else?"

I pulled a slip of paper from my shirt pocket and handed it to Jimmy. "Call this number," I said. "And tell the man who answers to make his move in five minutes."

"You expecting trouble in here, Tank?"

"Well, more like trouble is on its way to find me," I said, staring at the burly man as he moved closer. "And don't worry. If there's any damage done to your place, I'll see to it NYPD covers it."

Jimmy reached under the bar and rested an old, scarred police baton on the shiny wood, inches from my left hand. He then turned, walked toward the cash register, and picked up the landline to dial the number I gave him.

The burly man now stood inches from my face. "You see all sorts of shit up these parts, but I never expected to see a Tin Badge drinking a beer in a cop bar," the man said. "A guy like you, Tank, should know better. From what I hear, you like to do your eating and drinking with wops and spooks."

"You know, Calhoun, I heard about your father when he was on the job. He was a bit of an asshole and a racist prick," I said. "On top of that, he was dirty. Bought and owned by the East Harlem wiseguys like a cheap suit. I'm glad to see the rotten apple didn't fall far from the shady tree."

"There's a dozen cops in here," Calhoun said. "The ones who know you don't like you, and the ones who don't won't give a shit if you catch a beating. So say what you came to say. Then turn around and get the fuck out of here before we decide to make you crawl your way out."

"Does Gonzo give you beer money, too?" I said. "Does he pay you off in cash or with drugs? Not that it's any of my business. I'm curious, is all. Besides, all that wash will be hung out during the trial."

"How's your old partner doing these days?" Calhoun asked. He turned and smiled as he saw four cops in plainclothes circle me. "Do you go up to his nursing home and wipe his ass or do you pay some fat black broad to do it?"

"Pearl is a better cop in a wheelchair than you are walking on two legs," I said. I rested a hand on the bar, my fingers curling on the baton. "I'll make sure he takes a ride down to One Hundred Centre Street to sit in the courthouse the day you get sentenced."

"Where you coming from with all this trial bullshit?" Calhoun asked, rapping a knuckle on the bar, signaling Jimmy to hand him a fresh bottle of beer. "There's nobody going to jail in here. A hospital maybe. But no way a jail."

"I wish I could arrest you myself," I said. "Nothing would put a bigger smile on my face. But for me, those days are in the past. That job belongs to someone else."

"And who the fuck is that going to be?" Calhoun asked.

"That would be me," Chief Connors said. "I'm the one that's going to put the cuffs on you, Calhoun."

The bar became still and silent, and heads and eyes turned to the chief of detectives, standing ten feet behind me, close to the front door of the bar. Next to him were three heavily armed uniform patrolmen. "I want nobody to do anything stupid," the chief added. "The back of this place is covered and I have a dozen more cops waiting outside. Now, I want everyone's gun, badge, and ID put on top of the bar. I want it done slowly. And I want it done now. That goes for you, too, Calhoun."

"Are you serious with this bullshit, Chief?" Calhoun asked.

"No," the chief said. "I couldn't sleep, so I decided to round up a few dozen cops, leave a warm bed, and take a ride uptown to fuck around with a deadbeat and his deadbeat pals. You're shit on my shoe, Calhoun. A disgrace to the badge. Just like that creepy old man of yours. They didn't nail him. But I sure as shit am going to nail you."

"There is one thing I need for you to do before the chief slaps the cuffs on you," I said to Calhoun.

Behind and around Calhoun, cops were slowly dropping guns, shields, and IDs on top of the bar. Jimmy collected them and placed them in an empty cardboard box by his feet.

"And what would that be?" Calhoun asked.

I raised the baton and smashed it as hard as I could across the front of Calhoun's face. The force of the blow sent his head back and a stream of blood gushing out of his nose and mouth. He fell to his knees, his hands covering his face, blood pouring through them and onto the wooden floor. I bent over and whispered in his ear, "I wanted you to feel some pain. I know it was you that pointed Gonzo in Carmine's direction. You hear what I'm saying?"

Calhoun looked at me through glazed eyes.

"You're going away for a long time," I said. "To a place where cops are hated. And you'll probably die behind prison walls. But if by some miracle you make it out, there's going to be a very angry mob crew waiting to take a bite out of your ass."

I stood and handed the baton back to Jimmy. "Do me one last favor, would you, kid," I said to him.

"Name it, Tank."

"I appreciate you wanting to give me a beer on the house, but I'd like it better if you put it on Calhoun's tab," I said. "And ring one up for the chief and any of his boys if they want a quick one before they head back to work."

"My pleasure," Jimmy said.

I walked away from the bar and stopped in front of the chief. "He's all yours, boss," I said.

The chief looked down at Calhoun, still on his knees, resting his head against a side of the bar, blood flowing from his mouth and nose. "How do you suppose he got that injury?" the chief asked me, shaking my hand.

I turned and glanced at Calhoun. "Far as I can tell," I said, "he was reaching for his beer, slipped, and banged his face against the hard end of the bar."

"The harder they slip," the chief said.

"The harder they fall," I finished.

44.

THE WINTHROP

THE NEXT DAY

I SAT IN MY USUAL PLACE, UNDER THE SHADY TREE. PEARL WAS to my right, the wheels of his chair resting on the well-tended grass. Chris sat closer to Pearl, a can of soda resting next to one of his Air Jordan sneakers. I thought it time for Chris to get to know Pearl as more than a voice on a speakerphone.

Down farther to my left, the yellow police tape had been removed from the areas around last week's shootings. All that remained were blotches of blood that had seeped into the concrete path. In time, rain and sun would make them a memory, as well.

"Man, I would have paid major money to be there to see the chief slap the cuffs on that slimeball Calhoun," Pearl said. "That lowlife deserved to go down years ago. In fact, truth be told, he never should have been allowed to join the force. Given his old man's history."

"Was his father a cop, too?" Chris asked.

"They gave him a badge and a gun," I said. "That's as far as he covered the cop part."

"You name a criminal working Manhattan uptown or down and you could bet your balls Calhoun was collecting a weekly bag of cash from him," Pearl said.

"You bump heads with either one of them?" I asked Pearl. "The father or the son?"

Pearl shook his head. "Not directly. But I did hear the old man once crossed hairs with Floyd Carter back in the day. You know about him?"

"Not really."

"This be a good one for you to look up, Chris," Pearl said. "Floyd is a pretty amazing fella. He was one of the first African Americans to earn a detective's gold shield and was on the job just shy of twenty-eight years."

"That couldn't have been easy to do in those years," I said. "There couldn't have been that many black cops on the force."

"You could probably have counted them on the fingers of your hands," Pearl said. "But that's not all. Carter was one of the Tuskegee Airmen, the World War Two group of African American fighter pilots."

"I heard of them," Chris said. "I saw a movie about their group, *Red Tails*."

"On the money," Pearl said. "He didn't stop there, either. He flew and fought in the Korean and Vietnam wars and was one of the first pilots to take a plane over Berlin during the Cold War airlift in 1948."

"He got an award from President Bush, the second one," Chris said. "We talked about it in history class."

"Yes, he did," Pearl said. "Awarded the Congressional Gold Medal for cracking the color line at Tuskegee."

"Floyd and old man Calhoun shouldn't have been in the same state, let alone worn the same uniform," I said. "How'd they bump heads?"

"Way I heard it, Floyd was chasing down some crew around Calhoun's precinct," Pearl said. "The dealers must have asked the crooked badge to get the colored guy off their back. And if you think the son is a racist sack, the old man was twice as bad."

"I can see how this one played out," I said. "Calhoun tells Floyd to back his black ass up or he's going to find himself doing janitor duty at headquarters."

"Along those lines," Pearl said. "Got his red neck into Floyd's face, but it didn't go the way he figured."

"Floyd had him arrested?" Chris asked.

"Even better," Pearl said. "The two went at it late at night in one of those side alleys up around One Hundred Forty-eighth and Riverside. Floyd ended up with bloody knuckles and a few bruises. Papa Calhoun wound up in the hospital with all sorts of internal damage. The first and last time their paths crossed."

"We should give Floyd a call," I said. "Be nice to have him be part of our team."

"Since you brought up the subject," Pearl said, "it would be nice for me to be a part of the team as well."

"What do you mean? You've been part of the team since I first started doing this. Nothing's changed."

"I'm up here doing research," Pearl said. "Making calls, working the computer, hunting down names and leads. But now you got Chris to help do that. He's a hundred percent better at it than I ever will be."

"You do a lot more than that, Pearl, and you know it," I said. "Nobody, and I mean nobody, is better at breaking down a case. Without you, I would never have taken on these cases, and I sure as shit wouldn't have solved as many."

"I need more than that, Tank," Pearl said. "I need to be a part of the team. Not from up here. Up close, I mean. I want to be there when you tangle with Gonzo."

"Nothing would make me happier than to have you back by my side," I said. "But I don't see how I can make that happen."

"Because all you see is a man in a wheelchair," Pearl said.

"I see my best friend in that wheelchair," I said. "My best friend, who is confined to a rehab facility. My best friend, who, despite his wounds and his pain and his anger, has faced his battle with more courage than anyone could ever know. And I will do anything for my best friend. But I refuse to put him in harm's way."

"And you think putting me back out on the street during the takedown puts me in danger?"

"It puts the entire team in danger."

"It's a risk, Tank," Pearl said. "And I've never known you to shy away from taking one of those."

"You'd be a target," I said, practically pleading with him. "Look, last weekend, during the shoot-out, they were caught off guard. The last thing they were expecting was firepower from you. They see you out there again, they'll start blasting and you will be a sitting target, literally."

Pearl looked at Chris and reached into the pocket of his sleeveless hoodie. He came out with five singles and handed them to him. "Do me a solid," he said to Chris. "Go inside and get me a bottle of peach Snapple and get yourself whatever you want. I need a few minutes with your uncle."

Chris took the money, stood, glanced at each of us, and started to head toward the entrance to the snack area. Pearl and I waited until he was out of earshot.

"What's this all about, Pearl?"

"I'm done, Tank," Pearl said. His eyes were glazed over with tears.

"What the hell you mean, you're done? The doctors give you excellent reports. They say they can see the progress you're making week to week. You're far from done. Trust me on that."

Pearl lowered his head and his voice. "This ain't living, Tank," he said. "I'm never going to get out of this chair. I'm never going to be able to do the things I used to love to do. And I don't give a rat's ass what's in the reports. I know my body better than any doctor, and it will only get worse for me. Yeah, I'll stay stable for a year, maybe two, and then what? I'll need a full-time aide. I'll need somebody to take me for a walk, feed me, change my clothes, and wash up after me. And I'll still be missing the one thing I truly need."

"What?"

My emotions were also rising to the surface and I couldn't help but let them rush out. I loved Pearl as a brother and as a friend. It pained me to see him in his current condition, and I felt a sad weight each time I said goodbye to him, leaving him alone in a rehab facility.

"I need to feel like a man again," Pearl said. "I need to be with you on this job when you make your move against Gonzo. And if putting me out there gets me killed, so be it. I'll go out the way I was meant to go out. Shot dead on the street trying to bring down a crime boss sure as shit beats doing another thirty years in this chair."

I wiped the tears from my eyes and watched Pearl do the same to his. We sat in silence for a few minutes, each lost in our thoughts. "Would you do the same for me if the situation was reversed?" I finally asked.

"In a heartbeat."

"I don't doubt it," I said with a smile.

"So am I in or not?"

"You know your entire plan could backfire," I said.

"How do you mean?"

"You might surprise yourself," I said. "Surprise all of us and survive whatever it is that's going to go down. Make it through in one piece. Then where's that put you?"

"I'll live to fight another day," Pearl said with a laugh. "Right alongside you, partner. Long as I can take a breath, we're stuck with each other. That all right by you?"

"I wouldn't have it any other way," I said.

45.

NYU MEDICAL CENTER

LATER THAT DAY

I STOOD ACROSS FROM CARMINE'S BED. THE ROOM WAS DIMLY lit and quiet. He was off the machines now, sitting up, not yet at full strength but getting close. His face was still bruised, and under his hospital gown I could see the tight white bandage wrapped around his rib cage. Behind us, the blinds were pulled up and the curtains drawn back and the downtown skyline was visible in the early-evening light.

"That's great news about you getting out in the morning," I said. "What time are they setting you free?"

"Soon as the doc gives me a final look-over," Carmine said. "I'm packed and ready. Toss on some clothes, kiss a nurse or two goodbye, and then off I go. I figure I'll be on the street about ten."

"Connie is waiting down the hall," I said. "She looks upset. You have any idea why?"

"She's scared; that's the long and the short of it, Tank," Carmine said. "And worried."

"About you?"

"About me and you," Carmine said. "About what we're both planning to do."

"I've known you a lot of years, Carmine," I said. "And never once did I even hint at what you should or shouldn't do."

"But you figured what better time to start than now," Carmine said. "Say your piece, Tank. You've earned that right."

"I know you want to go at Gonzo," I said. "And I don't blame you one bit. I know while you've been in here recovering, you've reached out to some of your old crew, seeing who's available and who's looking to back your play."

"Let's say, for argument's sake, you're not far off," Carmine said. "Is that a problem for you?"

I shook my head. "No, not really. It would surprise me if you weren't doing that. And I'm not about to tell you anything you don't already know or haven't thought about yourself."

"Say it anyway," Carmine said. "We both might pick up a thing or two."

"I would love to have you by my side on this," I said. "Nothing would make me happier than to see us take Gonzo down together. But you've been away from the street end of the business a long time. And Gonzo won't see gangsters coming at him; he'll see a crew of past-their-prime old men. But that won't mean he'll take a step back. He'll come at you as hard as he's going to come after me."

"If you're trying to pump me up, then I have to be honest and say you really suck at it."

"I love your daughter," I said. "You know that."

"And she loves you," Carmine said. "Never been a doubt about that on either side since day one."

"She's tough," I said. "She's your daughter and I wouldn't expect otherwise. I think losing one of us would hit her hard but she'd come out of it in one piece. But I don't think she can handle losing both."

"In that case, Detective Tank, let's make sure she doesn't lose either one," Carmine said.

I stared at Carmine. I'd known it would be a waste of time to try to talk him out of going after Gonzo. He knew only one way to go—you get bit, you come back and bite back even harder. You bite him until he's on the ground, bleeding to death.

"If I can't convince you to sit this one out," I said, "then maybe I can convince you to come at it from another direction."

"Which would be what?"

"Team up with me," I said. "You and your crew work with me and mine. We plan it as one operation. And we go at them at once. He's expecting me; that we can count on. And he might figure you to take a peek in his direction. But he wouldn't plan on having us both reach out at the same time."

Carmine smiled and shrugged his shoulders. "And who would be calling the shots on this joint operation?"

"That would be me," I said. "If you want it to work, that's the way it's going to have to be."

"It would be a first, you realize that, right?" Carmine said. "Not just for me, but for my crew. Taking our marching orders from a cop isn't the way we're used to working."

"New world, Carmine," I said. "New rules."

"And if I can't sell it to them or to myself?" Carmine said.

"You go your way and I'll go mine," I said. "But it wouldn't be the smart play. And ever since I've known you, Carmine, you've always made the smart play."

I leaned over, and gave him a warm embrace, which he returned. "You'll know the plan going in," I said, turning and heading toward the door. "Add to it, modify it, change it any way you want. But once it's locked in, we move as one."

Carmine nodded. "And Connie?" he said. "What are you going to tell her?"

"What I've always told her," I said. "The truth."

46.

NYU MEDICAL CENTER—LOUNGE

MINUTES LATER

I HANDED CONNIE A COFFEE. SHE CUPPED HER HANDS AROUND the hot container. "The salads looked fresh," I said. "In case you're hungry."

"I'm not."

"But you are angry."

"What makes you think that, Tank?" she asked. "Just because you and my dad are determined to take on some heavily armed and drugged-out crew? Led by some crazed bastard who would kill you both and shrug it off a minute after it happened? Why should any of that bring my blood level to a boil?"

"You know me and you know your father," I said. "Did you think either of us could turn our backs and walk away from this?"

"Why would that be such a terrible thing to do? Walk away. Hand the case back and let the guys on the job handle it. And my father can pass this on to one of the younger mob crews working his old turf. They'd be more than happy to go after Gonzo."

"I couldn't stop Carmine if I wanted to," I said. "He was attacked, Connie, and he's hardwired to attack back."

"He's not in the shape he was in back in those years. Neither are you. I don't mean to be harsh. But the truth is what it is."

"I'm not here to argue about whether I can still hit a moving target or whether Carmine can still go toe-to-toe with a gangbanger."

"You walked over for a reason," Connie said.

"Two reasons," I said. "If I do go down, I would like you to take care of Chris. He'd be happy with you. I had my lawyer draw up papers naming you as his custodian. Just in case."

Connie nodded, tears sliding down the sides of her cheeks. She wiped at them with a tissue. "What's the second reason?"

"I'm sorry I've never told you enough times how special you are," I said. "And how much I love you. I remember the first time I saw you. I must have been twelve, maybe thirteen at most. It was at the old community pool. I was ready to dive in when I saw you come out of the water. You looked at me and smiled. I couldn't take my eyes off you."

Connie smiled through her tears. "You had on a bathing suit that was one size too big. You were thin and already had a tan even though summer recess had barely begun."

"Tar Beach," I said. "I used to go up to the brownstone roof, read Mickey Spillane novels, and work on my burn."

"It took a while before you asked me out," Connie said. "I figured it was because of my dad. Or maybe you just weren't interested."

"I was always interested. I carried a torch for you since that day by the pool. I was always afraid you would meet some guy, get married, have kids, and that would be the end for me."

"You weren't around much during that time," she said. "I kept up with you, though. In the papers or from neighborhood chatter. Everyone was proud of the cases you and Pearl were solving. My father was, too."

"I know why I took so long before I came around," I said. "But what about you? I know there were lots of neighborhood guys looking to hook up. But you never took the bait."

"I was working the restaurant and going to school," Connie said. "I learned the business from the bottom up, starting in the kitchen, working next to Mom. And then when she got sick, I needed to take care of her, bringing her to chemo, doling out her pills, making sure she had enough to eat. On top of that, I had to help dad run the place. He wasn't in the right frame of mind to do anything during that time. I don't think he's ever recovered from seeing her die the way she did. So the last thing on my mind was neighborhood guys asking me out on dates."

"That was a tough time for you and your family. Every time I came in the place for dinner or a glass of wine, I looked over and could see how sad you were and how hard you were working."

"Then one night, you came in, ordered a bottle of wine, a Biondi Santi. And you asked me to bring two glasses to the table."

"And you asked me why I needed a second glass," I said.

"And you said, 'I was hoping you would join me,'" Connie said. "And I did."

"It took a while for us to get together," I said. "And maybe that's how it was meant to play out. But I don't ever want to lose you. I have loved you for most of my life. From a distance and from up close."

"You're not going to lose me," she said. "You ever think one other reason I never went for any neighborhood guys was that I was carrying a torch of my own? For you."

"The thought might have crossed my mind," I said. "Plus, I always knew I had your dad in my corner. He never cared for those other guys and was not the least bit shy letting his feelings be known."

"He always looked out for you," Connie said. "When your parents died, he helped you make the arrangements. And when you and Pearl got wounded, he came to the hospital every day, even though the visiting area was crawling with cops."

I laughed. "He came into my room one night, snuck in a bowl of linguini with clam sauce, and had one brought to Pearl, as well," I said. "He told me he would have brought in fresh bread and roasted peppers but he was worried the uniform guys outside would do a stop-and-frisk."

Connie raised the coffee to her lips and held it there for a moment. "I realize that regardless of what I say, you're going to see the situation you're up against through," she said. "The same holds true for Dad.

There's no turning back for either of you, and no pleading from me is going to change that."

"I'm sorry, honey."

The tears were returning to the corners of her eyes, and her words were cracked and shaky. "If I lost both of you . . ."

I reached out and held her close to me, her head buried in my chest, sadness rushing out of her, her tears staining the front of my shirt. I put my lips close to her left ear. "I promise you, Connie," I whispered, "I will not let that happen. I'll make sure Carmine makes it back. I give you my word."

She lifted her head, cheeks flushed red, eyes rimmed with tears. "What about you?"

"Took a long time for me to reach out to you," I said. "A lot of years. But we got a lot more years ahead of us. Count on that. Forget about everything else and just count on that."

47.

WASHINGTON HEIGHTS

LATER THAT NIGHT

THE BEDROOM WINDOW WAS WIDE OPEN, THIN CURTAINS flapping up and down in rhythm with the mild late-night breeze. I could see the man in the bed, curled in a fetal position, breathing through an open mouth, facing me. He was shirtless, wearing slim black underwear and one white sock on his left foot.

I climbed off the fire escape and through the open window. I quietly made my way to the edge of his bed and pulled my gun from its hip holster. I looked around the small bedroom. A statue of the Blessed Mother was sitting on a bureau in a corner near a thin wooden door. There was a lit votive candle shedding a glow on her cream-colored face. There was a TV and a La-Z-Boy. A scrawny brown cat sat curled on a folding chair, her body nestled on top of a throw.

I tapped the man on the knee twice with the barrel of my gun. He moaned, eased up on his snoring, but didn't open his eyes. I tapped him again, this time with more force. He opened his eyes, saw my face, and sat up with a jolt.

"Hi, Gonzo," I said. "I don't believe we've met. Hope you don't mind my coming over at such a late hour."

"You looking for your life to end?" Gonzo asked. "I raise my voice and there will be four guns in here with four men hot to use them in less than a minute. Drop you like a fly against a windshield."

"Maybe," I said. "But not before I hit a triple."

"What the fuck's that supposed to mean?"

I raised my gun and pointed it at Gonzo. He had two pillows braced against his back. "One to the head, one to the heart," I said, "and one to the stomach. A triple. I'll go down, that might be true. But if you survive, and that's a big if, you'll spend the rest of your days sipping dinner through a straw."

Gonzo stared at the gun and then back at me. "What the fuck do you want?"

"We're going to bang our heads hard, you and me," I said. "There's no ifs, ands, or buts about that. And one of us will go down; that's also a pretty easy bet to cash in."

"And I cannot wait until I'm standing over your bleeding ass spread on the street out there," Gonzo said. He smiled, revealing enough gold in his mouth to strike a claim. "Watching you beg me to finish you off."

"That's one way it could end up. But I'm here to tell you I'm not planning just to end your life and clear the streets of your lowlife crew. I'm going to bring your entire operation to a close. After we're done, all you're going to be left with are those filthy clothes you tossed to the floor and that mangy cat on the chair behind me. And the odds are six-to-five against that even the cat takes a powder."

"I give you this, Tin Badge," Gonzo said, "you got a set of balls on you. Breaking into my place, putting a gun to my face. That takes major chops."

"I didn't break in," I said. "The window was open and you were talking in your sleep. I couldn't exactly make out what you were saying, but it sounded something like, 'Come in and make yourself at home.'"

"You a smart-ass on top of it," Gonzo said. "That's one more check I can put next to your name. But listen to me clear. There is no fuckin' way you or anybody you can dig up to take me on brings down my operation. No way. I'm major league, loser. You think I'm going to let a

Tin Badge and his friends come in and step all over what I built? I swear on the Madonna there, that will never happen."

I leaned in closer to Gonzo. "You see me now," I said. "Take a good look and tell me. Do you see me now?"

"Yeah, I can see you, fuckhead," Gonzo said. "It ain't like I'm blind."

"Next time you see me will be the last time you see me. You're over, Gonzo. The women, the drugs, the whole setup will be blown to bits. Even the Madonna knows you're fucked."

"You're blowing smoke, Tin Badge," Gonzo said. "My crew is going to Tarantino you. I hope you got your own teeth, because once we're done that's the only way they gonna be able to ID the bodies."

I pressed the nozzle of my gun into the side of Gonzo's right cheek. "None of that matters, dealer," I whispered. "All that matters is that I put you out. And out you will go."

Gonzo glared at me, his face flushed. "You better be as tough as you talk," he said through gritted teeth.

I pulled the gun from his face and stepped toward the open window. I leaned one leg out onto the fire escape and glanced back at Gonzo. "I had a drug dealer a few years ago say those very same words to me," I said.

"Yeah," Gonzo said. "How'd that turn out?"

"The way it was meant to," I said. "I took a flesh wound to the shoulder and got a nice promotion, and he ended up with a new place to call home."

"He in prison now, that what you're trying to tell me?"

"No, he's not in prison," I said.

"Where, then, Tin Badge?" Gonzo asked, tossing his feet to the wooden floor and reaching for an open pack of cigarettes. "Where this dealer now? Maybe I can dig him up and give him a chance to go a second round with you."

"Dig him up, is what you'll need to do," I said. I eased my other leg out and stood on the fire escape. "He's on Long Island. In St. Charles. The cemetery."

48.

GENERAL GRANT
NATIONAL MEMORIAL

THE NEXT DAY

I SAT WITH CHRIS ON ONE OF THE TILE-COVERED BENCHES that stretched along both sides of the mausoleum as well as along the rear. I had visited the tomb that houses the remains of both President Ulysses S. Grant and his wife dozens of times since I was a kid. It was nestled just above Riverside Drive, along West 122nd Street, the river on one side, the flow of the Drive on the other. I had sat on these benches for many hours, especially during my years as a cop, taking in the scenery, enjoying the peaceful solitude brought by the final resting place of the man who helped end the Civil War. It was one of those perfect places to clear my head, formulate my plans, and steel myself for the next task that stood before me.

"How long has this been here?" Chris asked.

"The tomb since 1897," I said. "And the mausoleum was finished in the 1970s. About two thousand people worked to get these benches finished for the opening. All volunteers."

"You come here a lot?"

"Not as much as I used to," I said. "It's a place gives you time to think. And it's a great spot to take in the view and the history."

"You ever come up here with Dad?"

I nodded. "More times than I can remember. He liked it more than I did. He was big-time into history, loved reading about presidents and military leaders. And Mr. Grant here filled both roles."

"He was halfway through a biography of Grant when he died," Chris said. "I saw it on his night table."

I let a few moments pass before I spoke again. "I have an important job I need you to do for me."

"What is it?"

"I want you to keep an eye on Connie," I said. "I'll be going against Gonzo soon. And Carmine will be doing the same. That means Connie's going to be worried. Be nice if you were around to keep her company."

"What makes you think I won't be worried, too?"

I glanced at him. "Guys hide worry better than women. At least I like to think so. But, if you're both going to be fretting over it, why not do it together?"

"I guess this is another way of telling me I won't be going with you," Chris said.

"What made you think there was even a chance of me letting that happen?" I asked.

"Well, I think I'm part of the team now."

"You are," I said. "And you're going to be plenty busy the next couple of days pulling together that information you and Joey dug up on Gonzo. That's where you come in and that's where you stay."

"I don't want to lose you," Chris said, words barely audible. "Even if we don't get along all the time."

"Most of the time."

"Do you know how he'll come after you?"

"I'll be going after him. On his own turf."

"How many men does he have?"

"About a dozen in his building," I said. "Maybe a dozen more in the area. How hard they fight and how long they stay in the fight is the key. They start seeing some of their own go down, they might peel off."

"Why would they do that?"

"They work for Gonzo not because they love the guy," I said. "It's because, for now, he is the guy. But if they get a sense he's going down, they'll step back. There will always be another guy."

"I keep looking at that picture of you in a police uniform standing next to Grandma," Chris said. "The one hanging in the den?"

"The day I graduated from the academy," I said. "Why's that one got your attention?"

"Because there aren't any pictures hanging of you with Grandpa or you with Dad," Chris said. "Just the one with Grandma."

"Your father didn't come to the graduation," I said. "And your grandfather couldn't make it, either."

Chris was quiet, his legs stretched out in front of him. "Did they not want you to be a cop?" he finally asked.

"Your dad was away, part of some student exchange program," I said. "And Grandpa wasn't keen on cops. Everybody's opinion is shaped by their own experience. All he saw was cops with their hand out, looking for a free this or a free that. It was the same for him back in Italy, surrounded by corruption. He felt if you went into a tainted business, you would be tainted, too."

"But you didn't let it stop you."

"There's dirty in every business," I said. "That doesn't mean you have to take part in it. I went in looking to do some good. Help people who were hurt by others. That may sound naïve. But it's what I believed and what I still believe."

"Is that why you're so hot to take Gonzo in?"

"That neighborhood where he hangs his hat," I said, "Washington Heights. The people who live there have seen a hundred like Gonzo come and a hundred like him go. All they leave in their wake is hurt and misery. And as soon as he's out of the picture, some other lowlife will pop up and take his place. It's the way of the streets. But there's good people living there, and they deserve better than what they're getting."

Chris stood and turned, looking at the fast currents of the Hudson River. "Are you like him at all?" he asked. "Your dad, I mean."

"In some ways," I said. "But I think both your dad and me were more like our mom."

Chris looked away from the river and back to me. "My dad used to say that, too," he said.

"Your dad was the clear favorite with Mom," I said. "In her eyes, he could do no wrong. She loved me, too. But she knew I would go my own way. She worried less about me. She sensed early on I could handle myself. She knew she could trust me not to let anything happen to your dad. I never much cared for bullies when I was a kid. I hated guys who went after other kids just because they could. Younger, weaker, the ones not looking for trouble. The easy targets. If I was around, I would try and make it not so easy for them."

"How do you feel about bullies now?"

"Hate them even more. Maybe that's why I'm going after Gonzo. He's just another in a long line of bullies making money off easy targets."

"You think he's afraid of you?"

"Sure as shit hope not," I said. The Henry Hudson traffic behind us was picking up in volume. "I'm counting on him not being afraid. It works to my advantage."

"It's dumb not to be afraid," Chris said.

"You can bet your life on that," I said.

49.

CIRCLE LINE CRUISE SHIP

TWO DAYS LATER

WE STOOD ON THE UPPER DECK, HEADING UP THE HUDSON River to Bear Mountain. Carmine was looking out at the New Jersey shoreline. He had been out of the hospital less than three days and had already gained a couple of pounds and added some color to his face and arms. He still had bruises and he walked with a cane, favoring his right leg. But all you needed to do was look in his eyes and you knew he had his edge back and was more than ready to fight the battle that waited.

I kept my back to the river and focused on the man standing between us. He was short and stocky and seemed out of place dressed as he was in a dark-blue Brioni suit. He had a leather attaché case squared between his legs and seemed less comfortable dealing with the choppy waves than either Carmine or I was. He was younger than I expected, late thirties at most, his brown hair razor cut and kept short. He had a calm exterior, and only the occasional twitching of his upper lip and the streaks of sweat across the back of his neck betrayed the nerves he was fighting to keep under control.

His name was Greg Bartoli. On the record, he was employed by a prestigious bank with branches in the United States, South America, the offshore islands, and Europe. He earned a high-six-figure salary,

was married, and owned a two-bedroom co-op in a full-service Upper
East Side building.

Off the record, he was the banker of choice for the major drug
dealers in the tri-state area.

Greg looked from Carmine to me and back to Carmine. "I understand you need help moving some money around," he said.

"That's close to being right," I said. "We do need help moving
money around. But just so we're clear, the money you'll be helping us
move doesn't belong to us."

Bartoli's eyes widened and he stayed silent for a moment. "You're
planning to steal it?" he finally asked.

"None of it will make its way into our pockets," I said. "We're just
looking to empty those of one of your clients."

"May I ask which client?"

"Gonzo," I said.

"And your reasons for clearing out his accounts?"

"Are my business," I said. "Yours is to show my computer guys
the routes they need to take to get his money—all of his money—
out of the banks and transfer it cleanly into one of ours. Once that's
done, you walk away and, if luck holds, you'll never set eyes on us
again."

"It's quite a lot of cash," Bartoli said. "I've never actually made
transfers in sums that large. If we're not careful, the rapid movement
could cause red flags to wave in our direction."

"Part of your job is to make sure they don't," Carmine said. "And if
you're not up to it, now is the time to let us know. Once this boat docks
in its berth, there's no turning back."

"I didn't say I couldn't handle it," Bartoli said. "I simply stated the
fact that it's a large sum of cash to move in a short period of time.
There are controls in place, and those need to be avoided. How that's
achieved will depend, to be frank, on how good your computer people
are."

Carmine and I exchanged a glance. "They'll get it done," I said.
"You show them the way in; they'll handle the rest."

"I assume you're both aware my usual fee is ten percent," Bartoli said. "The money wired into my private account."

"I gotta give it to you," Carmine said. "You're a ballsy little prick."

"How long have you been doing this?" I asked. "Moving money around for drug crews and sex traffickers?"

Bartoli shrugged. "That, as you would say, is my business. This isn't my first rodeo, if that's your concern."

"I'm not concerned," I said. "I was just trying to add up the federal charges that could land on your lap if I tossed your name to the U.S. Attorney. It would have to total out to, what, three, maybe four decades behind bars."

"At the very least," Carmine said. "And that's if you cooperate with the feds. But if you play hard-ass, feel free to tack on another twenty years."

Bartoli's eyes moved from Carmine to me and back to Carmine. "What the fuck are you two trying to pull here?"

His hands were trembling and his voice cracked, the veins on both sides of his neck bulging to the point where they looked ready to burst. "I'm asked to meet, and I showed for the meet. You toss some crazy scheme on my lap that will clean out one of my best clients. I lay out a few of the obstacles that could prevent us from doing that. And instead of trying to grasp the difficulty of such a task, you throw the threat of a federal rap my way. What the fuck kind of fool do you take me for?"

Carmine took two steps closer to Bartoli, his hulking body casting a dark shadow over the banker. "Let me be the one to fill you in on the kind of fool we take you for," he said. "The kind who will do exactly what he's asked to do. If any part of this operation goes south, I'm not going to be laying the blame on anyone we picked to work the computers. Or anybody who recommended you to me. I'm gonna lay it right on your fuckin' lap. And if and when I do cast my gaze your way, you're going to be on bended knees, begging us to let you go to prison. Am I getting through to you?"

Bartoli turned from beet red to ghost pale and barely managed the strength to nod his head.

"Okay then," Carmine said. "Sounds to me like we've arrived at an understanding. You do what needs to be done and you get to breathe free air. Simple as that."

"And while we're on the subject," I said, "I'm guessing you're going to donate your ten percent to our little operation?"

Bartoli managed a second nod.

"In that case," Carmine said, "there's nothing left to discuss. At least for the time being. So how's about we grab ourselves a seat and enjoy the boat ride."

"May I ask one more question?" Bartoli said.

"Make it a good one," I said.

"When do we begin the transfers?" Bartoli asked.

"Why do you need to know that?" Carmine asked.

"I need to clear my schedule of appointments," Bartoli said. "Out of fairness to my other clients."

"I wouldn't worry about your other clients," I said. "It's going to be done at night."

"After midnight," Carmine said. "At that hour there's no white and there's no black. At that hour every cat is gray. That's the time guys like me do our best work."

"And that better hold true for guys like you, too," I said to Bartoli.

50.

WASHINGTON HEIGHTS

THAT SAME DAY

GONZO LEANED AGAINST A LARGE OIL TANK. HE WAS IN THE basement of his building, surrounded by six of his crew. The large room was filled with thick clouds of cigarette and cigar smoke. The only light came from four overhead low-watt bulbs situated in the corners of the room.

"This motherfucker walks straight into my bedroom like he's got no worries in the world," Gonzo said. He was high, and none of the six had ever seen him this wound up, this filled with rage. "Comes in like this is his house, not mine. And where the fuck were my guys? In the living room, watching some stupid fuckin' movie."

"We didn't hear anything," one of the men said, and as soon as he spoke he realized he would have a better chance of surviving this meeting if he kept his mouth shut.

Gonzo took one step toward him and slapped him across the face with the back of his hand. "It's your fuckin' job to hear," Gonzo said, the muscles of his face rigid, his brown T-shirt damp with cocaine sweat. "It's why I fuckin' pay you. Not to watch my TV. Not to eat my food. Not to drink my beer. But to be in this building, keeping my ass safe."

The men kept their eyes on Gonzo but stayed quiet, aware they had made a monumental fuckup by letting a cop confront him in his own bedroom and knowing a price would need to be paid for such an error.

"This guy, this fuckin' Tank," Gonzo said, "is causing me a lot of grief. And grief hurts business. *My* business. Now, this guy ain't the type you buy off with a couple of bags of cash, and he doesn't look like he scares easy. He's putting together a move. Of that there is no doubt. That means we need to beat him to the fight, be the first ones out the gate. Now I need to hear some shit from you, some solid thoughts. If I don't, then I'll just kick up the boiler back there and toss every one of you motherfuckers in it. Go out and find me fresh crew bosses that can get the job done. Am I coming through or should I turn my back and talk to the fuckin' wall?"

"We need to clean our house before we move on the cop." It was the oldest of the six talking, the one who had been with Gonzo the longest, working with him since the two were moving swag for One-Eyed Sarullo back when they were teenagers.

Gonzo turned to face him. "Keep talking, J.J.," he said. "The rest of you, pay attention."

"This guy, this cop, got into our faces working off that break-in down in Chelsea, am I right?" J.J. asked.

Gonzo nodded.

"Well, you know my feelings on that situation," J.J. said. "I thought we should get rid of the girls and that fat friend of theirs same time we got rid of the two assholes who robbed and raped them. Had we gone that way, there would have been nothing for this cop to look at."

"You were on target with that, granted," Gonzo said. "But that boat ain't in the river anymore."

"Maybe not," J.J. said. "But I think we start there, at the beginning. Get rid of the girls and the black dude. They were the first ones the cop met, and we still have no idea what they told him that led him to sniff our way. So clear the decks with them."

Gonzo smiled. "I hear you. Toss the witnesses out of our way. And start building up a body count."

"That's what I'm thinking," J.J. said. "Now, we got Mano out of the picture before he could tell anybody more than he should. But that bigmouth fucker had three friends he was always bopping around with, telling them all sorts of God-only-knows-what. Make those three friends disappear."

"I'm okay with that," Gonzo said. "But it still ain't gonna make this guy turn tail and go back to his old way of life. He's still going to be looking to go hard at us. He's not stopping until he is stopped."

"We pile up enough bodies, it's going to get some attention," J.J. said. "Police attention."

"More cops?" Gonzo said. "Now, wouldn't that be the last fuckin' thing we all need?"

"On us, yes," J.J. said. "But if we start clearing the decks of folks this guy Tank had contact with, then the cops might start looking his way and wonder what he's up to. Toss a little blue heat in his direction."

Gonzo lit a fresh cigarette and stayed silent for a few seconds. "Might work," he said. "The cops must be pissed at him as is, him taking down one of their own, that moron Calhoun. It might buy us a little time, give us a chance to put together a battle plan."

"We catch a little luck," J.J. said, "maybe the cops will put him out of commission before we need to go down that road."

"That's not going to happen," Gonzo said. "He got put on the case by some cop, probably some guy with lots of brass on his chest. He didn't walk into it on his own. He was asked in. The cops might hassle him, but not enough to make him do a step-back."

"Still, be good for us to get these low-hangers off our radar," J.J. said. "The less of them around, less trouble comes our way."

"True words, my friend, true words," Gonzo said. He turned his gaze to a muscular man leaning with his back against a cement wall, arms folded across his chest.

Gonzo walked over to the muscular man, stopping a few feet away. Gonzo was a good three inches shorter and was outweighed by close to forty pounds of workout muscle. "You were in charge of my detail," Gonzo said to him. "Am I off base on that?"

The muscular man shook his head. "No," he said. "I was the one you left in charge."

"I'm guessing you're sorry about the big fuckup?"

"Very sorry," the muscular man said. He was having trouble catching his breath. "And I promise you, Gonzo, I will never let that happen again."

Gonzo looked up and stared into the muscular man's eyes. "Oh, you don't need to tell me," he said. "I know it won't ever happen."

Gonzo stared at the muscular man for a few more seconds, smiled, and turned away. He walked over to the oil tank and pulled out an automatic weapon from a side panel. He held the gun in his right hand, looked at the muscular man, and nodded his head.

"You will never let that happen again," Gonzo said, "because I won't give you a chance to let it happen again."

Gonzo lifted the gun and fired three shots at the muscular man. Two hit him in the center of his chest. The third ripped into his shoulder. His hands clutched his chest and he slowly crumpled to the ground. Gonzo walked over and gazed at him, listening for the death rattle he knew was coming.

"Let him bleed out," Gonzo said to the stunned men standing behind him. "Kick up the boiler in the meantime. Chop him up and toss him in. Then clean up the mess."

51.

ST. MARK'S CHURCH-IN-THE-BOWERY

WE WERE HUDDLED IN THE BASEMENT OF THE EMPTY CHURCH. It was closing in on one in the morning, and the only noise in the large room that could be heard was the scraping of chairs against a hard floor and the humming of the two computers next to Chris and Joey. Bruno stood off in the corner, sipping from a large bottle filled with his blend of vitamins, protein powders, and fresh-squeezed orange juice. Carl and Alexandra sat on hard-backed chairs, facing the door to the basement. Carmine stood by my side, each of us drinking hot cups of cappuccino fueled by double shots of Irish whiskey.

Bartoli stood in the center of the room, a confused look on his face. "How did you come to choose this place?" he asked. "Doesn't seem right to do what we're about to do inside a church."

"Look at it this way," Carmine said. "You won't have to venture far to seek forgiveness."

"This church has seen quite a bit during the time it's been here," I said. "We're just adding tech to the history of the place."

St. Mark's is the second-oldest place of worship in New York City, trailing only St. Paul's Chapel of Trinity Church in time of service. It was originally a Dutch chapel in 1660, located in the middle of Peter Stuyvesant's farm. Work on the current church was completed in

1799. For years it was home to the Poetry Project, where noted poets and writers ranging from Robert Lowell to Allen Ginsberg to John Ashbery and Frank O'Hara gave readings. There is a brass plate on one of the parish walls that contains a quote from W. H. Auden. It reads: THOUSANDS HAVE LIVED WITHOUT LOVE, NOT ONE WITHOUT WATER.

Bartoli pointed a bony finger at Chris and Joey. "Are these the computer wizards I'm supposed to work with?" he said. "Have they done anything other than crack a few passwords and hack into a porn site?"

"You do what you're here to do," I said. "They'll do the rest."

Bartoli removed a small notebook from the left pocket of his suit jacket. He flipped open a few pages and then ripped off a sheet and handed it to Chris. "That's the access code you'll need to get into the first bank," he said. "The money's deposited under the name Hugo Smith. But when you get in you'll see one name listed on the account. That will be Gonzo."

Chris looked at the sheet and started working the keyboard. "The bank?" he said to Bartoli, without glancing up.

Bartoli looked at his notebook, then tore off another page and handed it to Chris. I watched my nephew work the keys for a few minutes and then settle back into his chair, his eyes never wavering from the computer screen. "I'm in," he said.

"How much is in there?" Carmine asked.

"There are two accounts," Joey said, reading over Chris's shoulder. "Three hundred fifty-seven thousand in one, and four hundred seventy-six thousand in the other."

Carmine stepped in front of me and handed Chris a sheet of paper. "Transfer the cash from both to this bank," he told Chris. "Banco di Napoli. There's an account number there and a name, Antonio Felice."

I stared at Bartoli. "You never heard that name," I said to him. "And you don't know that bank. Clear?"

"Don't worry about him," Carmine said. "He'll stay quiet. Unless he wants to learn how to speak with his hands instead of his tongue."

"This guy Felice, you're locked-in certain he's good to go on this?" I asked Carmine.

"His family's been moving cash around Europe since World War Two," Carmine said. "He's the latest in a long line. We don't raise red flags on our end, he sure as shit won't on his. Whatever we send him will be washed and cleaned in less than forty-eight hours and deposited back in the States under the name and information we passed his way."

"How many more accounts does Gonzo have?" I asked Bartoli.

"Fourteen," he said. "Those are just the ones I manage for him. He might have a few more stashed with other bankers. But I doubt it. He seems like a one-stop shopper."

"Keep going, then," I said to him. "There are two computers in front of you and two young men who know how to use them. Dole out seven to each. The sooner we make these transfers, the better."

"Your plan isn't exactly perfect," Bartoli said.

"How so?" I asked.

"If Gonzo decides to check on his money, as he's been known to do, he'll know something's up," Bartoli said. "And he won't hesitate to put in a call to me and to the banks to see what's going on."

"Gonzo does monitor his accounts," Joey said. "Checks on them every three, four days. Last went in yesterday afternoon. He usually does all the banking in one sitting. But if he goes in today, he'll have some access issues."

"What kind of access issues?" Bartoli asked.

"For one thing, the Internet and phone service in his area will be down," Carl said. He checked the time on his watch. "Happened about forty-five minutes ago and should last through the night. Long enough for Chris and Joey to transfer all the money."

"And in the event his power comes back," Chris said, "I have his personal password, so he won't be able to get into his accounts."

"He'll just call the banks, then," Bartoli said.

"He'll have two problems if he goes that route," Joey said. "First, his computer screen will have a different number for each bank. It won't be the one connecting him to any of the branches."

"Where will the calls go, instead?"

Carmine looked at Bartoli and smiled. "Let's call him a family friend."

"You said two problems," Bartoli said. "What's the second?"

"They ask you to supply them with a secret question that only you know the answer to," Chris said. "It was easy to guess Gonzo's secret question, so each time I go into one of his accounts, I keep the same question but I add a different answer."

"What was Gonzo's secret question?" Bruno asked.

"The name of his mother's favorite pitcher," Chris said.

"Juan Marichal," I said.

"What did you change it to?" Carmine asked.

"Mariano Rivera," Chris said.

"Once a Yankees fan, always a Yankees fan," Carmine said.

I looked at Bartoli. "Out of the mouths of babes," I said.

"I'll admit it," Bartoli said, "I'm impressed. But you should give serious thought to what you're doing. You take Gonzo's money, he's going to come at you in ways you can't begin to imagine."

"It's what I'm counting on," I said.

"And you're planning to take him and his crew on with the ones surrounding me?" Bartoli asked.

"That's my business, Bartoli," I said, inching closer to him. "How, when, and with whom I go after Gonzo should be of little interest to you. You're just his banker, right?"

Bartoli wiped his brow and gazed over Chris's shoulder, watching the accounts move from one bank to another. "It won't take him long to figure out I was the one who helped you move his money," he said. "He's batshit crazy, but he's no fool. And he'll send someone to find me and he will do to me what he does to anyone that betrays him."

"So it's not really my team you're worried about," I said. "It's your ass you're looking to keep free of the fire."

"It's both," Bartoli said. "But from where I'm standing, I don't see you protecting them any more than you could protect me."

"If you have a place where you can lay low for a few days, keep out of sight, now would be the time to head there," I said. "If it goes our way, you'll be clean and in the clear. And if it doesn't, then what happens to you won't matter to me, because I'll be dead. And, as we know all too well, the dead don't give a shit."

"We have six more transfers to make," Joey said. "Shouldn't take more than twenty minutes to wrap it up."

Carmine walked over to Bartoli. "You know what I think?" he said. "I don't think you're worried about Gonzo finding out you tipped us off to where his offshore money was parked. What you are worried about is him thinking you were skimming from him."

Bartoli shook his head. "I'm a banker," he said. "Not a thief."

"A banker for a drug dealer and a pimp," Carmine said. "In my world, that combo translates to thief. Not a lot of open space between the two. You just hide it better than most."

"The boys have everything they need," I said to Bartoli. "It's time for you to take a powder. But remember our deal: What happened between us stays between us."

"I'm in enough trouble," Bartoli said. "I'll keep my end of the agreement."

"That's good to hear," Carmine said. "Because be it Gonzo or be it us, the last place you want to be is on a cold slab with two nickels over your eyes."

52.

EISENBERG'S SANDWICH SHOP

THE NEXT DAY

WE WERE AT ONE OF THE FEW TABLES IN A PLACE THAT HAS always, to me, seemed frozen in time. I was in my sophomore year of high school when I first set foot in the shop, on Fifth Avenue between 22nd and 23rd Street, and felt as if I was in the middle of a James Cagney gangster movie from the 1930s. There are no menus at Eisenberg's; anything you can order is written on wooden plaques lining the walls. If you came in alone, as I often did when I was on the job, you sat on one of the swiveling stools. If you had company and came just before or after the lunch break, you could snag one of the few tables in the place.

It's one of those New York City locations that's likely on its last legs and that would be a loss, to the city and to me. The food is straight out of deli heaven—from top-shelf pastrami to the best meatloaf in Manhattan and a matzo ball soup so good you'd be tempted to order a second bowl. And to wash it down there's Dr. Brown's cream soda. The only thing that tops the food is the service. The waiters are New York smart-ass, quick with a wisecrack, faster on the food order, and seem to know more about what's going on out on the streets of their neighborhood than the local beat cop. And to top it off, there's never a bill sent to your table. Once you're done, you walk to the register, tell the man or woman what you had, and they'll let you know what you owe.

I was sitting across from Chief of Detectives Ray Connors. He was munching on a thick brisket of beef on rye sandwich, yellow mustard dripping onto his fingers. He had a side of homemade coleslaw and two large dill pickles filling his platter and was on his third Dr. Brown's. Given the dire situation we both were about to confront, we were, at least for a few moments, content.

"My father used to take my mom here once a week," the chief said between bites. "They loved listening to the banter of the waiters as much as they loved the food."

I was halfway through a large portion of meatloaf served with an even larger portion of mashed potatoes and had attempted to order a root beer float. "Ducks float," the waiter informed me. "Not soda. That's fact. Not fiction."

"How about just a root beer, then?" I said. "In a large glass filled with crushed ice."

"If it makes you happy," the waiter said, walking off to fill the orders, "then it makes me even happier."

"Yeah," I said. "My folks used to come here, as well. Food's great, even if one meal kicks your cholesterol count up about a hundred points."

"On top of which, my pop smoked two packs of Camels a day," the chief said. "It's a wonder they both lived as long as they did."

I nodded. "I think their generation came of age expecting life to be hard. So they worked each and every day, and when they got a chance to go out—either to a movie, a trip to the country, or to have a meal in a place like this—they put all their worries aside and enjoyed every minute."

"My dad was a longshoreman down at the old Pistol Piers," the chief said. "The ones run by Tough Tony Anastasia, Albert's equally crazy brother. Worked four full days in the hole unloading cargo, then had two full days off. Made good money, at least good enough to pay for rent, food, and Catholic school for me and my brothers. And never once did I hear him bitch about the life in front of him."

"In many ways, as hard as they had it," I said, "they knew they were there to build something. For you and your brothers. For me and my brother. That was what drove them and why they were able to ignore the shit tossed their way. It was their only goal and they succeeded."

The chief set aside his platter and rested his elbows on the tabletop. "Your guys did top-shelf work locating the drop houses. I've got a team assembled to hit them day after tomorrow. It's a dozen of our best, including a few I pulled off a drug task force, major crimes, and Special Victims."

"Which ADA did you decide to go with?"

"Leslie Stuart," the chief said. "She's the best one in that unit, and like the rest of the cops chosen, she's someone we can trust. There will be no leaks or tips to Gonzo coming out of our end."

"You're getting Francine out of her place before the hit?"

The chief nodded. "She'll be taken to a safe house upstate. Her friend Reggie, too. And we'll have Gloria and her mom put under a protective detail."

"Gonzo's crew will be expecting fireworks," I said. "And he might even figure on a raid to hit maybe three, maybe five, of his drops. But he won't be looking for all of them to be hit at the same time."

"Where are you on the drug shipments?"

"They'll be taken off the road after you hit the drops," I said. "The trucks will be left over by Hudson Yards. That time of morning, there won't be much traffic down that part of town, so the trucks shouldn't attract attention."

"Just to be safe," the chief said, "I'll have a unit detour traffic, keep them clear of the area."

"Each truck is equipped with scanners," I said, "meant to notify them of any police presence in the area. Those scanners will be disabled by my computer guys soon as the trucks hit the road. They will be reactivated by the time your drug crew arrives on the scene."

"Based on Gonzo's weekly take, each truck should be good for at least a dozen kilos of heroin and cocaine," the chief said. "Not to mention any pills he's looking to move into the market."

"This breaks right," I said, "you're looking to bring in a ten-to-fifteen-million-dollar haul."

"How good is your truck crew?"

I gave him an easy smile. "Let's say this is not the first time they've taken down a truck route. But it might be the first time they didn't get to keep what's in the trucks."

"You and your guys have done an amazing job," the chief said. "I want you to know that."

"But," I said. "But . . . ?"

"Finding his safe houses, bringing in friends from the other side to steal his trucks. I figured once we knew how deep this operation ran, from a break-in and rape to a head butt with a prime-time dealer, I would still keep you on, because I knew there would be no one better to take it this far."

"But you're concerned about me and my team going into a gunfight with Gonzo."

"Bet your ass I am," the chief said. "Both as a boss and a friend."

"What's the worry?"

"It's been a while since you were in the middle of one," the chief said. "A cop, even a great one, loses his edge once he's off the job for some time. Add to that my concerns about your team."

"What about them?"

"Seriously, Tank," the chief said. "You have no idea how they'll react to the pressure and the heat that will be coming their way."

"I appreciate the concern, Ray," I said. "And believe me, the easiest thing in the world to do would be to hand this back and let you and your team deal with it."

"But you're not going to," the chief said.

I shook my head. "No. Now, I didn't expect it to fall this way, but this is the way it fell. I know the firepower coming our way. But that plays to my advantage."

"How so?"

"He has no idea what I have coming his way," I said. "He's seeing exactly what I want him to see. A retired cop, his crippled partner, an old wiseguy, and a team of amateurs. He's looking at an easy win. And that's exactly what I want him to think."

The chief looked at me for a few moments and then leaned closer. "Then tell me, Tank," he said, "what is it he's not seeing?"

"His world coming to a halt," I said.

53.

CHELSEA

LATER THAT NIGHT

IT WAS CLOSING IN ON THREE IN THE MORNING.

The side streets were quiet, surrendering to the late hour. A squad of large rats gnawed on open bags of garbage and containers of food left splattered on the sidewalk. A handful of homeless men and women lay against shuttered driveways, spread out on folded cardboard boxes, surrounded by grocery carts filled with their belongings.

I nudged Bruno when I spotted the battered Chevy pulling up next to Francine's building. The driver came in slow, headlights off, head hanging low behind the steering wheel. The man next to him lit a match, and from where we were standing, our backs shielded by a Whole Foods loading dock, Bruno and I could see their faces.

"Wait until they get out of the car," I said to Bruno. "Then we move."

Joey and Carl had wired Gonzo's building and were monitoring incoming and outgoing cell-phone calls and text messages. I had a hunch he suspected Francine of being the first to point me in his direction and he would look to bring further harm to the already damaged girl.

The two men, both young and in dark T-shirts and torn jeans, stepped out of the car and gently shut the doors. They glanced up and down the street and then walked to the trunk. They pulled out a red gasoline canister and a bag that appeared to be filled with rags.

"It's a torch job," I said to Bruno.

"They'll hit the basement, would be my bet," Bruno said. "Fire will spread in no time soon as the flames get close to the oil burner."

I tapped him on the shoulder, and we moved out of the shadows and toward the two young men. We caught up to them as they were about to open the gate leading to the basement stairs.

"Little early for a barbecue," I said. "Or too late, depending on your time preference."

The sound of my voice startled the two, and the sight of Bruno's hulking frame caused them to take several steps away from the gate.

"What the fuck are you talking about?" one of them managed to say. "We got no business with you and you sure as shit got no business with us."

"Put the canister down, and the rags, too," I said, "then step away from the building. Walk back to your car, hands where we both can see them, and be on your way. That is, if you'd like to get through the rest of the night without bleeding."

"If anybody's going to do any bleeding on this street, it's gonna be one of you fools," the man holding the canister said, trying his best to come off as tough.

Bruno never hesitated. He moved to his right, planted his right foot in front of his left, and landed a hard and vicious left hook to the side of the canister man's face. The blow caused the man's knees to buckle and his eyes to turn glassy. The canister slipped from his hand and landed on its side next to the basement gate. Bruno quickly followed with an equally powerful uppercut, and the man was lifted off his feet. He appeared to float for several seconds before landing on the cracked pavement, his head doing a double-bounce on the sidewalk.

His partner stood frozen in place.

"Your friend seems to be down for the count," I said to him. "Now it's on you. Take a few breaths before deciding. But while you're doing that, it would be best to take a look at your buddy on the ground. From the sound of those two blows, it might be weeks before he'll be able to eat solid food or tell time."

The young man glanced at his fallen friend. He caught the twitch in his right hand and saw the flutter of his eyes and heard the low moans coming from deep in his chest.

He turned back to me. "You're that cop, right?" he asked. "The one Gonzo is gunning for?"

"And you're the two pigeons he sent out to torch Francine and the rest of the folks in this building," I said.

"And he's gonna be looking to torch us if that don't get done," the young man said.

"You're not burning nothing tonight," I said.

"But we could make use of the gasoline and those rags," Bruno said.

"Then you might as well finish off my friend and kill me," the young man said. "Because if you don't, come sunup and that building's still standing, I ain't nothin' but a dead man."

"You got a place where you and your friend can disappear?" I asked.

"I live in Gonzo's neighborhood," the young man said. "Same as the guy on the ground. Our families, too. If this job don't get done, then, if not me or him, somebody we're close to will die."

I stared at the young man. If he was twenty he had just crossed into that decade, and he was scared. For guys like him and his unconscious friend, the street was the fastest route to steady money for their families. There were dozens of Gonzos putting cash out there, just to do what they asked and live by their rules. But there was a steep price to be paid in return.

I looked at Bruno and then back at the young man. "What's your name?"

"Felipe," he said in a low voice. "The guy on the ground is Hector. He's my cousin."

"You and Hector ever torch a building before?"

Felipe shook his head. "No. This would be our first."

"You know how many would have died tonight if you had burned it to the ground?"

He shrugged. "Gonzo told us the building was practically empty. Just the girl on the second floor and some fat black dude on the fourth."

"Did you believe him?"

"Not really," Felipe said. "From the outside, this place looks no different than the one my grandmother lives in, and there's at least twenty-five living in that rat trap."

"Still, you agreed to do it," I said. "You and your cousin were ready to burn down a building and burn people to death."

"We didn't have a choice," Felipe said. "You work for Gonzo, forget the word 'choice.'"

"Let me guess," I said. "Either you torched Francine's building or Gonzo was going to torch the building where your family lives. That the deal?"

"That's the deal," Felipe said.

"I have a better deal for you," I said.

"What?"

"First, you're going to give me the address where your family lives," I said. "I mean all your relatives. A girlfriend, too, if you got one. Same for Hector there."

"Then what happens?"

"I'll make a call," I said. "I'll have RMPs in front of their homes until my business with Gonzo is at an end."

"What's an RMP?"

Bruno smiled. "Shit, kid," he said. "You are a newbie. It's a patrol car. You know, the police."

"That protects them," Felipe said. "Doesn't do much for me and

Hector. He'll burn us for not torching the building and for ratting to the cops."

"That's where the second part of my deal comes in," I said. "This one will protect you and Hector."

"How you plan on working that magic trick?" Felipe asked.

"Simple," I said. "You and Hector are both under arrest."

54.

TRAMONTI'S

I WAS IN A REAR BOOTH NEXT TO CONNIE, BOTH OF US ACROSS from Chris, taking pleasure in watching him gorge himself on a platter of lasagna with a side of turkey meatballs. Chris was washing down his meal with a glass of Diet Pepsi. Connie and I were working our way through a 2012 Tignanello.

"This is the best lasagna I've ever had," Chris said.

"It's a family recipe," Connie said. "My mom got it from her grandmother when she was a girl in Italy. She passed it on to me."

"That means you have to pass it on to someone," Chris said. "Isn't that how it works?"

"It is," Connie said. "I have someone in mind."

"Vincenzo?" Chris said. "He helps you out in the kitchen. And he loves to cook."

I pushed aside my glass. "Vincenzo's a good guy," I said. "And a decent cook in his own right. But he has his own family recipes."

"I meant you," Connie said to Chris. "I was thinking of leaving the recipe to you. All of them, in fact. Carmine's, too."

"Makes perfect sense," I said.

Chris rested his fork against the platter and looked at me and Connie. "Thank you," he said. "You and Carmine have really made me feel at home since I got here."

"That's never going to change," Connie said.

Chris looked at me. "You don't need to go after Gonzo," he said. "You got his money. Cops are going to raid his safe houses and his drug supply will be gone. Isn't that enough?"

"Wish it were that simple," I said. "But if I don't go after him, he will come after me."

"Let me help," he said. "The rest of the team is going. And Carmine and his friends."

"You're going to monitor the computers and the transmitters. I didn't hand off a job like that to anyone. I gave it to you."

"I'm as scared about what could happen as you are, Chris," Connie said. "I love Tank and I love my father. But this is something they have to finish."

"What if your plan doesn't work?" Chris asked.

"You've grown up fast these last few weeks," I said. "If I go down, you'll have to grow up even faster."

Chris couldn't speak. He simply nodded.

I didn't look at Connie but could see her hand tremble as she lifted the wineglass.

"Of course, there is one thing you're both forgetting," I said. I grabbed a fork and reached over and broke off a chunk of lasagna from Chris's platter. I jammed the lasagna in my mouth and took a moment to savor the taste.

"What?" Chris asked.

"Gonzo is going into this fight with nothing to lose," I said.

"We know," Chris said, tilting his head toward Connie.

"But I'm going into this with everything to lose," I said.

"What does that make you?" Chris asked.

"The most dangerous son of a bitch Gonzo ever met," I said.

I looked at Chris and Connie and held the gaze for a few moments. Then I reached for the bottle of Tignanello and refilled my glass. I leaned back in the booth and took a slow sip of the strong Tuscan wine.

I closed my eyes and prayed I wasn't wrong.

55.

DEATH AVENUE

THE NEXT DAY

CARMINE WAS SITTING ON THE THIRD STEP OF A TENEMENT in the midst of a major reconstruction. He was sipping a cappuccino, a black silver-handled cane resting by his side. I had my back to the street, hands in the pockets of my jeans, one foot braced against the edge of a cracked stone step.

It was nearing sunrise, and the cars and trucks making their way up Tenth Avenue in the mid-20s still had their lights on as they navigated the damaged streets to Midtown, trying to dodge construction sites that held the streets of Manhattan hostage.

"They used to call this Death Avenue back in the day," Carmine said. "There were so many murders on this stretch, the city couldn't keep up with the body count."

"That's because they didn't have video cameras on every lamppost," I said. "This operation goes south, they'll not only have body counts, they'll have visuals of the shooters."

"I wouldn't worry much about that," Carmine said. "You're not the only one with friends at One PP. I got a few of my own. Team them with our computer geeks and all they're likely to get are grainy photos and no facial recognitions."

"I never met anyone from your crew," I said. "I figure you reached out to old running partners. Since it has been a while between drinks for them, a couple of decades give or take, 'walking partners' might be a better term."

"They might be grayer on top and fluffier in the middle," Carmine said, "but I'll still stack them up against anyone on Gonzo's end. When my guys played, they played in the majors, butted heads with the best. Gonzo's guys are shoot-first, think-later cowboys."

"It's the shoot-first part that makes me nervous," I said. "Let's keep this clean as we can. Your guys stop the trucks, toss the drivers and the keys, dump the drugs from the back on the sidewalk, and walk away. Simple as that."

"There's no such thing as simple in our lines of work," Carmine said. "We expect to take eighteen trucks, each carrying six figures of high-end drugs, from coke to heroin and who knows what the hell else. Gonzo will have pistols in the backs of those trucks guarding the stash, no doubt about it."

"They're not expecting it," I said. "That should work in our favor."

"We *hope* they're not expecting it," Carmine said. "Remember, they had a team of cops on the payroll. You nabbed the ringleader and the chief corralled some of his pad buddies, but who the hell knows how many more are out and about. And some of them could be riding shotgun in one or more of those trucks."

I shook my head. I thought I'd worked each step of my plan down to every angle that needed to be covered. But I hadn't given weight to the possibility that Gonzo might use dirty cops to do ride-alongs on his drug runs. I knew whatever team Carmine had put in place would not hesitate to raise a gun in the direction of any danger. They would shoot not to stop but to kill, and they would not believe someone hiding in the rear of a truck was a cop, even if he had a shield hanging off his neck.

"I see that look," Carmine said. "Ease up on the worry. The guys I brought on board are pros. They've been hijacking trucks since Ford switched from stick to automatic. They know their business. And they won't pull on a guy unless he pulls on them first."

"What if the guy who pulls is a cop?"

"If he's riding shotgun in a truck filled with drugs, then he's lost the right to call himself a cop," Carmine said. "He's a criminal, just like the guys on our side. Only difference is our guys don't hide behind a badge."

I saw a truck stopped at a red light three blocks away. "Here's the first truck," I said.

Carmine put an earpiece in his left ear and pulled a small cell phone from the pocket of his Yankees warm-up jacket. "It's top of the first," he said. "Time to move. Let's look to make it as planned—clean and fast."

I walked over to my car, which was parked in front of a hydrant, and stepped in behind the wheel. I started the engine and hit a speed-dial number from my list of cell-phone contacts. Chief Connors picked up on the second ring, his voice coming in clear through my radio monitor. "I'm a step ahead of you, Tank," he said. "We spotted two trucks turning up Tenth from Twenty-fourth. One driver in each. I expect there'll be a second, maybe even a third, in the rear."

"Carmine's guys are moving into position," I said. "They'll take the trucks and leave the drugs and the men in them behind for you to haul in."

"I have unmarked cars covering every area," the chief said. "They know to let the trucks get away."

"I hope to hell this works, Chief."

"By the time Gonzo pieces it together, we'll have the junk impounded and his guys in lockup," the chief said. "It's a batshit-crazy plan, but those are the ones that usually turn out best."

I smiled, the adrenaline flow easing my concerns. "What odds would you give this goes off without a hitch?"

"Six-to-five against," the chief said. "Just like life."

56.

THE SAFE-HOUSE RAIDS

THAT SAME DAY

THE RMPS, UNMARKED CARS, AND DARK VANS ARRIVED WITH the morning sun. Heavily armed and vest-wearing cops swarmed into twenty-four tenements, running from the West Village to Chelsea to the Garment District up as far as the West Forties. There were over one hundred cops assigned to the task of clearing out the safe apartments, led by a team of detectives chosen by Chief Connors. The chief oversaw the operation from a white van parked across from London Terrace, in communication with each unit.

A cop wielding a battering ram slammed open each door and then a team of six swarmed in, woke the women, and put guns in the faces of the dazed men attempting to shake off a night of drink and drugs. They cleared the rooms of drugs and weapons, cuffed the men, and escorted them to the buses waiting to take them to holding pens.

The women were checked for weapons, then handed over to a team from the Special Victims Unit, where they would be questioned to determine whether they were willing participants in Gonzo's prostitution ring or held against their will.

* * *

I WAS IN MY CAR when I got the call from the chief. "We got every-one," he said. "No casualties on either end."

I took a deep breath and closed my eyes. "Not bad for a washed-up third baseman, Chief."

"After the Yankees hear how smooth this job went down, maybe they'll give me another crack at it," he said.

"I'm afraid you're headed for the commissioner's office instead of the hot corner."

"If the truck raids go as smooth we're home free," he said.

"Listen, I was talking to Carmine and he pointed out something I should have thought of and didn't."

"Which is?"

"There could be cops inside those trucks, guarding the drugs," I said. "Carmine's guys pull their guns, they're not going to hold back."

"They shouldn't," the chief said.

"So nothing heavy gets tossed to Carmine's team?" I asked.

"Carmine and his men are part of our operation," the chief said. "Give me a solid old wiseguy over a bought-and-sold cop any day."

"Then we might as well go into this following Carmine's main sur-vival rule," I said.

"What's his rule?"

"Simple," I said. "You want to survive, then break every fucking rule you can. Just don't get caught doing it."

"A rule to remember," the chief said. "Now get those trucks. My guys are in position to confiscate the drugs."

I shifted my car into drive and steered out of its parking spot and made a left onto Tenth, moving against the light. "If I make it through this, Chief," I said, "remind me to ask you for something once the smoke and dust clear."

"Ask me now," the chief said.

"I want a raise," I said. "For me and for my team."

"Consider it done," the chief said. "I'll even find petty cash to toss to Carmine and his crew."

"Money, they got," I said. "But health insurance would be a nice gesture."

The chief laughed. "I never figured mob guys cared about health insurance."

"Sure they do," I said. "Same as everybody else. Except their policies are written a little different than the ones we have."

"Give me a for instance?"

"Their policies come with a two-bullet deductible," I said.

57.

THE TRUCK RAIDS

MOMENTS LATER

THE GRAY TRUCK MOVED SLOWLY UP TENTH AVENUE, AIR BRAKES hissing as it came to a stop in front of the red light on 27th Street. The driver was a young man barely out of his teens. He was wearing a crisp white T-shirt and chewing on a wad of bubble gum. He was alone in the cabin, window down.

The man with the gun and the black rider coat startled him. He seemed to come up from out of the pavement, standing inches from the young man's face, one hand gripping the side-view mirror, both feet on the doorstep. The barrel of a gun was pressed against the young man's neck.

"Slow and easy," the man said. "Head over to the far corner and then cut the engine."

"I got no money on me," the young man managed to say. His hands began to tremble and his shirt was stained with sweat.

"That's good," the man with the gun said. "Because I don't want any."

"Then what do you want?" the young man asked. "This truck ain't worth shit, if that's what you're looking to score."

"I don't want the truck, either," the man with the gun said. He waited as the young man eased the vehicle to the far corner, put the gears in park, and turned off the engine.

"What, then?"

"I want what's in the truck," the man with the gun said.

THE FIRST SEVEN TRUCK hijackings went off without a hitch.

The drivers did as they were told, and Carmine's wiseguys worked with calm and professional ease. They had the drivers place the packages of drugs and plastic bags of pills in neat piles on the closest corner. They then taped the driver and anyone else who happened to be in the truck to the first pole they could find. Once their task was completed, one of Carmine's men passed the word to the chief in his command van, who then set his designated cops in motion. RMPs, black vans, and unmarked cars raced to the corner to grab the drugs and arrest any members of Gonzo's team at the scene. By the time the cops arrived, Carmine's over-the-hill gangsters had taken the trucks and were on their way to Hudson Yards.

The plan was working to perfection.

Then we got to the eighth truck.

I was monitoring the situation from my car, careful to park a safe distance from the scene but close enough to observe the action. I stayed in constant communication with my team, parked in vans farther uptown, and with Carmine, around the corner from me.

His men approached the eighth truck at the corner of 31st and Tenth, half a block shy of a large building under construction. The driver was quick to step down from his cabin and stand with arms wide and feet apart against the side of the truck. He handed over the keys to the back, and while one of Carmine's men stayed with the driver, the other made his way to the rear of the truck and unlatched the dead bolt. He swung open the door, hands by his side, and leaned in to peek inside the dark cabin.

I jumped out of my car as soon as I saw the flash muzzle of a gun hit Carmine's guy in the shoulder, sending him sprawling to the ground. I ran toward the truck, pulling my weapon from my shoulder holster as I crossed against the light traffic flow. I could see Carmine get out of his car and move toward the truck. He had turned the corner and was walking as fast as he could on a leg and a lung not fully functioning.

I got to the truck first and saw the man with a gun stepping forward to confront me.

The man had a policeman's shield hanging on a silver chain over a gray hoodie. He had a gun aimed my way in his right hand. He was about twenty-five, well built, with sharp blue eyes and thick black hair combed straight back and gelled. "I'm a cop," he said to me in a voice that had traces of the Bronx in it. "Rest your weapon on the ground. Away from the bleeding guy next to you."

I knew Carmine was behind me, hiding somewhere between parked construction vehicles. I didn't make a move to drop my gun. "I'm a cop myself," I said, looking at the young man. "At least I used to be. Now, I did a lot of crazy things when I was on the job. But there was one thing sure as shit I never did."

"What would that be?" the cop asked.

"I never worked as a drug mule," I said.

"I'm not a mule," the cop said. "I think of myself as more of a bodyguard."

"Well, then, bodyguard," I said, "keeping that shit behind you safe might put you in an upstate cell block for ten years."

"No one's going anywhere," the cop said. "That guy bleeding on the ground, he don't look like a cop to me. And like you said, you're not on the job anymore. So the way I see it, the only one here with the power to arrest and bring charges would be me."

I could hear the sirens wailing in the distance, the chief having picked up the conversation on the cell dialed to his number in the back pocket of my jeans.

They were less than five minutes away.

I didn't know if that was enough time to save a life.

I glanced at Carmine's man, his tan jacket stained red with the blood oozing out of his shoulder wound. "You good down there?"

"Don't worry about me," he said. "Not my first bullet."

I looked back at the young cop. "I'm not dropping my weapon," I said to him. "Not for you and not for anyone else."

The young cop tilted his head toward the sirens, which now sounded only a couple of blocks away. "The police posse is almost here," he said. "I put a pin in you, jump off this truck, and I tell the boys in blue I took down a drug-dealing ex-cop and his mobbed-up pal. Sounds pretty ironclad, don't you think?"

"Sounds like bullshit," Carmine said, stepping in next to me. "Now it's your turn, punk. Toss the gun or I put a hole next to your navel. Your call. But you got less than ten seconds to make it."

I didn't look at Carmine. I didn't need to look at him. Men like him pull a gun, they have every intention of working the trigger until their opponent drops. But I did look at the young cop and saw one second of hesitation, unsure of whether to pull on me or on Carmine.

It was one second too many.

He aimed his gun at Carmine but never got a chance to get off a round. Carmine's aim was steady and accurate. He hit the young cop in the lower abdomen, just below the rim of his bulletproof vest. The blast sent the cop sprawling on his back, gun falling from his hand, head and shoulders landing on a large stack of cocaine packets.

I grabbed the gun from Carmine's hand and holstered mine. An unmarked car screeched to a halt next to the truck and inches from my right leg. Two men jumped from the car—one rushed toward me; the other jumped on the truck to check on the wounded man.

"Which one of you is Tank?" the detective next to me asked.

"That would be me," I said. "The guy on the ground needs medical attention. The sooner the better."

"So does the one up here," the second detective said, leaning his head out of the rear of the truck. "Gut shot. Looks serious."

"Except the one in the truck needs to ride with cuffs on," I said.

"He's a cop, as he'll be the first to tell you. He also works for Gonzo, the guy whose drug supply we are currently fucking with. He might fail to mention that part."

"And we're supposed to let you walk?" the first detective said to me.

"My day's just getting started and me and my partner here have about a dozen more of these trucks we need to bring in," I said. "That's a lot of drugs to take down before breakfast. But let me put your mind at ease. What's your name?"

"Allison," the detective said. "Frank Allison."

I reached into the rear pocket of my jeans and removed my cell phone. "Chief, you still with me?" I said. "You mind giving a call to Detective Frank Allison and explain the situation?"

I listened and then slid off the phone. "Chief Ray Connors will be calling in to your unmarked in a few seconds. I hope you don't think us rude, but we're not going to stick around to listen. Just make sure our wounded friend here gets to a hospital. Under the care and supervision of the NYPD."

I nudged Carmine and we turned and started to walk toward my car.

The detective's car phone began to chime, and as he reached for it, he looked up at me and Carmine.

"Where are you heading?" he asked. "We're going to need statements from the two of you."

"You know Tramonti's Restaurant?" I asked, still walking as I talked.

"The one in the Village?" the detective said. "Yeah, been there a few times."

Carmine smiled. "Thank you. I'm starting to think not every cop is an asshole."

"Run it by the chief first," I said. "He'll tell you what charges to pin on the dirty badge. Then, if he gives the green light, you meet us there in a couple of days. Dinner's on us. If we're still alive."

58.

GREENWICH VILLAGE

LATER THAT DAY

I WAS COMING DOWN THE STEPS OF MY BROWNSTONE JUST AS Chief Connors pulled up in his car. He double-parked, killed the engine, and came out holding two large cups of Starbucks. I sat on one of the middle steps and waited as he approached.

He sat next to me and handed me one of the coffees. "Interesting task force we had working for us today," I said to him.

The chief smiled as he swallowed a sip of his still-hot coffee. "And an effective one. Narcotics hasn't finished totaling out the drugs taken from the trucks, but my guess is we're looking at a ninety, maybe closer to a hundred-and-a-quarter-kilo score. Lord knows what the street value of that junk is; these dealers cut it up and flake it with everything from baking soda to roach spray."

"What's the deal with the dirty cop that took a bullet?"

"On the way to the hospital he said one of the old guys shot him," the chief said. "I'm guessing he's not talking about the guy spread out on the sidewalk. So that leaves Carmine."

"You believe him?"

"I never believe a word that comes out of the mouth of a crooked cop," the chief said. "On top of which, the driver standing with his arms up told one of the uniforms the first shot came from inside the truck. He wasn't sure who fired the second shot, but when he looked toward the back of the truck he saw you holding the only gun. In his mind, that makes you the shooter."

"Makes sense, doesn't it?"

The chief held the smile. "Internal Affairs will come around and ask a few questions, which I'm certain you know how to answer. Besides, that bastard has more to worry about than a gut shot. He'll be laid up in the hospital for a few weeks and then he'll be put through the system. He's going to need a dozen lawyers to deal with all the charges he's going to be hit with. I wouldn't waste any worry on scum like him."

"I'm not," I said.

"So now we've impounded Gonzo's drugs," the chief said. "Plus, we have about forty members of his crew spread out in cells throughout the city, which reduces his manpower. But I'm certain that even a dull-normal guy like Gonzo would have a rainy-day fund set aside. Aside from what he kept in the offshore accounts."

I tilted my cup toward the chief. "He's tapped out. Gonzo doesn't have enough to buy these two cups of coffee."

"Where's the money headed?"

I rested my coffee container next to my left foot. I reached into my jeans pocket and pulled out two folded sheets of paper and handed them to him. "It totaled out to about four million in laundered cash," I said. "For the moment they're in safe accounts under safe names. In a few weeks, they'll be moved to the charities listed on those two sheets. The donations will be significant and anonymous."

The chief scanned the list, refolded the papers, and put them in his jacket pocket. "You've crippled this guy, Tank," he said. "He's running on fumes. It's only a matter of time before somebody realizes he's a loser and takes him out."

"Happens to all of them," I said. "No reason he should be the exception to the rule."

"Then there's no reason for you to go and butt heads with him," the chief said. "He's going to fade away. Just let it happen."

"It needs to be finished," I said.

"I can order you to steer clear of Gonzo."

I looked at the chief. "I love you like a brother, Ray. And I respect you. But that's one order you know I will never follow."

"What about your team?" the chief asked.

"I'm going to keep them away from the action. Same as I did with the trucks."

"And Carmine?" the chief asked. "He's not planning to go in with the same goodfellas he used this morning? Those old-timers were winded getting out of their cars."

"They were hired for the trucks," I said. "They've been paid and are on their way back to their bocce courts. I fronted the money. I'll get it back when I submit my expense account."

"What are they filed under, I wonder?"

"Private security," I said. "And I won't bother listing their names, since I never asked for their names."

"Carmine had top-tier shooters working for him, as I recall," the chief said. "I ran into a few back when I was on the OC task force. They never went looking for trouble, but when it came their way they buried it."

"That they did," I said. "Dead and alive. If any are still around, I'm sure Carmine reached out."

The chief stood and faced me. "I'll be on the phone, ready to move in at any time. If I feel it getting too hot for you and whoever goes in with you, I'm sending my guys in to pull you out. I'll play it your way as long as your way works."

I stood and shook hands with the chief. "No arguments from me. If it gets out of hand, I'll count on you to get my guys out of the soup."

"And where does that leave you?"

"I'll be there until the end," I said. "I'll be staring down at Gonzo's body or he'll be staring down at mine. It's the only way for this dance to come to a stop."

59.

THE BROWNSTONE

THAT NIGHT

MY TEAM WAS WAITING AS I WALKED INTO THE LIVING ROOM. Bruno was sipping a large bottle of VitaminWater and sitting next to Joey, who had an open laptop on his knees. Carl stood with his back to a window. Alexandra sat with Connie, chatting quietly, each holding a bottle of Snapple. Pearl was next to the couch, his wheelchair lodged along one of the bookcases. Chris was sitting on a barstool, showing Pearl something on his iPad. Carmine followed me in. He was joined by a tall, sinewy man in his midfifties. He was neatly dressed, nodded a silent greeting to the people in the room, and stood off to the side.

"This is Paulie," Carmine said, to me as much as to everyone else. "He's here to help."

I moved to the center of the room and gazed at each of them for a brief moment. "You thought this would be like any other case," I said. "We find the bad guy, hand him over to the PD, collect a check, and go back to our lives. Only this didn't turn out like the others."

"And it's about to get dangerous," Carmine said. "Life-and-death dangerous."

"You've done excellent work," I said. "Running down the phones. The bank transfers. Monitoring the audio on the drug operations. Me and Pearl have worked with top-tier teams, but none could stack up to the people in this room."

"We still got one piece left to the puzzle," Carl said.

"You're right," I said. "Gonzo needs to be taken down. But that falls to me and Carmine."

"We're not going to let the two of you go in alone," Joey said. "We came in at the start and we're going to stay to the finish."

"You'll need us, Tank," Bruno said.

"And you know how much a gypsy loves a good fight," Alexandra said. "I've already lined up some friends to lend a hand."

"And we've stayed on Gonzo's phones," Joey said. "Me and Chris are plugged into his devices and have been picking up lots of chatter."

"Such as?" I asked.

"He's freaked about having his drugs confiscated," Chris said. "He left a dozen voicemails to a man in New Jersey. With each one, Gonzo promised to make good on the drug money."

"You get a name?"

"His name is Bono," Joey said.

"I hate hearing that," Paulie said, speaking for the first time. "I really like Bono."

I turned toward Paulie. "You know him?"

Paulie shook his head. "Never met him, no," he said. "But I love his music. Guy's a great musician. And he gives so much to charity. With all his dough, who would think he'd need to go into the drug business?"

"You're thinking of the guy from U2," Chris said. "It's not the same Bono."

"That's a relief," Paulie said.

I glanced at Carmine, who shrugged. "He's not in this to take a Regents exam, Tank," Carmine said. "He's here to do damage. You'll be glad I brought him along."

I paced the room. These weren't just my friends sitting around me. This was my family. Except for Carmine and Paulie, none had any business going into a battle with Gonzo. But I knew I couldn't talk them out of coming with me. In that respect, they were no different than Pearl insisting on being part of the action, just to get a taste of being a cop again.

"I'm not going to waste any more breath trying to talk you out of coming into this," I finally said. "So why don't we map out a plan that might help us pull this off."

I was met by smiles. "Don't tell me," I said. "You already have a plan."

"And a damn good one, if you ask me," Pearl said.

60.

WASHINGTON HEIGHTS

THE NEXT NIGHT

I STOOD ACROSS THE STREET FROM GONZO'S BUILDING, WATCH-ing the sun disappear over the tenement structures that lined the block. It was just past seven o'clock and the night was unseasonably warm. I had parked my car farther down the street and my team had split up and occupied two vans, each a safe distance away. We were able to communicate with one another and there were eyes not only on me but on the street and on Gonzo's building. Carmine and Paulie were in a dark-blue sedan, parked around the corner.

We had been picking up surveillance footage from Gonzo's build-ing for four days, more than enough time to tell us who lived where, what their connection to the drug boss was, and where they stood in his pecking order. On the way over, I called an old friend in the narcot-ics unit and asked for a background check on Bono, working off the assumption it was a nickname.

"Want me to run down info on The Edge, too, while I'm at it?" my friend asked.

"Save any U2 jokes for later, Patrick," I said. "This Bono works out of Jersey."

I was heading toward Riverside Drive when Patrick phoned back. "He was a heavy dealer once upon a time," he said. "Got a jacket long as LeBron's arm span. Done a few spins in federal and one in state. All drug-related. These days he's more of a middleman, working with dealers from the tri-state area. Takes twenty percent off the top and moves the junk to its next destination."

"He got himself a crew?"

"If he does, they are under our radar," Patrick said. "My guess would be three, maybe four bodyguards, including a driver. He lives in a big house in Englewood Cliffs. Doesn't venture out much."

"Thanks, Patrick," I said. "I owe you. Anything I can do from my end, say the word."

"Hook me up next time U2 hits the Garden," Patrick said, laughing.

I WALKED TOWARD THE entrance to Gonzo's building. There were two men blocking the front door. Each reached a hand toward the back of his jeans as I got closer. I stopped at the base of the cracked steps and looked up at them. "I'm here for Gonzo," I said.

"He's inside," one of the men said. "But he didn't tell us to keep an eye out for any friends who would be stopping by."

"I'm not a friend," I said. "But I'm pretty sure he'll want to see me anyway."

"Why?" the second man asked.

"Because I have all his money," I said.

The two exchanged a quick glance. One of them opened the wooden door leading into the tenement and stepped inside the vestibule. I could see him talking to a third man, half hidden by street shadows. I moved up the first two steps of the building. The young man left in front of the door pulled his gun and held it close to his right leg. "You come up when we say you come up," he said.

I shrugged and then I heard Carmine's voice come through my miniature earpiece. "We're in," he said. "On the roof. Door leading down is unlocked and unguarded. We'll stay put until we hear from you."

"Tell Gonzo he's got five minutes," I said. It was a message meant as much for his men as it was for mine. "If he wants to see his money again, he needs to see me."

I heard shouting coming from the halls of the tenement. The windows fronting each apartment were open to let in the breeze from the distant river. I looked up and saw an elderly woman with her arms folded across the crease of the windowsill glancing down at me. She had a toothless smile and vacant eyes. There was a large ashtray next to her, a smoldering cigarette resting in one of the slots.

The wooden door swung open and the man who had initially stepped in now stepped out. He gestured for me to come up. "He'll see you," he said. "But first I have to frisk you."

I shook my head. "You put one hand close to me and I'll drop you like a hot match," I said. "I walk in the way I am or I walk away."

"But I need to check and see if you carrying," the young man said, more a plea than a demand.

"Let me save you time, Einstein," I said. "I'm an ex-cop. There isn't a chance in hell that I'm *not* carrying. Just like you and your compadres. Why should I be the only guy at the party without a weapon?"

The young man glanced over at the older and bigger man next to him, who shrugged and waved me up. "Just remember, smart-ass," the young man said, "there are more guns aimed your way than you could ever aim our way. You hear what I'm sayin'?"

"Be hard for me not to," I said, coming up to the top step of the building. "I'm standing right next to you."

"Go in," the young man said. "Third floor, off the landing. The door will be open."

"Nice and easy, Tank," Pearl said into my earpiece. "Nobody's going to make a move until you meet with Gonzo. So no need to worry about one of these cowboys putting one in your back."

I crossed the second stairwell, guarded by two men sitting in straw chairs. Neither bothered to look up as I passed. "The thought hadn't crossed my mind," I whispered, waiting until I approached the third set of stairs before I spoke. "Until you mentioned it."

"You got three minutes alone with him," Carmine said. "Then me and Paulie make our move. Try and stay alive until then."

"You guys need to stop trying to cheer me up," I muttered.

GONZO WAS SITTING IN a black leather La-Z-Boy, footrest up, feet splayed out. He was wearing knockoff designer jeans and a short-sleeve button-down shirt. He had on a pair of brown moccasins and white socks. I stood less than five feet away and took in the room. There were two shooters by an open window and two more by a door behind me. Toss in the ones I counted on the steps and guarding the halls and it put the total at fourteen visible. There might be three, maybe four more stragglers hiding behind closed doors.

"So, you gonna tell me or you gonna wait for me to ask?" Gonzo said.

"About your drug money?"

"Why the fuck else you here, Tin Badge?" Gonzo asked. "You must think yourself pretty slick, walking tall up in my crib like you're fuckin' Eliot Ness. You been fuckin' with me, with my business, for too long."

"You're out of business, Gonzo," I said. "Those apartments where you were stashing your drugs and the women you forced to play for pay, they're memories. Up in smoke. And let's not forget the truck routes, all the drugs and pills stashed inside. They're in the wind, too. Along with the drivers and the muscle hiding in the rear of the trucks. You might as well put a 'Closed Forever' sign on your window. You're finished. If Bono hasn't filled you in yet, then I will."

"Bono?" Gonzo asked. He jumped up from his La-Z-Boy and stepped toward me. "How the fuck you connect to Bono?"

"That's beside the point," I said. "You asked about the money. All that dough you squirreled away in offshore accounts. That's a lot of scratch for a guy like you."

"More money than you will ever see."

"Normally, that would be true," I said. "But since you were kind enough to switch the money from your accounts to mine, well, I do have a lot more than I ever imagined I would."

"What the fuck are you talking about?" Gonzo said. His anger was mixed with confusion and concern.

"You check your accounts lately?" I asked. "If you want I can tell you exactly how much is in there. Zero. That's what you're down to. Zero."

Gonzo lunged for me, swinging a right fist toward my head. I dodged the blow and shoved him to the ground. I turned my head and saw the two by the window move toward me and the two at the door pull their weapons. "Five against one, Tin Badge," Gonzo said, getting on his feet. "Ain't no way you walk out of here. It's down to how much I want you to suffer before you die."

"My grandmother used to say, 'You got to die of something and you got to die somewhere,'" I said. "But I don't think she would want me to take my last breath in this shithole."

"You got no other choice."

"Wrong again, Gonzo," I said.

THE THREE SHOTS RANG out from the hallway.

Carmine and Paulie had made their move, coming down from the rooftop and catching the men on the third floor off guard.

Now I needed to make mine.

The men in the room turned to look through the open door to see why shots were fired and at whom. I shoved Gonzo aside and reached for one of the men who'd been near the open window. I caught him chest high, and he wrapped his arms around my waist. I turned him, his back to the other men in the room. One of the two gunmen by the door aimed his weapon in my direction.

He never got off a shot.

Paulie stood in the doorway and shot him in the center of his back.

His body hit the floor face-first, gun held limp in his right hand. I eased the man I was grappling with closer to the open window, knowing that Paulie had my back and Carmine was covering the stairwell. The man had about thirty pounds and two full inches on me, his gun hanging low in his right hand.

I leaned him halfway out the open window, my right hand raining hard punches on his chest and stomach. I felt him sag, his breath coming in short spurts, and I let him go just as the second man grabbed me from behind and shoved me to the floor. I didn't see the man hit the ground, but I heard the thud and knew he was done fighting for today.

I looked up and glanced at Paulie.

He had his gun on the lone guy by the door, turned him around, and started to walk out the door, using him as a shield. "Me and Carmine got the place covered," he said. "You worry about this prick and his buddy." He nudged his head toward Gonzo and the one near the window.

"You can't take the whole stairwell by yourselves," I said. I pulled my gun from my hip holster and aimed it at Gonzo and his guardian. Both seemed frozen in place, not sure what was happening around them or what to do next. Gonzo had a gun wedged in the back of his jeans but had yet to make a move to reach for it.

"No shit, Sheerluck," Paulie said. "Your pal Alexandra sent some of her family to help us. I always heard gypsies were good with knives. But until I saw it with my own eyes, I never believed it. They're cutting these bastards like they're beef on a hook."

Paulie and his shield disappeared into the hallway, leaving behind a trail of gunshots and smoke.

I moved my gun between Gonzo and the man by the window. He was on his feet now, a shaky hand aiming his gun in my direction. Gonzo glared at me and then turned to the man. "Shoot him, Angel," he shouted. "Put every bullet you got into his ass."

I looked at Angel. I had a fraction of a second to decide if he was the real deal or if he was a reluctant brawler. "You don't need to die," I said to him. "Not for this fool."

"Shoot the motherfucker," Gonzo screamed. "Shoot him now!"

"You don't need to listen to him anymore, Angel," I said. I had my gun aimed at the center of his chest. "He's not top dog anymore. He's just another guy on his way to prison or the morgue. You can save yourself. But you need to do it without a gun in your hand."

Gonzo ran across the room toward Angel and shoved him. Angel landed with his back against a tattered wall. I got to my feet and swiveled behind Gonzo. I reached for the gun he had wedged against his spine, pulled it out, and tossed it out the open window.

"Now toss your gun out, too," I said to Angel. "You do that, you get out of this alive. Use the stairs to the roof. Get off the block that way."

Angel looked at me and then back at Gonzo. He took a deep breath and then casually tossed his weapon out the window. "Sorry, Gonzo," he said.

"Go," I said to him.

Angel, drenched in a cold sweat, brushed past Gonzo and made his way out of the room, heading toward the stairs that would take him to the rooftop and freedom.

Gonzo lowered his head for a few moments and then turned to me.

"Looks like it's you and me, Tin Badge," he said.

"Alone at last," I said, and holstered my gun.

61.

GONZO'S APARTMENT, WASHINGTON HEIGHTS

MOMENTS LATER

Gonzo landed the first punch. A right to my rib cage. It was a hard blow, but I managed to blunt some of the force with my elbow. He then swung a wild left I ducked under.

"I'm gonna beat you like a fuckin' drum," Gonzo said. He was sweating so much that small puddles of water were forming around his feet.

"You'll need to commit a homicide," I said as I circled him. "I would rather be found dead than lose a fight to a scumbag like you."

Gonzo lowered his head and charged me. I braced myself, waited, and then raised my right knee, catching him hard on the left side of the head. The force of the jolt slammed him against the nearest wall, and I moved in. I crouched down and landed solid blows to his chest and stomach. He was breathing with his mouth open, and I scored with several hard punches to his gut.

Gonzo had spent too much time sitting in a La-Z-Boy, giving orders. His body had once been rock-hard—the muscles were still visible. But he hadn't worked them in a while and the rust showed. He had enough strength to push me and clear himself from the wall. He grabbed a Little League baseball bat off a coffee table and started swinging it at me.

I took a few steps back, ducked under the bat, kicked at the back of his right leg, and watched as he slipped to the floor. Then I was on him, landing blows with both fists to his face, neck, and throat. I was fueled with pent-up anger and was relishing the chance to release it. I thought that side of me—the violent, dangerous part of me that I'd fought for so long to suppress—had been put to rest. But standing there in front of Gonzo, punishing the man who had brought pain and anguish to so many for no reason other than to profit from it, made me realize that my anger and violent side would never go away. It would remain a permanent part of me. And on this day, in this apartment, in front of this man, I was glad that it was so.

I stepped back, glancing down at Gonzo. His face was bruised and one eye was closed. Thin lines of blood flowed out both sides of his mouth. He coughed up even more blood and spit a thick wad on the floor, wiping the sides of his mouth with his right arm. The bat was on the ground, beyond the reach of his left hand. He looked at me and smiled. "That all you got?" he asked. "If it is, then you are completely fucked."

I reared back my right leg, kicked Gonzo square in the chest, and sent his body crashing against the side of the La-Z-Boy. "There's more if you want some."

I moved to the open window and checked the street outside. There was a small crowd gathered in front of the building. There were five of Gonzo's men lying facedown on the pavement, Carmine and Paulie keeping them in place. I spotted Alexandra's crew watching the side streets. "Anybody hurt on our end?" I asked.

"We're feeling no pain," Carmine said. "Can't say the same for Gonzo's guys."

"I'll be down in a couple of minutes," I said. "Gonzo will be with me. Is the stairwell clear?"

"You'll need to step over a few bodies," Carmine said. "But other than that, good to walk."

I heard the click of the gun before I saw it. I turned, and Gonzo had pulled a snub-nose .38 from the side pocket of the La-Z-Boy and was aiming it at me. His blood-soaked face broke into a smile. His hand was shaking and he was working with only one good eye. He squeezed the trigger and got off a round. It landed against the wall to my right, missing me and the open window by several feet. I fell to my knees, rolled on the ground, and flipped open my holster.

Two seconds later, I was standing above Gonzo, my gun pointed at his head. His gun was still in his hand, but I could tell he was struggling to focus and aim his shot.

"You can die," I said to him. "Right here. Right now. Or you can let me take you downstairs and hand you to the NYPD. Your choice. Facedown in your shitty apartment. Or a prison cell. Whatever way you want to go, decide now."

Gonzo gazed up at me for several seconds, his eye glassy and red. The gun slipped from his hand and dropped to the floor. I kicked it to the wall. I reached down and grabbed him by the back of his shirt. "Let's walk, dealer," I said. "You lead and I'll follow."

We were heading toward the open door when I glanced out the window and saw four gunmen coming out of a far corner tenement, heading toward Carmine, Paulie, and Alexandra's crew. I held Gonzo in place. "We got company," I said into my mike. "Get the van moving. Do a one-eighty soon as you come into the street. There are four men, guns exposed. Carmine, Paulie, find cover. For you and the others."

"I see them," Carmine said. "We're low on ammo. Not sure we can take all four. And the gypsies have knives, not guns."

"Don't worry about the gunmen," I said. "Just find a safe place for you and the others."

"What about the shooters?"

"We got a nice surprise for them."

I leaned Gonzo against the side of the open window. "Try and keep your eye open," I said to him. "This is not something you'll want to miss."

62.

WASHINGTON HEIGHTS

MOMENTS LATER

THE BLACK VAN WITH CARL BEHIND THE WHEEL CAME CAREENING
around the far corner of the street. He came in at an angle, broke
sharply, and did a full U-turn, the back of the van facing the oncoming
gunmen. The double doors of the van swung open, and Bruno jumped
out and slid a ramp down to street level. He then took cover at the side
of the truck. I saw a sawed-off shotgun hanging on a belt around his
neck. He slid into position and cradled it in both hands.

The gunmen were about twenty feet away. They had guns in both
hands and were ready to rain fire down on the van. I figured them to
be the last of Gonzo's crew, his backup in the event his end of the job
went south.

"One guy with a shotgun against those sharpies," Gonzo sputtered
through a mouthful of blood and cracked teeth. "Your boy won't match
up. He'll be dead before he gets off a shot."

I slammed Gonzo's head against the window frame. "Shut your
mouth and focus," I said. "You're about to see a real cop in action."

From out of the van, Pearl's motorized wheelchair came sliding
down the ramp, moving at full tilt toward the gunmen. He had a gun
in each hand, a determined look in his eyes, and a smile on his face.

Once again, my friend, my partner, was doing what he was always meant to do—be a cop.

The gunmen stopped when they saw the wheelchair and the man in it. Pearl did not hesitate. He fired one round after another in the direction of the gunmen. The one on the far left was the first to go down, taking a full load to the chest. A second grabbed his shattered knee and dropped his gun. Pearl swiveled his chair to the left and right, dodging the return fire coming his way.

Then Bruno made his move.

He stepped forward, pumping shells from his shotgun at a rapid pace, taking down the third of the four shooters. Pearl was a few feet from the last one standing and brought his wheelchair to a halt.

"You can live or you can die," Pearl said to him. "I'll let you decide."

Bruno stepped in next to Pearl. "You weren't good enough to take down one of us," he said to the gunman. "Means you got no chance to take down both. I would give up. Then again, I'm not you."

The gunman looked at Bruno and Pearl. He then bent down and rested his weapon on the ground.

"Smart move," Pearl said, keeping his guns aimed at the man. He turned to Bruno. "Make sure our friend doesn't make a run for it. I'm not allowed to shoot a fleeing suspect in the back."

Bruno walked toward the young man, towering over him, and landed a vicious right hand to his jaw, sending him sprawling to the ground, knocking him out cold. He walked back toward Pearl and shrugged. "I didn't have cuffs," he said.

Pearl smiled. "Works for me."

I pulled Gonzo from the window. "Show's over," I said, holding him by the back of the neck. "Let's get the hell out of this dump."

We walked slowly through the hallway and down the stairwell, passing moaning and groaning bodies, some on their last breaths, others destined to be taken to the nearest hospital and then off to arraignment.

"The chief is on his way," Joey said into my earpiece. "He said to tell you he's coming in with a full boat, ready to take them in."

"That's music to my ears," I said.

"I'm going to clear out before he gets here," Carmine said. "I'll take Paulie and the gypsies with me. If we're not seen, we couldn't have been on the scene."

"I didn't even know you were here," I said.

As I stepped out of the front of the building, still holding Gonzo in front of me, I could hear the sirens and see some RMPs, buses, and unmarked sedans making their way toward us.

I pulled Gonzo down and sat next to him on the top step of the stoop, leaning my back against a black railing. "I don't know about you, Gonzo," I said, "but I could go for some Brunello right about now."

"Fuck you and Brunello," Gonzo said.

63.

WASHINGTON HEIGHTS

MOMENTS LATER

I WATCHED AS A PLAINCLOTHES DETECTIVE SLAPPED CUFFS on Gonzo and started to lead him to the back of a squad car. Their first stop would be the hospital, to stitch him up and tend to his wounds, and then, after that, the start of a journey that would culminate with him on the receiving end of a long prison sentence. The chief was standing next to me.

Gonzo lifted his head from the rear of the patrol car. "We got unfinished business, you and me," he said. "Soon as I get paroled, we're going to meet up. You hear me, Tin Badge?"

I moved closer to the car. "By the time you get out of prison, I'll be dead," I said.

"I'll need your reports by the end of the week," the chief said, turning to me. "And you and Pearl will need to talk to the IA guys about the shootings. At least the ones you were involved in."

"Not a problem," I said. "Even though I have no idea what went on in those hallways up there. I could guess, but it would be just that. A guess."

"I'll clean up the mess," the chief said. "Just stick to the facts as you know them and we should be good. I'll process your final payment tomorrow."

"What about expenses?"

"If you can itemize them, I'll put them through," the chief said. "If not, I'll beef up your payout to cover the ones you can't explain."

"This was more than I bargained for," I said.

"I put my best teams on the hardest cases," the chief said. "And you and this insane crew you put together are one of the best."

"I smell more work coming our way."

"I've got stacks of open cases I'd like solved shoved in a corner of my office."

"Any of those open cases out-of-town jobs?" I asked. "Wouldn't mind getting out of the city for a bit."

"What do you have in mind?"

"Bermuda would be nice," I said. "But I'd settle for Malibu or Canton."

"Canton, Ohio?" the chief said. "What the hell would you want to go there for?"

"It's where the NFL Hall of Fame is," I said. "Always wanted to see it. And it would be sweeter to go there on NYPD's nickel."

I SHOOK HANDS WITH the chief and started to walk toward my car. I spotted Joey at the far corner, heading my way, smile on his face. "Shouldn't you be in a van going back to base?" I said into my mike.

"Figured I'd ride with you," Joey said. "And I could use the walk. My legs were getting cramped sitting in front of those monitors."

"I'm parked around the corner," I said. "Let's meet up by the car."

Joey lost the smile and began to run, arms and legs pumping at full speed. "Tank!" he yelled. "Get down! Quick! Man with a gun behind you! Get down now!"

I rolled to the ground and pulled my gun. A gunman I had seen stretched out on the sidewalk had managed to maneuver away from the crime scene and move in my direction. He was dragging a wounded left leg and held a semiautomatic in his right hand. He fired off three rounds.

I didn't get a chance to fire my weapon.

Two uniform officers, standing to the shooter's right, drew their weapons and took him down. I caught their eye and nodded my thanks. I got to my feet and holstered my gun. "We're all clear, Joey," I said.

I turned and looked up the street and saw Joey on the sidewalk, faceup, hands at his sides. "Joey!" I shouted into my mike. "Joey's down!"

I ran in his direction, nearly tripped on a chipped piece of pavement, and fell to my knees when I got to him. He was bleeding from a chest wound, blood coating his mouth. His eyes were closed, tears flowing down the sides of his face. I clutched his hand in mine.

"I need a truck!" I shouted without looking behind me. "Now!"

Joey opened his eyes. "I'm sorry, Tank," he said in a low voice.

"You got nothing to be sorry about," I said. "Not a damn thing."

"Did they get the guy?" Joey asked.

I nodded. "Stay with me, Joey," I said, reaching for his hand and holding it tight in mine. "I know it hurts. Just look at me and breathe. It's not easy. But you can do it. I know you can, kid."

"It hurts too much to breathe."

I lifted his head and cradled it in my arms. "Help is going to be here soon," I said. "All you need to do is keep breathing and keep talking."

Joey raised a hand and rested it against my face, his fingers drenched with blood. "I wondered what this would feel like," he said, his voice losing strength. "It's different than I expected."

"What is?"

"Dying," Joey said, looking at me through tear-streaked eyes.

"I should have never let you get into this," I said, fighting to keep my emotions in check. "I fucked up."

"Getting into this was the best thing to happen to me," Joey said. "I loved every minute."

I wrapped my arms around him, his head and neck buried against my chest. An ambulance, sirens running, was backing up toward the two of us. One of the team vans came careening around the corner, braking to a sharp stop. The rear doors opened and Chris was the first one out. He ran to Joey's side and reached for his left hand.

"Is he going to be okay, Tank?" Chris asked. He was trembling as much as Joey.

I looked at Chris, my eyes coated with tears, and didn't respond. I didn't have to. The look told Chris everything.

"There he is," Joey said, turning his head and smiling at Chris. "My main man. Make sure he stays on the team, Tank. Make sure."

"There's no team without you" was all I managed to say. I gazed at the wound, the blood forming a dark pool around the three of us, and knew there was little chance for him to survive the bullet that had been meant for me.

Joey lifted his head and stared at me. "There has to be a team," he said. "Promise me, Tank. Please. Promise me that."

Chris had his head buried against Joey's shoulder and was squeezing his hand so hard he was cutting into his skin. I looked at Joey and nodded. "I promise," I said.

The rest of the team stood around us now in a semicircle, heads down, shoulders sagging.

Joey took in a final, painful breath. His upper body sagged and his eyes closed. His feet shook for several seconds.

Then he was gone.

Two EMS workers stood above us. "We can take it from here," one of them said to me in a gentle voice, a hand resting on my shoulder.

I moved some locks of hair away from Joey's face and stared down at him one final time. I then stood, walked over to Chris, and gently nudged him away from his friend. The boy's face was wet with tears. Chris lifted his head. "Is Joey . . . ?" he asked.

I nodded and we turned, each of us walking slowly toward the van.

We had lost one of our own.

64.

WASHINGTON HEIGHTS

MOMENTS LATER

WE STOOD IN FRONT OF THE VAN AND WATCHED THE EMS team lift Joey's body onto a gurney and wheel him toward the open doors of their truck. They would take him downtown and keep his body there until his funeral arrangements were made.

"He had the best heart on the team," Alexandra said.

I looked up and down the street; the second van—the one with Bruno, Carl, and Pearl in it—was still parked in the middle of the avenue, front end facing us. I began walking down the avenue.

I passed the crime scene, cops and EMS personnel taking in the wounded and cuffing the remaining members of Gonzo's team. I walked around the van and saw the back of Pearl's wheelchair. Bruno was leaning against the van, a bulletproof vest dangling off his right hand. I noticed he was still wearing his vest.

"You just take that off Pearl?" I asked.

Bruno shook his head. "Didn't have to," he said. "He never put it on."

Bruno handed me Pearl's vest. "Me and Carl will ride with the others," he said, his voice cracking. "You need me to make any calls for Joey, just say the word."

"No need, Bruno," I said, taking the vest from him. "We were the only family he had."

I walked toward Pearl's wheelchair and gently spun him around. "What the hell's going on?" I asked, holding up his vest. "Why the hell didn't you wear your vest? Were you hoping to catch a kill shot? Was that your plan all along? Like losing Joey isn't painful enough. We needed to lose you, too."

Pearl's left arm was coated in blood, a flesh wound the cause of the damage. "I'm very sorry about Joey," Pearl said. "He was a great kid. If only Bruno or I had seen the gunman before he did."

"Why weren't you wearing the fucking vest, Pearl?" I shouted.

"You know the answer to that as well as I do," he said.

"Tell me anyway," I demanded.

"I wanted them to take me down," he said. "I wanted my pain to go away. I knew it was only going to get worse. We both did. And I needed it to stop."

"But you weren't ready to go down, were you?" I said. "At least not as ready as you thought you were. You took those shooters dead on and came away with only a flesh wound. If you wanted to be taken out, you were in a position to let that happen."

"I felt alive, Tank," Pearl said. "For the first time in years. Alive and lucky. And you're right—I fought like hell not to get taken out."

"Damn it, Pearl," I said, "you are the most stubborn, thickheaded bastard I've ever met." I wrapped him in my arms, his head resting against my right shoulder. "And I'm so fuckin' glad you're still here for me to let you know that."

"I love you, too, my brother," Pearl said.

"You can't fuckin' leave me now, Pearl," I said.

"I'm not leaving you," Pearl said. "We've always been together, from day one. Partners and friends forever."

"Partners and friends forever," I whispered into Pearl's ear. I kissed his cheek and cupped a hand around his face.

I rested my head on top of his and let the emotions of the day drain out of me.

65.

WEST SIDE PIERS

ONE WEEK LATER

I STOOD NEXT TO CHRIS, LOOKING OUT AT THE ROILING WATERS of the Hudson River. We hadn't had a chance to spend time together the last week. It had been an emotional few days, saying goodbye to Joey. At his funeral, he'd been given an NYPD escort and a line of officers to salute him as his casket was brought down the steps of our local church.

Connie stayed close to Chris during the entire time, holding him when he needed to be held and giving him his space when required. He had seen far too much death for one so young. And he and Joey had been close friends by the end.

"Me and Jack used to come here with your grandfather on Sunday mornings," I said. "It was a lot different back then."

"How?"

"There weren't as many tourists down these parts, for one thing," I said. "The area was a lot rougher, not as developed."

"Why did you come here, then?" Chris asked.

"We loved the water, and this was as close as we could get to it in those days," I said. "And it gave us time to spend together. Talk things out. Or just take in the view."

"Is that what we're going to do?" Chris asked. "Talk things out?"

"If you want," I said.

"It hurts," Chris said.

"I know," I said. "I miss them, too. And, yes, even your dad."

"I never want to not miss them," Chris said. "I know that might sound crazy."

"It's not crazy," I said. "There won't be a day goes by we won't miss them. They were a part of us when they were alive and they'll remain a part of us."

"It's not the same as having them here," Chris said.

"No," I said. "It would be better if you were here with your mom and dad and Joey was back at the brownstone, drinking coffee and getting me free cable."

"So we just go on?"

"That's right," I said. "We're together now. We bumped heads at first and no doubt we'll do it again. But we won't be doing it as strangers. We'll be doing it as family."

"I guess then Dad was right," Chris said.

"About what?"

"I told you when we met that he'd mentioned you to me only one time," Chris said.

"You were holding out on me?"

"I wasn't sure if us living together would work," Chris said.

"But now you think it's okay to tell me?"

Chris nodded. "He talked about you one other time. Dad told me that if anything ever happened to him and my mom, he wanted me to come live with you. That you would be the one who would take care of me. The way you once took care of him."

"When did he tell you that?"

"Three weeks before he died," Chris said.

The morning sun brought sparkle to the water and warmth to our faces. A light spray splashed against our sneakers and coated the front of the pier.

I stared out at the horizon, my nephew close by my side. We were quiet during the rest of our stay, both of us thinking of the ones we lost and would never see again.

66.

MEMORIAL SERVICE

JUNE

WE WERE GATHERED IN THE BACKYARD OF TRAMONTI'S. THE trampled garden had recovered from its near destruction, and I could see basil starting to sprout and tomato plants easing their way toward full growth. I was holding a glass of white wine, leaning against a whitewashed brick wall, listening to the jazz quartet playing a somber tune in one corner of the large yard.

A crisscross of overhead bulbs glowed in the summer night, and each table was warmed by lit candles. Framed photos of Joey rested on the tables. I glanced around and made eye contact with Alexandra, who raised a glass in my direction.

Paulie and Bruno sat across from one another at a corner table, engrossed in a game of chess. Carl was at a table with three of the fighters recruited for our battle with Gonzo. I was sitting with Pearl, just watching the scene. Carmine and Chris came up next to us.

"Great work on the garden, Carmine," I said. "A couple more weeks and you'll have enough fruit and veggies to feed the locals."

Carmine nodded. "Everything I learned about taking care of a garden I learned from my honey. She was the one with the green thumb. I was the one with the shovel."

"I never thanked you properly for stepping in the way you did," I said. "Without you and Paulie, we would have come out of it a lot more damaged than we did."

"We lost more than we should have," Carmine said. "But that's on that miserable lowlife Gonzo. Not on you."

"True words, Carmine," Pearl said. "I always thought you would have been a terrific cop."

Carmine laughed. "Let's not get crazy," he said. "I would look ridiculous in a uniform. Besides, I'd much rather give orders than take them."

"So would we," Pearl said. "I imagine that's one of the reasons neither me or Tank ever rose above a detective's rank."

"And I would wager tomorrow's trifecta that Chris here is cut from the same cloth," Carmine said. "He came through in ways no one could have ever imagined."

"That's no lie," I said to Chris. "You told me when we met that you read the books and watched the shows and movies. I figured that was what a kid your age did. But you got skills and you know how to use them."

Chris gave us each a hug. Then he started to move toward Bruno and Paulie's table. "I get to play the winner," he said.

"That'll be Paulie," Carmine said. "May not be the brightest guy in the room. But he's the best trigger man I've worked with, and when it comes to chess he's like a beaten-down Bobby Fischer."

I walked toward the garden and reached out an arm for Connie. "We'll have a chance to share our memories of Joey before the night is out," I told her. "But that's not what I came over to say."

"Let me see if I can guess," Connie said. "You want to compliment me on the food? Or the choice of wine? Or for remembering to ask your favorite jazz quartet to play in his honor?"

"I love you, Connie," I said. I took her in my arms and held her close. "I've loved you since I was a kid and I'll love you until I'm a senile old man."

I leaned in and kissed her, embracing her, feeling the warmth of her body rubbing against mine. She then rested her head against my chest and we both swayed to the music. "Lucky for you, I feel the same way," she said in a low and tender voice.

I looked up and glanced around at all the faces in the garden. These were my friends. This was my family. These were the ones I loved.

"'Lucky' is the right word," I said.

67.

THE BROWNSTONE

THREE NIGHTS LATER

I WAS RESTING ON MY BED, ON THE SECOND FLOOR. IT WAS late on a Tuesday night and I had just returned from a meeting with the chief of detectives. I had been interviewed several times the past few months by various members of the Internal Affairs Bureau, but their focus was on dirty cops and not on a Tin Badge and his team that helped put away a major drug dealer.

On top of that, the chief had covered our tracks and we'd taken no credit for the arrest or the takedown of Gonzo and his crew. As far as the NYPD was concerned, the matter was closed and bad people were lined up to be sent away for long prison stretches.

Joey was given a plaque and we were working toward having a neighborhood park named in honor of the brave young man who'd saved the life of a cop who happened to be his friend.

I leaned against the headboard and stared at the thick yellow folder that rested in the center of the bed. Chris had left it there. It was a detailed look at the deaths of his mother and father.

I'd read through it three times and was impressed by the details he had uncovered and his ability to piece them together.

I rested my head back and closed my eyes. It was clear from what Chris had compiled about Jack and the company he worked for that not all was as it was meant to appear. The firm was manipulating accounts, skimming money from clients, and charging for work that wasn't being done. They also were involved in financial dealings with shady individuals and several pump-and-dump operations. There was far too much cash floating in and out of the firm for it to be anything but a front for a number of illegal activities.

And Jack had been on the verge of exposing it all.

Somehow, the higher-ups got wind of what he was about to do—turn whistleblower—and figured the best way out was to end his life. Which they did, on the night he and his wife got into that car and drove to a dinner in a blinding snowstorm.

Chris had details of the car and the condition it was in, and he was right. My brother had always treated his cars as prized possessions. He was as obsessive about their maintenance as he was about their appearance. Chris had enclosed mechanical reports on the car before and after the accident. Based on his findings, the car had clearly been doctored.

Which could lead me to only one conclusion. The conclusion Chris wanted me to come to: His mother and father did not die in a car accident.

They were murdered.

Chris had built his case and now he was looking to me to solve it. To find the ones who had killed my brother and his wife.

It was a case I did not want to take.

It was a case that frightened me more than any other. It would spring loose the demons of my past while I chased the ones who had brought harm to my brother and his wife. The ones who had stripped Chris of his parents.

It was a case that could alter my life. It could do damage to relationships and affect friendships that had lasted for decades.

I reached for the folder, clutched it in my hands, and stood up from the bed. I opened the door to my room and walked down the hall toward Chris's room.

With each step, I knew this was one case I needed to solve.

* * *

I KNOCKED ON CHRIS'S door and didn't wait for a response. I opened it and walked in. He turned and looked at the folder.

"Did you read it?" he asked.

"Several times."

"What did you think?"

"Based on what's in here, there's only one thing to think," I said. "Your parents were set up and murdered."

Chris pounded a fist against a pillow to his left. "I knew it," he said. "And now you do, too."

"That's right," I said. "We both know it now."

"Are you mad at me for looking into it?"

"You had no choice," I said.

"What are you going to do?" Chris asked.

I walked over to his desk and rested the folder next to his computer. "You're going to keep digging," I said. "Go as deep as you can go into that accounting firm. And get me all the financials as far back as they go. Go through personal records of every member, top to bottom. Can you do that without anyone finding out?"

"Yes," Chris said.

I started to walk out of the room. "Once you have everything lined up, bring it to me and I'll start working on a plan."

"You think you'll be able to solve it?"

I looked at him and nodded. "Yes," I said. "I think I can solve it. Even if it kills me."

68.

TRAMONTI'S

I STARED AT CONNIE AND WATCHED AS SHE SIPPED HER WINE and took in what I had told her. "You're certain they were murdered?" she asked.

"I wouldn't be moving in this direction if I wasn't," I said.

"Then I don't see you have any choice but to take it on. I know you and your brother didn't speak. But despite that, he's still your brother and Chris's dad."

"You never asked me why he and I didn't talk," I said. "Why we chose to live our lives as if the other didn't exist."

"Tank, I figured if you wanted me to know, you would have told me," Connie said. "I know how complicated families can get. My dad doesn't speak to many of his own relatives. It's not uncommon."

"Jack and I were close when we were kids and even beyond that," I said. "There was nothing he wouldn't do for me or me for him. He was a kind kid and an honest one. We loved sports and movies and we both loved to read. I turned him on to *Classics Illustrated* comic books, and he got me hooked on Sam Cooke and the Rolling Stones."

"Was he a jazz buff like you?"

"Jack loved any kind of music," I said. "From classical to heavy metal, he listened to it all. He taught himself to play the guitar and learned songs in Italian to play for our parents. Nobody could ask for a better brother."

"He sounds a lot like Chris."

"I'll look at Chris at times and he moves and talks like my brother did when he was that age. Even has the same mannerisms. Having Chris around makes me feel like I have Jack in my life all over again."

"It sounds to me like you miss your brother," Connie said.

"Every day," I said. "I missed having him in my life when he was alive and miss him more now."

"So what happened, Tank?" Connie asked. She reached across the table and held my hands in hers. "Why did you stop speaking to one another?"

I looked at her and took a long and deep breath. For a moment I had difficulty forming words. After several seconds that felt like hours, I gripped Connie's hands tighter and then leaned deeper into the booth.

"Jack saw me kill a man," I said.

ACKNOWLEDGMENTS

IN BADGES IS MY TENTH BOOK AND TOOK MUCH LONGER TO bring to your table than I expected. But, as so often happens, life and death sometimes get in the way.

This is my first book written without my wife, Susan J. Toepfer, working as my first read. She died on Christmas Eve 2013 and missed the publication of *The Wolf* in the summer of 2014. That entire year remains a bit of a blur to me. I very much miss the articles and notes Susan would leave on my desk or listening to her tell me about a movie or a play I should see or about a book or a TV series I would love as much as she did. But most of all, beyond missing my wife, I miss talking to my best friend. And I always will.

Our two children, Kate and Nick, are always around to check in to see if I'm okay, to grab a meal, take a trip to our beloved island of Ischia in Italy, or simply sit and talk over a glass of wine and watch an action movie or a dumb comedy. Okay, maybe over many glasses of wine.

Kate has her mom's curiosity to learn all she can and see all that there is to see. She has her mother's spirit and her soul.

Nick has his mom's charm, is laugh-out-loud funny, and is there in any situation that calls for someone to take the lead. He has his mother's sense of humor and her smile.

My son-in-law, Clem Wood, is a good friend with a great heart, and he is as smart as he is kind. No father could ask for more from the man his daughter loves so much. Amy Plaut has shared in a number of our adventures. She is smart, funny, attractive, and she and my son balance each other perfectly.

I have been fortunate to have had so many great people in my corner these many years. Gina Centrello has been there for me since we first met more than twenty years ago. She is much more than a publisher. She's got a heart as big as Manhattan and it is an honor to call her my friend. I have been a member of the Ballantine family since my first book, and I would be lost without them by my side. Jennifer Hershey, Kara Welsh, Kim Hovey, Greg Kubie, and everyone else who has worked so well and so hard across so many years for my books—my warmest thanks.

And to Anne Speyer—I can't thank you enough for riding to the rescue and in warp speed turning *Tin Badges* from *my* story into *our* book.

Thank you all so very much for your patience and kindness. It will never be forgotten.

I would be lost without the great doctors in my life, and they have earned my respect and gratitude: Drs. Lombardi, Cantor, Schlegel, Palagi, Syrop, Loo, Reily, Lisa L., and the amazing Dr. Lori—they are simply the best at what they do. And to Joyce and Charmaine, friends for life.

My thanks to the friends who have been there for me during the happiest and saddest of days: Hank, Leah, Otto, Paolo and Costanza, Dorothy and Guido, Antonio, Angela, Leo, Liz, Adri and Tim, Tina J., Irene, Martha B., Len and Louise Riggio, Lorenzo Di, Jerry B., Larry Zilavy, Alban, AJ, Andy G. and Lynn, Peter and Carol, Sandi M., Andy and Jerry. The next glass of wine is on me.

To the fabulous Keatings—Timothy J., Annie, Tommy, Beth, Rose, Kathy, Frannie, Sean, Nina, Connor, Patrick, George, Ryan, Little MEK, and last but never least—Tommy Keating, future studio chairman. Thank you for the warm embrace and for taking me in from the cold.

To my team—they are indeed the best any writer could hope to have on their side. Jake and Ruth Bloom and Lou and Berta Pitt have had my heart since we first met decades ago. And they will always have my love.

Dave Feldman, Lee B., and Ashley Silver work hard for me on every deal, big or small. I can never thank them enough for all they do.

Suzanne Gluck is a great agent and an even greater friend. I owe her more than any words could cover. To her husband, Tom D.— I hope your Blackhawks take it every year. And Andrea—you are indeed a rock star.

To Frank S. and P.J. and the entire crew at AGS—thank you for all you do each and every day and have since day one. I would be lost without you.

And to Luigi from La Villetta and Alex from DiNardo's and Vincent, Ida, and Anthony from Manducati's and especially the great Giuliano and the crew from Primola—thanks for keeping me well fed throughout the year.

To my best pal and the coolest Olde English Bulldogge on the planet—my boy Gus. Life changed for me when he died on September 28, 2018. No one, and I mean no one, has ever had a better buddy. He got me through many dark days and nights, and, yes, he did sometimes drive me crazy, but I loved him more than he'll ever know. There will always be a full bowl of treats for Gus. Always.

And a tip of the cap to his posse—Siena and Georgie, the Butch and Sundance of dogs. And to Dr. Farber and Dr. Homan and the great team at West Chelsea, thank you for taking such good care of my pal Gus (and yes, Melvin, that means you).

Mary Ellen Keating walked into my life on a miserably cold January night. She has the greatest heart, biggest smile, and the most beautiful eyes you can ever hope to see. Thank you for the laughter, the love, the kindness, and for putting up with me these past few years. Here's to more—travel, adventure, romance, and, yes, wine.

Rocco—goodbye, my old and dear friend. I miss you each and every day.

And to Mr. G.—a great man who helped me in more ways than anyone will ever know. I never left his company without a smile. He will always have a special place in my heart.

ABOUT THE AUTHOR

LORENZO CARCATERRA is the #1 *New York Times* bestselling author of *Sleepers, A Safe Place, Apaches, Gangster, Street Boys, Paradise City, Chasers, Midnight Angels,* and *The Wolf.* He is a former writer/producer for *Law & Order* and has written for *National Geographic Traveler, The New York Times Magazine,* and *Details.* He lives in New York City and is at work on his next novel.

ABOUT THE TYPE

This book was set in Caslon, a typeface first designed in 1722 by William Caslon (1692–1766). Its widespread use by most English printers in the early eighteenth century soon supplanted the Dutch typefaces that had formerly prevailed. The roman is considered a "workhorse" typeface due to its pleasant, open appearance, while the italic is exceedingly decorative.